predator

Books by Terri Blackstock

Intervention
Double Minds
Soul Restoration
Emerald Windows

Restoration Series
1 | *Last Light*
2 | *Night Light*
3 | *True Light*
4 | *Dawn's Light*

Cape Refuge Series
1 | *Cape Refuge*
2 | *Southern Storm*
3 | *River's Edge*
4 | *Breaker's Reef*

Newpointe 911
1 | *Private Justice*
2 | *Shadow of Doubt*
3 | *Word of Honor*
4 | *Trial by Fire*
5 | *Line of Duty*

Sun Coast Chronicles
1 | *Evidence of Mercy*
2 | *Justifiable Means*
3 | *Ulterior Motives*
4 | *Presumption of Guilt*

Second Chances
1 | *Never Again Good-bye*
2 | *When Dreams Cross*
3 | *Blind Trust*
4 | *Broken Wings*

With Beverly LaHaye
1 | *Seasons Under Heaven*
2 | *Showers in Season*
3 | *Times and Seasons*
4 | *Season of Blessing*

Novellas
Seaside

Other Books
The Listener
The Gifted
The Heart Reader of Franklin High
The Gifted Sophomores
Covenant Child
Sweet Delights

TERRI
New York Times bestselling author
BLACKSTOCK

predator

ZONDERVAN®

ZONDERVAN.com/
AUTHORTRACKER
follow your favorite authors

ZONDERVAN

Predator
Copyright © 2010 by Terri Blackstock

This title is also available as a Zondervan ebook.
Visit www.zondervan.com/ebooks.

This title is also available in a Zondervan audio edition.
Visit www.zondervan.fm.

Requests for information should be addressed to:
Zondervan, *Grand Rapids, Michigan 49530*

Library of Congress Cataloging-in-Publication Data

Blackstock, Terri, 1957 - .
    Predator / Terri Blackstock.
      p. cm.
    ISBN 978-0-310-25066-1 (softcover)
    1. Murderers—Fiction. 2. Cyberstalking—Fiction. 3. Online social
networks—Fiction. I. Title.
    PS3552.L34285P72 2010
    813'.54—dc22   2009053281

Any Internet addresses (websites, blogs, etc.) and telephone numbers printed in this book are offered as a resource. They are not intended in any way to be or imply an endorsement by Zondervan, nor does Zondervan vouch for the content of these sites and numbers for the life of this book.

Published in association with the literary agency of Alive Communications, Inc., 7680 Goddard Street, Suite 200, Colorado Springs, CO 80920. www.alivecommunications .com

Cover design: *Jeff Gifford*
Cover photography: *Imagesource*
Interior design: *Michelle Espinoza*

Printed in the United States of America

10 11 12 13 14 15 • 23 22 21 20 19 18 17 16 15 14 13 12 11 10 9 8 7 6 5 4 3 2 1

This book is lovingly dedicated to the Nazarene.

predator

one

They would find her sister today. Krista had felt it in her gut all morning as she'd assembled the volunteer search teams to comb the acres of wooded land behind the high school. Their search was for her little sister's body— not a living, breathing Ella—but she'd clung to the hope that Ella hunkered somewhere unharmed. Elizabeth Smart, Shawn Hornbeck, and Jaycee Dugard had all been found alive. Even after two weeks, Ella could be too.

Security video near the place where she was last seen showed Ella riding her bike up to the curb across the street from a convenience store. As she waited to cross the street, a black van had driven up beside her, blocking her image for a moment. Then, when the van moved, Ella was gone, and her bike lay toppled over in the street.

In the days that followed, hundreds of volunteers had

searched the area around the store, gone door-to-door in the neighborhoods nearby, and trampled every field or wooded area within a five-mile radius.

And they were still looking, hoping beyond hope ...

But when the police car arrived and pulled up to the registration table, Krista's throat tightened. News vans had followed the squad car, and as the officer got out, reporters flurried around him.

Krista froze in the field, staring at the activity, unable to move. Her phone rang, startling her. Her hand was clammy as she pulled the phone out of her pocket and flipped it open. "Hello?"

"Hon, there's a policeman here," her friend Carla said. "He wants to talk to you."

"I see him," Krista said. "I'm coming." She stood there a moment as she flipped the phone shut, carefully slid it into her pocket. Then she stepped through the tall weeds, no longer examining every blade of grass for any sign that her sister had been here. She kept her eyes on the officer as she slowly made her way toward him.

The volunteers who hadn't yet been deployed to look for Ella stood motionless, silent as she approached. Cold wind whipped her hair into her face, and she hugged herself to stop her shivering. "You found her, didn't you?" she said through chapped lips.

The officer hesitated. "Krista, I'm Lieutenant Baron. Is there somewhere we can speak privately?"

"In my car," she said and pointed out her Kia on the curb. She glanced at the reporters, wondering what they knew. Pulling her keys out of her pocket, she headed for her car. Lieutenant Baron followed.

As they got in, Krista swallowed the knot in her throat. Ella wasn't dead. She couldn't be. It was all a big mistake. Maybe they'd found her alive. Maybe she was okay.

Lieutenant Baron closed the passenger door and looked down at his hands.

"Tell me," she demanded. "What's going on?"

"We found a girl's body."

Krista stared at him, numb. "Is it Ella?"

"We're not sure. She didn't have identification on her ... We need you to come and identify her."

Now the numbness gave way, and a slow, burning rage climbed in her chest. "Where?"

"In a wooded area on Chastain Boulevard, behind the old Martin Lumber building."

"That wouldn't be her," Krista said quickly. "She would never go to that area." As she said it, she knew it wasn't rational. Ella was abducted. She had no control.

"She was clearly taken there," he said.

Taken there. The rage faded into nausea. She pictured her little sister fighting some killer for her life. Ella, who trusted everyone. The shock of betrayal would have been the precursor to murder.

"It may not be your sister at all, but we have to make sure. We tried to reach your father, but he didn't answer his phone and he isn't home."

"He's at the other search site, over by Lake Lora."

He made a note. "We'll get somebody over there."

Krista's voice came out hoarse. "Where is she?"

"She's still where they found her. The crime scene investigators are still working the scene. We could have waited until she was at the morgue, but Detective Pensky knew you had all these volunteers out searching. He didn't want you broadsided by reporters who got to you first."

She looked down at her hands. They were dirty, damp with sweat, even though it was forty degrees.

She nodded then, trying to make her brain work in systematic steps. Step one, breathe. Step two, go to the site. Step three, look at the body. Step four, tell them it's not Ella.

But she couldn't seem to move.

"Ma'am, would you like for me to drive you to the site?"

She tried to think. Could she even drive? Her mind veered off, touching on places where she could reach her father. Why wasn't he answering his phone? He'd kept it with him day and night since Ella's disappearance. Then again, phone reception was spotty at the lake.

"Ma'am?"

"Yes," she said, not sure what she was answering. "I mean, no. I'll drive myself."

"All right," he said. "I'll escort you." He opened his door, started to get out. "Ma'am, are you sure you can drive?"

Her face burned, though her body shivered. She wiped the perspiration from above her lips. "Yes, I'm fine." She started her car.

"I'm not going to talk to the reporters," he said, "but should I tell the volunteers to stop searching?"

Krista looked out her windshield. Most of the volunteers had returned to their starting point and were huddled in a crowd, staring in her direction. The teens from the Eagle's Wings girls' center, where Krista worked, had come in a van to help. She had so wanted these inner-city girls to see their fragile prayers answered for Ella. They stood in a huddle with Carla, the ministry's director, expressions of dread on their faces.

"It might not be Ella," she said aloud. "Tell them to keep searching."

Lieutenant Baron got out of the car, and she sat staring as he said something to the crowd, then walked away from the curious reporters and got into his car. He pulled out, and she followed him.

That flame of hope still flickered inside her. Maybe Ella was hiding somewhere, scared to death, afraid to answer the calls for her. Maybe if they just searched a little bit harder . . .

The police officer turned on his blue flashing light, and she followed him through Houston traffic. She glanced in her rearview mirror and saw reporters' vans following behind her. Like vultures hunting down corpses, they were going to record this nightmare no matter who claimed the body.

Krista thought of trying to call her father, but it might be better if she waited until she saw the girl. There was no point in crushing his hopes if it wasn't Ella. He was already distraught enough. Besides, they'd have a policeman at his search site in no time.

In minutes they were at the site—a patch of woods on a lonely, rural road—where a dozen police cars and a couple of television news vans sat haphazardly in front of a roped-off area. She double-parked next to a police car and got out, pushing through the crowd at the crime-scene tape. A reporter was taping a stand-up before a camera.

"Police say the body was found by two ten-year-old kids who were walking through the woods. The girl was partially buried, but part of her head was exposed. We're waiting to hear if this is the body of fourteen-year-old Ella Carmichael, who went missing two weeks ago."

Buried? Dizziness swept over her, sweat beaded on her face. Krista looked past the reporter, into the woods where all the activity seemed to be. Through the trees, about fifty yards away, she saw people moving around. Though she strained, she couldn't see the girl.

The reporter noticed her and led her cameraman over. "Krista, can I have a word with you?" she asked, sticking a mike in Krista's face.

"No." Krista ducked under the tape.

"Is it your sister?" the reporter called behind her. "Have they asked you to identify the body?"

Krista ignored the questions and shot toward the activity, but a cop stopped her. "Ma'am, you can't go back there."

She was about to shake him off and push through, when Lieutenant Baron came to her side. "It's okay. They asked for her."

He took her arm and walked her toward the investigators. When she reached them, she realized the body was another twenty-five yards beyond them. "You can't go any closer," the Lieutenant said in a soft voice. "There could be footprints or trace evidence. We can't risk disturbing the site. Only the CSIs are allowed near the body right now, but they'll give you the chance to see her soon."

Nausea rose, but she stood paralyzed, staring toward the mound of dirt where the girl lay. She couldn't see a thing. Not what she was wearing or the color of her hair ...

The girl was still in the hole where she'd been buried. Images flashed through Krista's mind of Ella being buried alive ...

No, she told herself. *It isn't Ella. It isn't Ella. It isn't Ella.* When would they let her see her, so Krista could set things straight and go back to search for her sister?

Icy wind whistled through the trees, and Krista thought of Ella out in the elements, crushed by dirt, and freezing rain pouring down on her. Who could do such a thing?

Not Ella. Not Ella.

She heard thunder. The sky had grown appropriately dark, as if it mourned the passing of this young life. It was going to rain. They would have to move the girl soon, or whatever evidence was still on her body would be washed away.

Krista waited, willing back the numbness, certain she wouldn't recognize the girl. As the first raindrops fell, a man in a medical examiner's jacket took in a gurney, and Krista watched as they pulled the body from its shallow tomb. She saw the pink-striped shirt that Ella was wearing that last day. Blonde hair matted with blood and earth.

Her knees went weak, turned to rubber. She dropped and hit the ground. At once, a crowd of police surrounded her, asking if she was okay. She blinked and sat up, let them pull her back to her feet.

Ella!

She heard footsteps pounding the dirt.

"Aw, no! No! It can't be her!" Her father's voice, raspy and heart-wrenching, wailed out over the crowd. She wanted to go to him, comfort him, but it was as though her hands were bound to her sides and her legs wouldn't move.

As they brought the girl closer, Krista saw the bloody, bruised face. Ella's face.

The search was over. Her sister was dead.

two

The limousine was cold. Krista stared at the careening raindrops on the window. Her father sat next to her, wiping the tears from the folds of his mouth. She'd only seen him cry once before Ella disappeared. That was the day they buried her mother, fourteen years ago. Three days after Ella's birth.

How would he survive this? How would she?

Her gaze strayed through the windshield, to the hearse just ahead of them, holding her sister in a shiny black coffin with pink roses blanketed across it. Ella had always loved pink. Her room had been painted that color since she was ten, and the comforter on her bed had the same flowers.

Anger bludgeoned Krista's chest, coiled up like smoke, burned her heart, her throat, her eyes. She needed to say something to her father. The right thing.

"Dad, I'm going to find him," she whispered. "Somehow, I'll track him down. He was following her GrapeVyne page. He's there, somewhere, in that long list of her friends."

"Hush, Krista." Her father's tone was devoid of spirit, but stern and final. The silence that had permeated their home for over two weeks fell heavier over them, stifling out her breath. She closed her eyes, free-falling through that silence, unable to catch herself.

When they reached the gravesite, Krista slid out and stood stiffly next to her father, as the pallbearers—boys from their church's youth group—carried Ella to the tent. For all she knew, one of them could be the killer, masquerading as a trusted friend.

Every tear was suspect, every pained face questionable. She shivered in the cold, thankful that her father had decided to inter Ella in an above-ground tomb. Neither of them could stand to watch them lower her back into the ground—and bury her again. It rained all around them, wind blowing mist under the tent. Still, at least three hundred people had turned out.

Even some of the girls from the center where Krista worked had come. Though many of them had lived through murders of family members, as well as rapes and terrors of their own, they had piled into Carla's van to give their condolences.

The pallbearers walked up one at a time, putting their roses on the coffin. The mourners stood shuddering in the rain, wiping their noses and hugging. She hoped they never forgot.

From the depths of her pain, a purpose emerged. She would make it her business to remind them.

three

The house filled up quickly with friends, relatives, and strangers armed with casseroles and offering hugs and tears. At twenty-five, Krista had had little experience with funerals, except for her mother's. She supposed they'd done the same the day they'd buried her, when Krista was eleven, but she hadn't been expected to host them then. When she'd locked herself and the newborn Ella in her bedroom to insulate them from shattering condolences, no one had forced her to come out.

Today she felt an obligation to welcome people in and help them when they didn't know what to say. Their struggles to make sense of such a senseless death drained her, and she longed for them all to go home and leave her and her father to their grief. But relatives had traveled long distances and were determined to stay, and the teen girls from the Eagle's Wings ministry needed some reward for coming. Most of these teens were middle-school dropouts, their parents in prison or on the streets with needles in their arms. Those who were privileged to have at least one parent who loved and cared for them were alone most of the time, as their parents worked two and three jobs just to provide a moldy apartment for them to live in. Some were pregnant, some tattooed, some were on drugs themselves. They didn't fit in with Krista's relatives, but she was moved by the fact that they would come. That meant that all the seeds she and Carla had planted in their lives were beginning to flower. It moved her to tears that they would risk their own discomfort in order to comfort her.

She didn't want to break down in front of them. They needed to see her strong, courageous. They needed to see a peace that passed all understanding.

But inside, a silent rage boiled, threatening to ruin her ministry and her image. Worse yet, it threatened to ruin *God's* image.

When the girls finally left, she breathed relief, no longer feeling she had to be the mature, settled one. While her relatives talked quietly among themselves, she slipped into her bedroom and turned on her computer. As soon as it was fired up, she navigated to GrapeVyne.net, the online community that had occupied so much of her sister's time. Signing in with her sister's name and password, she brought up her page.

Friends had posted hundreds of notes to her dead sister, so many that they'd pushed Ella's final Thought Bubbles far down the page. Krista scrolled down and found her sister's last public thoughts.

Thinking about becoming a brunette.

Krista smiled. Ella was never satisfied with herself. A

real blonde dyeing her hair brown? Her friends responded
by telling her she was crazy.

The Thought Bubble before that made her smile fade. It
was the statement that might have cost Ella her life.

> Riding my bike to Sinbad's. Dying for a soda,
> and Dad won't keep them in the house.

Ella had never come home from Sinbad's. Her bike had
been found overturned in the street near the convenience
store, her cell phone and purse lying on the ground. Some
of the contents of her purse had scattered out, and her hand
mirror was shattered into dozens of pieces.

Any predator with a computer would have been tempted
by that Thought Bubble. Why had Ella felt compelled to tell
everyone where she was going and when?

Krista scrolled down as she'd done so many times since
her sister's disappearance and saw Ella's habits and schedule posted in various Thought Bubbles throughout the day.
She'd posted dozens of pictures of herself, some with her
school jersey on. Some of her posts mentioned her school,
her teachers, her after-school activities, her friends. She
posted often during the day, using her cell phone.

The killer had access to this information, and he was
somewhere here, hidden among her GrapeVyne friends.
Krista clicked on Ella's Friends and saw a list with pictures
of over eleven hundred people. What had her sister been
thinking, to post private thoughts to over a thousand strangers? Why hadn't Krista realized it and stopped her? She'd
tried to give her sister her space, but she should have been
spying on her, demanding to be added to her Friends List so
she could monitor what was going on.

She scrolled down through the faces, searching for someone who looked evil. Someone who could stalk and rape and bury alive a young girl in a shallow grave out in the woods.

The friends all looked benign and young, but it was subterfuge, she knew. He was there, somewhere. He was watching, enjoying the fallout. He may have even added his condolences to the others on Ella's Vyne.

Then it hit her. She could talk to him. If she posted a note to him, he would read it.

An inner fire hit her face, burned her eyes, tightened her lips. Her heart kicked against her chest. She put the cursor in Ella's Thought Bubble, and typed,

> You think you got away with this, but I'll find you. I'll hunt you down like the animal you are.

She hit send. There was a 140-character limit, but she had more to say. She waited for the box to empty and her note to flash up on the screen. Then she added,

> You'll wish you'd never heard the name Ella Carmichael, and you'll suffer the way she suffered.

Then she signed it, *Krista Carmichael*. She hoped he was reading it already.

four

Ryan Adkins tapped his pencil on the sole of his tennis shoe, wishing he could bring this meeting to a close and get back to the other work piling up on his desk. There weren't enough hours in the day.

His director of legal counsel droned on about the newest lawsuits filed against GrapeVyne. There was one after another, blaming his company for everything from kidnapping cases to Nigerian money schemes.

"This latest came from the attorney general of Connecticut, charging that we're not protecting children from typo-squatting."

One of the attorneys looked up with a frown. "Typo-squatting? What is that?"

"It's when porn sites buy up domain names that are one letter off from the name of a popular site. They rely on typos to get their hits."

Ryan's temples were beginning to throb. "So let's buy up the typo sites they have for GrapeVyne. Let's offer them enough to make them sell. What else have we got?"

"The Internet Safety Task Force has issued a paper called 'Enhancing Child Safety and Online Technologies.' You should probably take a look at it. They want us to appoint a director to sit on the task force. Apparently, Twitter, MySpace, and Facebook have done that already."

"All right," Ryan said. "I appoint you."

"With all due respect, I have a little too much on my plate as it is."

Andrew was right. Ryan turned to the security director, a fortyish man whose hair had turned gray since he came to work at GrapeVyne. "How about you, Jim? Can you do it?"

"Guess I'd better."

"Good." Ryan slid his chair back and stretched out his jean-clad legs. "Guys, you carry on here. I've got a million things to take care of."

"Just one more thing," Jim said. "Have you seen the news about the note that was posted on Ella Carmichael's GrapeVyne page yesterday?"

"Yesterday? She died over two weeks ago, didn't she?"

"Yes. They're saying her sister posted this note to her killer."

Now he was interested. He swept the hair out of his eyes and leaned forward on the mahogany table. "What did it say?"

Jim tossed a printout of the message to him.

> You think you got away with this, but I'll find you. I'll hunt you down like the animal you are.
>
> You'll wish you'd never heard the name Ella Carmichael, and you'll suffer the way she suffered.
>
> Krista Carmichael

Ryan sighed. "Oh, man."

"It's been on the twenty-four-hour news cycle since she posted it after the funeral yesterday. The FBI is working with us to find the killer. We've taken a snapshot of her account so none of her Friends can delete."

Yes, that could be a problem, Ryan thought. If the killer deleted his account, all of his past posts would disappear. "If the guy does delete, that would be a major clue."

"Frankly, he's probably too smart for that," Jim said. "He's no doubt feeding on the drama on her site."

Ryan had never believed it was possible, but sometimes he hated his job. "Give the FBI whatever they want. We don't need them breathing down our necks." He stacked his papers and shoved them into the soft briefcase on the floor. He picked it up and slung the strap over his shoulder. "Have we sent condolences to the family?"

"Bad idea," Jim said. "If we start that, we'll play into the idea that GrapeVyne is to blame. We're not responsible for this."

"Guess you're right." That was why he had attorneys and former law enforcement people on his staff. "I have a meeting. Gotta go."

He pushed through the mahogany doors and stepped out onto the conference floor of Willow Entertainment, the company that owned GrapeVyne. He always felt out of place here, like a trespasser who'd walked in off the street. There was a strict dress code in this part of the company, whereas the GrapeVyne building housed people who wore jeans and sweats to work.

Bypassing the elevator, Ryan trotted down the stairs and out into the cool air. Crossing the soft lawn, he went into the GrapeVyne building.

By most people's standards, GrapeVyne was still in its

infancy. What had begun as a dorm-room idea had turned into a billion-dollar company in a matter of five years. Who would have thought?

"Ryan, look alive!"

He turned, saw a basketball flying over the rail of the second floor, caught it, and looked up. Ian Lombardi, his best friend and chief nerd of GrapeVyne, had a hole in the knee of his jeans and was wearing the same green thread-bare T-shirt for the third day in a row.

"What are you, sleeping here?" he called up.

Ian rubbed the bags under his eyes. "Lots to do on the upgrade before deadline. Hey, thanks for not making me go to that meeting. I'd rather be shot and thrown over a cliff, then torn to pieces by a rabid leopard."

"You've given this a lot of thought, haven't you?" Ryan grinned and tossed the ball back to him and headed for the stairwell. Ian joined him on the second-floor landing and trotted with him to the eighth floor, where the real talent of the company worked.

"I was thinking of getting a pizza. Want to share it while I go over the upgrade with you?"

"Can't. I have to meet with Geico."

"You're meeting with the lizard?"

"No, the advertising executive."

"Bummer."

"No kidding." They got to Ian's office area, their rubber soles squeaking on the floor.

"Hey, remember what it was like before the suits took over?"

Boy, did he ever. Those were GrapeVyne's best days. But he couldn't complain. Not with a hundred-million-dollar nest egg sitting in the bank and a seven-figure salary for staying on as CEO. And he was only twenty-five.

He walked through the maze of cubicles on the floor he called the Rumpus Room. His inner circle—the twelve most valuable computer engineers and designers who'd helped grow the Vyne from a college-only social community into a site used by every first-world country on the planet—created their magic here. These weren't people who liked structure, and they weren't impressed by corporate underpinnings. They liked open offices where they could get a question answered quickly by stepping a few feet across the room or yelling over their desks. Much of the work done here was collaborative, so the open floor fed their creative juices.

Ryan reached his office area and glanced in the waiting room to see if the Geico man was there. He saw GrapeVyne's advertising director, but Geico hadn't made it yet. Good. He might have the chance to return a call or two before the meeting.

As he rounded the glass wall, he saw a young woman standing at his secretary's desk. He couldn't see her face, but her hair was long and blonde. Her long, flowing skirt and blouse were a little too big, as if she'd recently lost some weight, and she wore flat shoes. "I won't take but ten minutes. Five, if it's all I can have. It's very important."

The urgency in her voice made him pause before going into his office.

"I'm sorry, ma'am," his secretary said, "but he's booked solid all day today. I'll be glad to give him a message."

"Tell him it's life or death." He heard her voice wobble. "People are dying, and there's something he can do. Please ..."

He met his advertising director's eyes across the waiting area, saw him roll his eyes. Ryan dropped his briefcase inside his office door and, sliding his hands into his jeans pockets, strode toward the girl.

"Betty, it's okay. I have a minute."

The girl turned to him and slammed him with her eyes. They were blue — not the fake, contact lens kind of blue — but a grayish blue that made her skin look porcelain. She was cheerleader pretty, but he saw intelligence in her eyes.

"I'm Ryan Adkins."

She gave him an up-and-down look, as if she didn't expect the CEO of a major corporation to be wearing jeans and sneakers. At least he had worn a button-down shirt today.... though the tail hung out.

She shook his hand. "Krista Carmichael."

The name sounded familiar, but he couldn't place it. He motioned toward his office. "Betty, call me when Mr. Xavier gets here. Larry, entertain him for a minute, will you? Give him a tour or something."

"Will do," Larry said.

Ryan led the girl into his glass-enclosed office, closed the door, and sat on the edge of his desk. "So," he said, "is someone holding my mother hostage? Did my urine sample come back cancerous?"

She seemed disgusted. "What?"

"You said life or death. Sounded pretty important. Have a seat."

She ignored him and kept standing. "Actually, I should have left out 'life,' since it's only about death. My sister's death."

His eyebrows slowly drew together, and he stood up. "Ella Carmichael? You're her sister?" He couldn't believe he was so stupid. Had he really made a joke about her life or death comment? "I'm sorry; I didn't make the connection."

"Then you know that she was kidnapped, beaten, raped, and buried alive." Her voice broke. "We searched for her for two weeks. She'd used your site to post details of her life and her whereabouts, and a brutal killer took advantage of it. Have you looked at her GrapeVyne site?"

He didn't want to lie. "Actually, I haven't. Not yet."

"Of course not. Busy man like you." She crossed her arms and took a step toward him. He saw a strength in her eyes, strength that impressed him. She wasn't a weeping willow.

"My sister dumped her life out there for everyone to see. Every move she was going to make, she posted on Grape-Vyne. Any online predator could have found her with the click of a mouse. And one did."

He thought of telling her that her sister wasn't the only one. That his security team logged reports of such events several times a day, whenever police needed their help to find missing persons. It was a hazard of online communities across the board—not just his.

Instead, he stayed quiet and let her rant.

"I wanted to come and appeal to you—as a human being—to do something to stop this madness."

He went around his desk and sat down. "Look, Krista, I run an online community. It's a place where people can stay in touch with their friends, make new ones, keep up, share pictures. It's not evil. We're not a clearinghouse for stalkers and murderers."

"You might as well be. My sister's killer is still one of your members, scouring Thought Bubbles for his next victim." She leaned down, palms on his desk. "Do you care, Mr. Adkins?"

"Ryan," he said softly. "Everybody calls me Ryan."

"I couldn't care less what everybody calls you."

He sighed. Behind her, through the glass, he saw that the Geico executive had arrived. "Look, I'm really sorry about your sister, and I hope they catch the killer. We have a team that does nothing but work with law enforcement to help them solve crimes related to our site, and they're on this, working with the FBI."

"There's more you can do. Two things you could do right now, today, that would keep people safer. Remove the Thought Bubbles. People could still blog; they just wouldn't be tempted to do it so often."

"Is that all?" he said with a laugh. Thought Bubbles, the one-liners that people posted throughout the day, were one of the reasons the company had grown exponentially since it was created.

"No, actually. That's not all. You could also use the advertising sidebar on your pages to tell your subscribers of all the cases of missing people connected to contacts they made on GrapeVyne. Show them the news stories about women who were stalked, women who vanished after posting things they shouldn't have ..."

"Those sidebars are for advertisers. It's how we stay in business."

Still bent over his desk, she locked into his eyes. "So you lose a little bit of advertising revenue to save a few lives," she said through her teeth. "Instead of touting Jennifer Aniston's latest wrinkle remedy, you could actually scare kids into being a little more private."

He tried to keep his voice calm. "It's not my job to scare anyone into doing anything. We're providing a service. That's all."

"That sounds really good," she bit out. "Except that it's a service for predators."

His phone buzzed. His secretary was probably trying to offer him an escape. He didn't answer it. Getting to his feet, he came back around the desk. She was small—maybe five-four—but her cause made her seem much bigger.

"Look, I know you're grieving," he said. "And what

happened to your sister is horrible. But GrapeVyne didn't cause that, any more than the phone service did, or her school, or her neighborhood. This is a community, like every other community. It's up to individuals to protect themselves. And if the subscribers are under eighteen, then it's up to their parents."

"They could protect themselves better with more information. That's all I'm asking." She dug into her purse for a flyer with Ella's picture on it, thrust it at him. "Get to know my sister. Go to her GrapeVyne page. See how easy she made it." Her mouth trembled, and she compressed it. "She loved taking pictures. See how talented she was. Look at the smiles on her friends' faces. The laughter. The silliness. And then pick up a newspaper and read about what he did to her."

He looked down at the flier, into the face of the dead girl. She looked like Krista.

"I'm on a crusade," she said. "You haven't heard the last of me. I'm going to find the killer. You can help me find him faster."

"Krista, you should let the police handle it."

"The police don't have as much expertise with online communities as you do. You have profile information, email addresses, personal data about every one of your fifty million users. I've done my research. You have all the complaints that have been filed about members who have predator-like tendencies. Some of the comments on her site seem questionable. You could track down those members and see if they're really who they say they are."

"We don't do that, Krista. We're not law enforcement. We can't spy on people. We're just running a business. Besides, Ella's not the only one who's been ..." His voice trailed off as he realized that wasn't the right thing to say.

She swooped in. "So she's just one of many, and if you

hunt for her killer, you might have to hunt for all of them. And heaven forbid, if you find these killers, lives might be saved."

"We just don't have the staff for that."

"You have a forum. At the very least, you could make changes to your site that will educate your members about the brutality and evil of social networking."

"But there's a lot of good to them too. In fact, I remember hearing on the news that you used your own GrapeVyne page to get the word out about where volunteers could go to join the search for your sister ..."

"There *are* some good things, but if membership increases your chances of death, the good's pretty much overshadowed. With or without your help, I'm going to find my sister's killer and make sure that others aren't killed by people like him. And if I have to take GrapeVyne down to do it, I will. Because as far as I'm concerned, you're a predator too."

His mouth dropped open. "Wait a minute!"

Turning, she opened the door and shot out.

Ryan drew in a long breath and opened the flyer. It was a program from Ella's funeral.

five

Though Krista's boss had offered her time off to mourn for her sister, Krista's concern for the girls she counseled drew her back to the center sooner. She'd awakened this morning with a burning sense of urgency, as though she were single-handedly responsible for the safety of everyone who used online communities.

She'd gotten nowhere with Ryan Adkins, but she could still help the girls at Eagle's Wings. She headed to the teen center, the albatrosses of fear and anger ever with her as she drove through the inner city, where gangs prowled and bullets flew to the score of sirens at all times of the day and night.

She passed the tattoo shop and the liquor store and the pawn shop on the corner, where drug dealers loitered, watching her drive by. She pulled onto the cracked concrete of the Eagle's Wings' parking lot. No one was here yet, since it was only eleven. They didn't open until noon, so she'd beaten Carla to work.

She glanced up at the sign as she went to the front door. Someone had thrown an egg at it, and it had splattered over the second line of the sign: *Where Young Women Soar.* Already, the egg smelled rank and rotten. She'd have to remember to get a ladder and clean it up.

She unlocked the glass door, stepped inside, locked the deadbolt back. She turned on the light and looked around at the front room that she and Carla had painted so meticulously, to make it look like an elegant home rather than a storefront ministry. On the wall facing the door, she'd painted the words, *Be Strong and Courageous! Joshua 1:9,* in gold script.

She walked through the sitting area to the computer room, turned on the light. Her chest tightened as she looked at the dozen computers that had been donated by local churches and businesses. They were the biggest draw of the ministry. These at-risk girls who faced a future of poverty and abuse would come here to get on GrapeVyne or do email or Twitter, and then they'd hang around for counseling services and Bible studies. The computers were the tools through which Krista and Carla built relationships with the girls.

But as she'd learned with Ella, each computer could be a gateway for evil. She had to stop it.

She went to Carla's office, unlocked the door, and stepped inside. The cable modem and wireless router sat on a table in the corner, next to the jack in the wall that fed them the Internet. She unplugged the router, took off the cable connecting it to the modem. Then coiling the cable up, she went to her own office and shoved it into her desk.

It would knock the Internet out of commission until she could convince Carla that this part of their work needed to end.

She heard the front door open, the welcome bell chime. She stepped out of the office.

Carla was coming in with a box of supplies. "Krista, you're back!"

"Yeah, I needed to come by and get something."

"What, hon?"

Krista hedged. "Um ... Just something I left here ..."

"Then you're not staying?"

"I don't know. I don't think so."

"Good. You need more time." Carla put the box down and kissed her like a mother. "You can't give to these girls if you're sapped for strength yourself. Give God some time to heal you. Don't come back until you're ready."

"Thanks, Carla."

Carla's eyes misted over. "Is there anything I can do for you or your dad?"

"No, I don't think so." She drew in a ragged breath and suddenly felt guilty. Carla was so compassionate, such a loyal friend, that she couldn't deceive her. Krista stepped into her office again, and got the cable. "Carla, I can't lie to you. I really came here to do this."

Carla frowned and stared at it. "What is that?"

"It's the cable connecting the wireless router to the modem. I took it off to disable the Internet connection."

Carla's face changed. Her voice softened a degree. "Sweetie, you know that's going to make the girls crazy. It'll keep them from coming here. And it won't keep them off the Internet. They'll just go to the library to get online."

Krista blinked back her tears. "Maybe not. Maybe they'll still come."

"Hon, I know what you're thinking. You think that Ella would still be here if it wasn't for the Internet."

"She would be, Carla. It's not just what I think. It's a fact."

"But there are good uses of the Internet. The girls are learning important skills. They're learning how to write to express themselves, how to read better. They're making friends who have higher ambitions than anyone they know. On GrapeVyne, everyone is equal. There's not an upper class and a lower class. They can have relationships with people who would never give them the time of day. They're communicating, which is something some of them couldn't do before. And they're on *your* GrapeVyne page and mine every single day, reading the Bible studies we post, interacting with us about Christianity. It's too useful a tool to do without."

"They don't understand how dangerous it is," Krista said. "At least let me disable it until I have time to talk to them about predators and what happened to Ella."

"They all know what happened to Ella. And Krista, some of these girls are prostitutes. They live in horrible danger every day, from people in their neighborhoods ... or their own homes."

"But they haven't been stalked by murderers, or they wouldn't still be here. What if we got them off the streets into this safe, comfortable, caring place ... only to be exposed to predators ... maybe even the same one who killed my sister?"

"We educate them so that they won't be."

"But can't we just let the computers be about taking GED prep classes and Bible studies?"

"We can, Krista, but I don't want to. We can't throw out all the good with the bad. They come because of the computers. What we're doing here is working."

Krista's face twisted, and pain throbbed through a vein on her temple. "But it won't matter if they're dead!"

Carla wiped her own tears and took the cable from Krista. "All right, how does this sound? What if we just keep it shut down until you have the chance to talk to them about the dangers? Then we connect it again. At least what they're doing can be monitored here. We can guide them, just like we're doing in all the other dangerous areas of their lives."

Krista shrugged. "Okay, if that's all you'll agree to. Guess it'll have to do."

"So when do you want to talk to them?"

She sighed. "This afternoon, I guess. As soon as possible, before they have the chance to go get online at the library."

Carla took Krista's hands and studied her face. "Are you sure you're up to that so soon?"

"It doesn't matter. It's not about me, it's about them."

Carla nodded with resignation. "Then you'll tell them. And they'll know."

Krista knew what Carla was thinking. They would tell the girls how to stay safe on the Internet, but then they'd walk home on streets filled with drug dealers, rapists, and every other kind of predator. Some would come to the center with black eyes and broken noses tomorrow; others would come with wounds so deep that there was no emotion in their eyes.

She couldn't be everywhere with all of them. She couldn't save them from all the dangers and terrors in their lives. But if it was at all within her power, she would protect them from *this* evil.

It was the only way she'd ever be able to sleep again.

six

The Geico meeting dragged on too long. Ryan was glad his advertising director drove the conversation, because his mind kept going back to Krista Carmichael's words.

He'd been called a lot of things in the last few years. But "predator" wasn't one of them.

He told himself she was still grieving, that he needed to extend some grace to the woman who must still be in shock over her sister's death. But shocked or not, she was angry enough to make trouble. He could feel it. Already the press had gone wild over her note to her sister's killer. If she wanted to, she could go on every major news program and run GrapeVyne into the ground. It would be a PR nightmare. Parents across the country would shut down their kids' accounts. He would have to get creative, be proactive.

"Our data is irrefutable, because we can measure results in numbers of hits on these ads," Larry was saying. "The average ad on our sidebar gets three million hits."

The Geico man shifted in his seat. "But is this the right demographic for us? Teens aren't interested in insurance."

"Teens are about sixty percent of our demographic," Ryan said. "Adults between the ages of twenty-five and fifty-five make up about forty percent of our members."

"And of course, we can target the ads to those clients," Larry added. "That's the beauty of our service. We scan the profiles of the members to learn their interests and passions, and only shoot the ads to the ones who are most likely to buy that product."

"You can do that?"

Ryan nodded. "That's what Willow Entertainment's Internet Division brought to the table. They have amazing resources collecting that data. Before they bought us, our ads were hit and miss, based on educated guesses. Now we have hard data to support our decision making. After the first month of advertising with us, we'll have numbers on how many people click on your ads. If the results are bad, you'll have the option to pull your advertising. But you guys have to think outside the box these days. TV commercials don't cut it anymore, because so many people are TiVoing and fast-forwarding past them. But a lot of our clients spend hours a day staring at their computer screens. Putting the Geico gecco on the page they're staring at is a sure way to sell more insurance."

By the end of the hour, they'd convinced Geico to give it a try. Since most of the revenue of GrapeVyne came from their ads, Ryan breathed a sigh of relief. His job could be terminated if GrapeVyne ever ran in the red. As long as they had big clients like this, they'd all be fine.

Ryan checked his phone's calendar as he headed back to

his office. What was next? He had half an hour before he was due in a meeting with Financial. He needed some caffeine before that.

He told Betty to hold his calls, then slipped back into his office. He took another Excedrin for his headache, then turned on his computer. Curiosity compelled him to go to Ella Carmichael's GrapeVyne page.

The pretty, young face came up on the screen. He looked under her picture and saw the number of GrapeVyne Friends she had. There were 1143.

Krista's message to the killer was at the top of the page, followed by hundreds of condolences from readers. Had the sicko who killed Ella seen the message? Even if he hadn't logged in lately, he most certainly would have seen it on the news. He might have even responded to it here, just to get his kicks.

He scanned the messages, looking for something inappropriate, something that raised a red flag, but saw nothing. He clicked on Friends, and rows of pictures came up. They all looked like teenagers. Had another kid committed this horrible crime? Or was it someone masquerading as one?

He went back to her home page, read through the Thought Bubbles for the last few days of her life. Krista was right. Ella was amazingly detailed. She started first thing in the morning, telling what kind of cereal she was eating, what she intended to wear that day. Sometimes she even took pictures of herself in different outfits and let people vote on them.

She posted via her phone every class she was in, what her teacher was saying, what her friends had quipped. Where she was going after school, who she saw, what stores she shopped in, where she was sitting at ball games, when she went to bed.

Nothing in her day was sacred.

He read back over Krista's note again, and remembered the heaviness of pain and despair and that steely resolve he'd seen in her eyes. Then he typed in Krista's name, and her personal GrapeVyne page came up. She was twenty-five, and most of the blogs she'd written on her site were Bible studies. He scrolled down her Vyne and saw that dozens of teenaged girls engaged with her about living the Christian life. As he checked out some of those girls' pages, he discovered that many of them were minorities from the inner city. There were pictures of them with Krista, and he could see that she had earned their respect.

She was impressive ... gutsy and determined. Yes, she was going to be trouble.

He picked up the phone and buzzed his secretary. "Hey, Betty, make a note to remind me to issue a press release with some new security measures we plan to implement to protect our members."

"Sure, Ryan," she said.

"Also remind me to come up with some."

She laughed, and he hung up, checking his watch. Time for the next meeting. Maybe he'd think of something to give to the press between now and the end of his meeting, something that would hold off her smear campaign and make them appear responsible, without admitting responsibility.

It would be a tough balancing act, but he knew he could pull it off.

seven

Tuesday afternoon, dozens of the girls who frequented
the Eagle's Wings center came to hear Krista's talk,
and they wept with her as she told them how Ella's killer
had found her. By the end, she hoped she had them scared
to death. She stayed afterward, hugging the girls and listening to their awkward condolences, trying to be a bastion of
Christian courage and peace.

Their Internet access restored, some of the girls got
online to check their profiles for any dangerous information
they may have given out. Krista noticed one girl who hadn't
rushed to the computers. She sat in the corner, staring out
the window. Krista crossed the room and sat down beside
her.

"Jesse, what's the matter?"

Jesse was a girl she'd had a hard time getting to know.

She came and sat through Bible studies with a glazed, distant look in her eyes, and rarely interacted with anyone. The fact that she'd stayed behind after the meeting was unusual.

Jesse shook her head, shrugged.

"Was it something I said?"

Jesse met Krista's eyes. The girl had once had the potential to be pretty, but a scar that split across her eyebrow and eyelid, making that eye droop more than the other one, had robbed her of that potential. "I know what you feel like," Jesse said. "My brother, he died too."

Krista swallowed. "I'm sorry, Jesse. I didn't know. When did it happen?"

"Last summer. Got shot in his head."

Shot. The girl had been coming here for six months, and she'd never told them.

"My mama died before that. Got beat up, cracked her skull. Willie, her boyfriend, he in jail now."

The horror of what this girl had endured washed over Krista. She put an arm around her to hug her, but the girl was stiff, unresponsive.

Jesse tilted her head. "How you still believe?"

"What do you mean?"

"In God? Why he let this happen to your sister?"

The question took Krista to a dark place, a place she'd been trying to avoid. She didn't want to ask that question for herself, because she didn't know how to answer it. But Jesse waited, so she dug deep and found her answer ... the rote one that came naturally, because she had said it so many times.

"We live in a fallen world, Jesse. Sin messes everything up."

"But if he is God, and made the earth and everything in it, why he didn't stop some gangsta's bullet from killing my brother? Why he couldn't stop Willie from bashing in my mama's head? Why he couldn't protect your sister?"

Krista cleared her throat, wiped her mouth. For a moment, her mind went blank. She groped for the answer. "He could, because he's sovereign, Jesse. He controls everything—"

"Everything 'cept killers?"

"No, I don't mean that. I mean he was there ... he did have the power ... he could have stopped it ..."

"Then how can he be good if he didn't?"

Krista closed her eyes. Her storehouse of biblical knowledge seemed empty. "He just is ... He's good." Her words trailed off as she realized she didn't really know what she was talking about. The things she'd always said in response to others' suffering seemed like empty, flat platitudes now. They fit like trapezoids into little square holes.

She saw the disappointment on Jesse's face. "At night," Jesse said, "I hear a little girl down the hall screamin'. Her daddy beatin' her. Her sister's twelve and pregnant. Everybody says it's her daddy's. He doin' the same to that little girl. Why don't God see that?"

Krista dug inside her soul, rummaged around in all the dusty files she kept there, and tried to find something meaningful to say in reply. But again she found nothing. She should never have come here today. She should get up now and call Carla, and let her finish this conversation.

But Jesse hadn't asked Carla. She had asked Krista, who had a point of reference. A dead sibling. A horrible evil that had changed her life forever.

Krista fought the tears pooling in her eyes. "Maybe ..." she whispered. "Maybe it's so you and I will find the miracle of courage, and God will use us to help those others who still have a chance. Maybe you're talking to me because of what happened to Ella, and someone will talk to you because of what happened to your brother and mother, and that someone will talk to that little girl ..."

Jesse's brown eyes glistened. "What will we say?"

Krista paused and thought. "We'll tell them that this life isn't all there is."

It wasn't good enough. Jesse rolled her eyes and got up. "First we got to believe that." She pushed through the glass door, and Krista watched through the window as she walked back into enemy territory, where violence ruled and people served drugs rather than God. Where cruel fathers raped their own children.

Where evil stalked.

These girls lived in war zones where young men didn't live past their twenties and young women were abused until they turned mean themselves.

What had made Krista think her family was favored, immune to that evil? What made her think the same God who watched over these girls would give extra care to her sister?

Why had she believed that God owed her better?

She looked through the glass, her gaze following Jesse until she turned down a street, disappearing from view. She hadn't given her a reason to hope. She wasn't sure she had one.

Instantly, she banished that thought from her mind. Of course there was hope. She knew it in her gut, in her heart, in her soul. It should have brought her peace.

But that rage that simmered beneath the surface was foaming over, burning her beliefs like acid. She didn't know how much longer she could hold it in.

eight

Daylight gave way to twilight as Krista pulled into her garage. Her father's car wasn't there. She couldn't imagine what he'd been doing with his time since Ella's death, but he was rarely home. She went into the dark house but didn't bother turning on the light. She got her laptop and opened it, letting the screen provide the only light in the room.

She typed her way to GrapeVyne.net and clicked on the link to open a new profile. Though it was against the rules to have two profiles, she entered information for a fake persona — Maxi Greer. The name sounded sassy and young. She tabbed to the Age box and typed *15*.

Using Ella's taste as a reference, she entered her favorite bands, her favorite songs, her favorite books, and even typed in a few quotes that she thought a fifteen-year-old might use to express herself.

Finally, she opened another browser window and went to a site where she could download photographs of models for a small fee. She paged through the faces until she found one that would work. The photo was in profile, mostly hair and nose and teeth. Not enough for anyone to recognize it and say, "I know that girl." She paid the fee and downloaded it, made a few changes to it through her photo program, then uploaded it to Maxi's GrapeVyne profile. Then in the School box, she typed, *Homeschooled and lonely, and really interested in making friends.*

When she finished designing her page, she made it active. Immediately, it was there, open to anyone she "Friended."

She spent the next hour clicking on Friends she found on Ella's site. Within minutes, some of them had accepted her friendship, and their faces began springing up on her page. It looked like the page of a normal fifteen-year-old girl.

Maybe the predator would find it soon. She hoped he didn't just watch the interactions, but that he would engage enough for her to draw him out.

She could make herself bait for the sake of her sister ... and for the sake of Jesse and all the young people who had no one to fight for them. She would risk her life if it meant bringing him down.

She wasn't even afraid.

nine

Standing in line at airport waiting for cab. Flight
was good. Home soon.

Megan Quinn sent her Thought Bubble and dropped her
Blackberry back in her pocket, hoping to protect it from the
rain. No one had warned her that it was pouring in Houston, so she hadn't brought an umbrella or raincoat. The red
coat she'd gotten for Christmas was somewhat waterproof,
so she stood with her hands in the pockets, shivering and
trying to stay warm.

How much longer for the cab?

New York had been cold during winter break, but she'd
hoped it would be warmer when she returned to Houston.
But this rain was miserable.

There were several people in line in front of her, waiting

for cabs. Hopefully it wouldn't be too much longer. She took
her Blackberry back out of her pocket, turned it around,
held it at arm's length. Making a sad face, she took her own
picture. Then she sent another Thought Bubble.

> Me at Houston-Hobby in freezing rain, waiting
> for the cab.

She clicked Send, and it rocketed through cyberspace.

A cab came and four people tumbled in. She moved with
the line. Only five or six more groups in front of her.

"Miss, can I give you a ride?"

She turned and saw a man with an umbrella. He was
wearing a long black raincoat and looked clean-cut and dry.
"No, that's okay. I'm waiting for a cab."

"I have my town car right over there." He pointed to
a black sedan parked across the street. "Where are you
going?"

Thunder clapped and lightning flashed. "Rice University," she said over the noise.

"That'd be forty bucks," he yelled back. "A cab would
cost you the same."

She realized he was a professional and not just some
doofus trying to pick her up.

"It's very comfortable," he added. "Much better than a
cab."

She regarded the line in front of her. It could be a while.
"Okay," she said. "Deal."

He grabbed her suitcase and her carry-on bag and rolled
them across the street. She followed behind him. He opened
the back door, let her in. As she heard him putting her suit-
cases in the trunk, she got out her Blackberry again.

> Got a cab. Really a town car, woo-hoo. Can't

wait to get back to the dorm and change out of
these wet clothes.

The man got into the car. His brown hair was too long
in the back for a man his age. He needed a haircut.

"All right. Where at Rice do you live?"

"Just off-campus, at Bard Apartments on Shakespeare
Street. I'll show you when we get there."

He pulled the car out and didn't say anything else. That
was fine with her. She preferred quiet in a cab. Nothing was
worse than trying to make conversation with a stranger. She
checked her text messages, saw Thought Bubbles from several of her friends.

I'm at Walmart looking for cough drops.

••••

Just got out of the shower — an hour before
Rod comes. Will I ever make it?

••••

Trying on the pale blue blouse with the high
collar, but thinking my black blouse might be a
better choice.

She texted her roommate Karen, who had the clothing
issue:

I like the black one. Go with that one.

Karen texted back immediately:

You always say that.

••••

But it makes u look classy.

••••

R u saying I need help with classy?

••••

Yes, that's what I'm saying. And that you're fat.

Megan almost laughed aloud at herself.

Then came the answer:

Ur so funny. How long before ur here?

....

Thirty minutes or so. Should be there by six.

She looked at the man in the front seat, caught his eyes in the rearview mirror. Had he been watching her? She glanced out the window and realized he was getting off at the wrong exit.

"Um ... this isn't the right way. It's the Broadway Boulevard Exit onto I-45."

"I know, but my GPS says there's traffic ahead. This is a quicker route."

"Oh, okay." She went back to her messages. Brennie had found her cough drops. Jill was drying her hair. She navigated to her GrapeVyne page, to see if anyone had left comments on this morning's blog post. There were a few responding to her thoughts about the stress of being with family during the holidays.

She glanced back up. The night lights were fading now, and the car was moving rapidly through some rural area. She frowned. "Excuse me, but could you tell me what route you're taking? We're not going in the right direction."

He chuckled then. "Trust me. We are. There's a turn-off in about a mile that will turn us back in the right direction. We'll be at Rice in ten minutes."

That didn't sound right. Uneasy, she looked down at her phone.

"Is that a Blackberry?" he asked, looking at her in the mirror again.

"Yes."

"Mind if I look at it? I've been thinking about getting one."

"Sure." She handed it to him across the seat. He looked down at it as he sped down the rural road. Was he going to miss the turn-off? She watched out the window for him, but there didn't seem to be any roads to turn on. Surely they'd gone a mile by now.

He looked back up, caught her eyes in the mirror again. "Nice phone." As he spoke, his automatic window lowered. "But you won't be needing it."

He tossed it out the window.

She gasped. "What are you doing?" She looked back. "Stop. I have to go get it!"

The car rocketed faster down the long, lonely road as his window slid back up. She leaned up on his seat.

"Why did you do that? Why won't you stop?"

She saw through the rearview mirror that his eyes had grown hard.

Her heart thudded. Why had she gotten in this car with him?

"Stop, I said! Let me out!" When he didn't slow down, she tried to roll down her window, but she couldn't. He must have locked it. She could jump out. She might break something, but at least she could go for help. But the door wouldn't budge. There must be a child lock on it.

Terror came over her as she rammed her body against the door. She was going to be a news item—a missing person who was later found raped and murdered on an abandoned road. She'd be just like that Carmichael girl.

"Let me out!" she screamed. "People know where I am. I've been texting them every step of the way. They know what kind of car picked me up. They know what you look like."

"Car's not registered in my name. They'll never find it," he said in a steely voice. "You didn't tell them what I look like. I'm one of your followers, Megan. I get all of your Thought Bubbles. I saw what you posted, right here on my own phone."

The blood drained from her head, and she thought she was going to faint. She looked around frantically for an escape. "What do you want from me?"

"I just want to have some fun with you, Megan. You're always having so much fun."

"I'm a black belt in karate," she blurted out. "I can defend myself."

"No, you aren't, Megan. I'd know if you were. I know when you wake up in the mornings, what was on your last test, what you got for Christmas, what you gave everyone else ... I've been tracking you for the last six weeks. No karate, sweetheart."

She grabbed the back of his hair and screamed into his ear. "Let me out of here, you psycho!"

He lifted his hand, pointed a gun at her. "Get back! Now!"

She fell back on the seat, tears burning her eyes. "You won't get away with this. I have people who love me. They'll come looking for me."

He laughed.

She put her hands over her mouth, trying to muffle her crying. *Think*, she told herself. *Think!*

She saw a dirt driveway up ahead, and she searched through the wet windows, looking for a house. He'd have to stop sometime, and when he did, she'd need to know where to go for help.

But she couldn't see any houses anywhere.

He turned onto the dirt road, the back end of the car

sliding on the slick street. She heard gravel under the tires, saw trees, thick and tangled as they went deep into the woods.

God, please help me ...

She grabbed her purse and dug through it, searching for anything she could use. She pulled out a pen that she might be able to stab into his eyes, stuffed it into her coat pocket. Listerine spray ... maybe it would burn his eyes. Keys ... She stuck them between her fingers and balled her hand into a fist.

The car stopped, and he reached over the seat and grabbed the purse off her lap. He dropped it on the front seat. "You can scream if you want, Megan, but nobody will hear you. There's no one for miles and miles."

She screamed anyway as he got out of the car, unlocked the back door. His eyes were gleaming as he opened it and started to climb in. Sliding back against the opposite door, she tried to open it again. Still locked. She kicked at him, he grabbed her legs and pulled her out of the car. Her shoe came off, but she kept kicking. Her elbows hit the dirt before her back and head. She lashed, screaming, as he dragged her through the mud.

"Help me! Somebody help me!"

He dragged her in front of the headlights, cold, wet mud sliding through her hair, down her neck, her back. He smiled as rain glistened on his skin. She tried to sit up and kick free, but the more she fought, the more he enjoyed this. She tried to hit him with the keys in her hand, scratched at his chest, his arm. He grabbed her hand and almost broke her fingers getting the keys, shoved them in his coat pocket. He wrestled her red coat off of her, cast it aside, so she no longer had the pen or the breath spray.

Think, she told herself. *Fight.*

Her arms and legs flailed, her teeth bit, her body rocked. His fist cracked across her jaw. She felt it dislocate. Saw stars. Rain. Black clouds.

Heard thunder.

Another crack across her forehead. Then her mouth ... her ribs, her kidneys.

She pulled herself into a fetal position. *God ... please God ...*

She heard the man's heavy breathing as he bent over her. "You good Christian girls ... so innocent ... so naive. I'm going to enjoy getting to know you, Megan. And then I'm going to bury you alive... No one will ever find you."

She tasted blood and balled herself tighter ... bracing herself for what was to come.

ten

Megan wished she were dead, so she pretended to be. She lay limp, her face and lips swelling, her sides an agonizing blend of splintered ribs and bruised kidneys, her knee torn, her legs bloody. She opened her swollen eyes and saw him, his back to her, as he shoveled into the wet soil.

Was he digging her grave?

She couldn't just lie here, waiting for him to bury her. Somehow she had to get away. She sat up quietly, wincing at the pain, but not making a sound. She pulled her wet clothes back into place. Silently, she got to her knees, gritting her teeth to keep from crying out, then got her feet under her. Only one shoe ... one foot bare ... She managed to stand up, to take a step, pain slicing through her ... then another.

He heard her and swung around, reaching for his gun.

Her last reserve of adrenaline shot through her, and she

stumbled into a run, deep into the woods, searching for a branch that could be used as a weapon, or some place to hide. A shot fired, missing her, and she kept going. Either she would die running, or she would escape. She pounded through the brush, tearing it back and ducking under. She heard his breath and the sucking of his feet in the mud as he came closer.

She saw a fallen log, about two feet in diameter, and eight or nine feet long. Could she squeeze inside? Would he look for her there?

She threw herself to the ground at the opening and went in headfirst, sliding into cobwebs across rotten wood, fearing the creatures inside less than the one outside. She heard his footsteps as he ran past, cursing. His voice faded as he ran farther away.

She lay still, trembling in the tomb of the tree trunk. He could still come back.

Nausea worked through her digestive tract, threatening to spew out. Would she have to lie here in her own vomit? No, she had to hold it back. She tasted blood in her mouth, and felt hot and cold at the same time, dizziness whirling in her head.

God, help me survive.

Something slimy crawled across her leg, and she tried to shake it off. *Think about something else.* She forced her mind back to her Sunday school days, when she'd memorized passages of scripture. She tried to remember Psalm 27.

> *The Lord is my light and my salvation; Whom shall*
> *   I fear?*
> *The Lord is the defense of my life; Whom shall I*
> *   dread?*
> *When evildoers come upon me to devour my flesh,*
> *My adversaries and my enemies, they stumbled and*
> *   fell.*

She couldn't remember what came next, so she silently repeated those words again and again. She heard him coming back, lumbering through the woods, pausing near her log. Was she far enough in that he couldn't see her feet? She dared not move. Her mind sought distraction, so she groped for more of the Psalm.

> For in the day of trouble He will conceal me in His
>   tabernacle;
> In the secret place of His tent He will hide me;
> He will lift me up on a rock ...

Again, the next words failed her, and she struggled for more snippets of the passage she had once known.

> Hear, O Lord, when I cry with my voice,
> And be gracious to me and answer me.

She heard the man moving past the log, heard the crackle of brush and the whisper of leaves. Was he going back to his car?

She waited, listening, heard nothing. She wanted to crawl out of the log, but knew the silence could be a trap. Where was he?

Moments dragged by, moments that seemed like an eternity, moments that gave way to deeper night. She went through the Psalm again, focusing her thoughts, trying not to think about what awaited her. That shovel ... that hole. That gun. That darkness.

Finally, when she thought she could bear it no longer, she heard the sound of his engine starting up, heard the car pulling away, heard it passing this place on the road, distancing itself from here.

Was he really gone?

She crawled out, looked around, saw only what the moonlight illuminated through the trees. He wasn't here.

She got to her feet, feeling weaker than she had before. Blood pooled in her mouth. She spat it out and stumbled through the brush and trees, trying to reach the road. There had been no lights down this long, barren road. Maybe if she went the other way, farther down, she would find help.

She made her way to the road and looked to see if headlights searched the trees. She saw nothing. Staying close to the trees, she limped down the road, praying for rescue.

eleven

Megan limped for what seemed like a mile and still saw no lights. Maybe she should go back in the other direction. Her phone had been thrown out the window somewhere along that road. Maybe she would hear it ringing or see it lighting up in the darkness. Then she could call for help.

She turned and went back that way, her feet slogging in mud. When she saw headlights coming, she thought of running out into the road and waving the car down. But something told her that it was her assailant, coming back to look for her. Knowing she could be passing up her only chance for help, she slipped behind the trees and hid as the person drove by. The car drove too slowly. Yes, it was him, all right.

Had anyone missed her yet? She was due back at her

apartment hours ago. Maybe someone had called the police. Maybe someone would come.

As she walked back along the tree line toward civilization, she spat out more blood. She couldn't move her jaw, and the pain of broken bones racked through her sides. Her weight on her knee ripped tissue with each step. What if she dropped right here in the dirt? How long would it take for someone to find her?

She kept going, not able to give up, walking what seemed like miles until the rain stopped and the clouds split, constellations marking the passage of time. She heard movement, the breaking of twigs, breath coming just on the other side of the trees. Could he have found a way to come at her from inside the forest? Or was something else stalking her?

And then she saw it. A deer, stepping gingerly out of the trees a few yards ahead of her. He grazed in the grass, then heard her and started. He peered at her through the darkness, his eyes locking with hers. Then he ran back into the woods, as if she were something to fear.

The knowledge of such gentleness just inside the trees gave her the feeling that all along that path was not evil. Maybe it was a sign.

Finally, she saw lights up ahead. A house, far back from the road behind acres of land—a house she hadn't seen as they'd driven past earlier. One lamp burned in some room in the house. She caught her breath, thanking God, and dragged toward it, each landing on her right leg shooting anguish up her leg. She ducked under a fence and stumbled across damp earth until she reached a dirt driveway. Dizziness threatened to drop her as she got to the front door.

She reached the stairs and wobbled up them, banged on the door. What time was it? Was it the middle of the night? Would she wake someone from a sound sleep? Was anyone even home?

She saw a light come on upstairs, heard footsteps across the floor. She looked back toward the road, praying the predator wasn't here somewhere, waiting for her. Dizziness came over her, and her mouth filled with blood again. She spat on the doormat and wilted to the floor.

"Who is it?" a woman asked through the door.

"Help," Megan cried. "I need your help ... phone."

The porch light came on, and she knew they stared out at her, trying to decide whether to open the door. Finally, it cracked open, and she saw a kind-looking elderly woman, and a man with a rifle aimed right at her.

"Roy, she's bleeding! Call 911!"

Megan didn't allow herself to drift out of consciousness. "He ... he was looking for me," she said without moving her jaw. "He might come."

The woman dropped to her side. "Honey, who did this?"

"A man ... black town car. Please call."

She lay in the shelter and security of that home, wrapped in a blanket and resting on the couch, as she waited for the police and ambulance to come. The kind couple paid no attention to her blood on their upholstery. For the first time since her attack, her mind sank into the exhaustion of her fight.

.....

Megan stirred when the house filled with EMTs, and as they attended to her wounds and took her vital signs, she tried to give the police the information they needed. "He had a round face, brownish-gray hair, longer in back, touching his collar. I couldn't see the color of his eyes. Black town car, leather seats."

"Was there a name on the car? A company that he worked for?"

"No, he wasn't a real driver. He'd been following me from my posts on GrapeVyne. He told me it wasn't his car."

As they put her on the gurney to take her to the hospital, she thanked the couple for helping her. As she was wheeled out, she saw the woman crying, the man comforting her.

Would they be able to go back to sleep, knowing a killer lurked so near? She prayed for their safety.

"Is there someone you need to call?" one of the EMTs asked her as they flew through town.

"Yes." She thought of her parents, but then a more pressing concern rose to her mind. Her roommate.

"Oh, no, he has my purse and my suitcase. He'll know my address. He has my keys. My roommate is there. I have to warn her."

The EMT gave her his phone, and she called Karen's cell phone. It rang until her voicemail picked up. Megan waited for the beep. "Karen, this is Megan," she said. "A man picked me up at the airport and almost killed me. I'm going to the hospital, but he has our address. You need to get out. Go stay with Brennie or something. Don't stay there. It's not safe."

She got off the phone and smeared the tears, touched one of the split places on her face. She didn't even want to look in the mirror. "Please ... could you ask the police to go by the apartment to check on her, and tell her to leave? She didn't answer. She could be there asleep. He'll go there and hurt her."

The paramedic nodded. "I'll talk to them as soon as we get to the hospital. What about your parents? They need to know what's happened to you."

She thought of her mother hearing of this. It would destroy her. The stress of this might do her parents in. Still, she knew it had to be done. They couldn't hear about this from someone else.

"Okay." Her dirty, blood-stained hands trembled as she took the phone and dialed their number. Her mother answered on the third ring.

"Mom?" She crumbled to pieces as she broke the news.

twelve

The boy was brooding. Either he was mourning Ella's death or guilt weighed him down.

David Carmichael, Ella and Krista's father, wasn't sure which it was. From his vantage point behind the wheel, hidden among the other vehicles in the Walmart parking lot, he watched the kids assembled around their cars, smoking, flirting, and gossiping, as if life went on.

For them, he supposed it did.

He rubbed his raw eyes, knowing he should have taken the sleep medication his doctor gave him after Ella was found. For the two weeks leading to her discovery, he had hardly slept a wink. How did a dad sleep when his little girl was lost? How could he even close his eyes, knowing she was out there somewhere with some maniac?

He'd dozed a few times in his chair, sitting with the

phone and the laptop as he'd pored through her Grape-
Vyne Friends' profiles, trying to figure out who might have
abducted her or harmed her in some way.

In that two weeks, he'd lost ten pounds and aged ten
years. But he hadn't been able to bring her back.

Since that time, he'd dreaded the mockery of nightfall.
Each time he dozed, he had terrible dreams. He would jerk
out of sleep and find himself covered with sweat, shaking
like a drunk with the DTs.

The dreams bombarded him with images of suspects'
faces. Last night's face was Tim Moore's, Ella's ex-boyfriend,
whom she'd been forbidden to date. He'd cruelly dumped
her, David had learned from her emails. Ella had fallen apart
and chased him as if he were her lifeline. As if she had no
one else.

Had he killed her to get her off his back?

He watched the eighteen-year-old who should never
have had access to a fourteen-year-old girl. The boy leaned
against his car, feet crossed at the ankles, looking down at
the pavement as he smoked a cigarette. A girl breached the
distance between him and the others and sidled up next to
him.

He didn't offer a smile. David wished he could hear what
they were saying.

The girl looked young—too young to be with a guy
that age. Maybe David would find her picture on Ella's page
when he got home. He could call and warn her parents that
she might be flirting with a killer. He could tell police that
Tim Moore was . . .

. . . was what?

The police had already ruled Tim out as a suspect, even
though David told them that he and Ella had a relationship
that ended badly. The kid wasn't at work the night of her
disappearance. So why hadn't the police arrested him?

The girl said something to him, and the boy laughed.

Rage roiled up in David's chest. He thought of getting out of his car and beating that grin off his face. He pictured himself grabbing the boy by the neck, dragging him into his car, and taking him out to that place where he'd buried Ella.

Help me, God. I'm not going to survive this.

Tim pushed off from his car and walked around to get in the driver's side. The girl went to the passenger side.

"No," David whispered. "Don't get in."

But the girl did. The car started up, and he saw Tim wave good-bye to the kids in the cluster. Then they pulled out.

David started his car and backed out of his space, watching to see which way they turned. He almost hit someone coming out of the store, slammed on his brakes.

When the person passed, he hurried to the exit and pulled out onto the busy road. He saw the old white Bonneville a few cars ahead and changed lanes to get closer. The car turned off and he followed, keeping two cars between them.

Where was he taking her? He thought of calling the cops, but they would just demand to know what the boy had done.

He followed them down several streets, until they came to a residential neighborhood near David's house. Tim's car pulled up to the curb of a small house with a well-groomed yard. The girl got out, bent back in to say something, then pushed the door closed.

David pulled into a driveway a few houses down, turned off his lights, and watched as the girl ambled across her yard and went in. Tim pulled away.

David waited until he was out of sight, then pulled back out of the driveway and followed him. He caught up to him as he pulled from the neighborhood back onto a busy street. His heart pounded as he followed him down some back streets ... and finally to Tim's own home.

David drove past as the kid got out and headed in.

But would he stay there for the night? He drove around the block, then came back and parked at the curb a few houses down. A light had come on at the back of the house. That was probably Tim's room. He'd wait here a while and see if he went out again. If he did, he'd follow him.

Krista would tell him he was crazy to do this, but what else could he do? If the police had any leads, they hadn't told him. Someone had to do something. Ella was dead. Her murder was brutal, her last hours torture.

What kind of father would he be if he let that go unpunished?

Hours passed, and his head began to ache. He hadn't eaten since ... when? He couldn't even remember. Grief hung heavy in his throat, blocking out any appetites, except for revenge.

He wouldn't rest until Ella's killer was dead.

thirteen

Ryan was in another meeting when the FBI called and insisted that they had to talk to him right away. He went to his office and picked up the phone.

"Ryan Adkins."

"Ryan, this is George Carter, FBI."

"Agent Carter, you probably need to talk to our team that works with law enforcement. They've been collecting the information your agency asked for about Ella Carmichael."

"This isn't about her. It's a new case. A Rice student named Megan Quinn was abducted and attacked last night, here in Houston."

Ryan closed his eyes and drew in a deep breath. Not another one. "Don't tell me. The attack is linked to GrapeVyne?"

"That's right. She says the man told her that was how he

knew where to find her. He'd been following her Thought Bubbles, and they led him right to her."

"Wait. She *told* you? She's not dead, then?"

"No, she managed to escape. She's been able to give us some details about the perpetrator. But we need your help."

Ryan woke up his monitor and typed in her name. *Megan Quinn* brought up five entries. He found the one from Houston and pulled her account up. She looked young, perky, cute, like Ella.

"Agent Carter, do you think this is the same person who murdered Ella Carmichael?"

"Could be. He told her he liked Christian girls, and Ella was a Christian too. It's our strongest lead for the Carmichael case."

"So what do you need from us?"

"I'm asking your security team to lock down her account, take snapshots of it, and give us a list of everyone who viewed her account for the last forty-eight hours, whether on the computer or on their cell phones."

"All right. I'll get my team working on it immediately."

"I wanted to talk to you personally because we've got a real problem here. Guy's still out there, and he has a voracious appetite. If we don't catch him, there will be others. We'll need full access to Megan's account, and we're going to set up some decoy accounts to lure him."

"Have you compared the Friends the two girls have?" Ryan asked. "Ella was fourteen but Megan's older, so they wouldn't be likely to move in the same circles. Common Friends could be clues. But don't trust your eyes. A predator would have a fake profile so he couldn't be caught. The profile of a sixteen-year-old girl could really be that of a killer."

"Yes, we have our cyber crimes agents working on it with us. We appreciate your help. Maybe we can get both of these cases locked up today."

Ryan got off the phone and went back to Megan Quinn's account, took snapshots of the days the agent asked for, then went back to the day of Ella Carmichael's murder. Using code he had written to help his security team filter out bogus profiles, he ran a comparison of both girls' Friends. Twenty common Friends came up.

He scrolled through the Friends, looking for evil, someone who would bury a young girl alive after beating her bloody. But everyone looked innocent and young.

Maybe Ryan could use GrapeVyne to help them locate this killer. And if it brought some peace to Krista's family and to the girl who'd escaped last night, then it would be worth his time.

fourteen

H e's here somewhere. I know he is."
Krista whispered the words aloud to her computer
screen. She hadn't slept all night. She hadn't even tried.
Instead, she'd sat at the computer, taking copious notes
about Ella's GrapeVyne page. She'd filled three legal pads
with details she'd gleaned from Ella's Friends' comments
over the last year. Whenever she thought someone had
posted something questionable or suspicious, she'd gone to
their sites to see who their Friends were and what they were
saying.

Out of Ella's eleven hundred Friends, she'd screened
about two hundred of them. That wasn't nearly enough.
But the details she'd learned about these teenagers' lives was
enough to curdle her blood.

The girl whose face was up on the screen—a sixteen-
year-old girl named Sara Miles—had given her Friends

enough information to bring a predator right to her door. He would know the hours that she was home alone each day, what street she lived on, her parents' names, her school and classes, her younger siblings' names and activities. He would know that she was vulnerable and gullible, how she felt about her parents' divorce, how intimate she got with her boyfriends. She was an open target for anyone with evil intentions.

Krista tried to think like a predator. He'd be like a lion in a butcher shop with this kind of information. He could literally shop through millions of targets, stalk his next victim, and hit when she was most vulnerable.

And none of these people realized they were playing into his hands.

The thought made her sick, literally. She felt her stomach churning, roiling, rising . . .

She got up and ran into her bathroom, vomited into the toilet. She flushed, then sat on the floor, waiting for the next wave. Leaning her head back on the wall, she thought of that stalker reading the things her sister had posted, driving by their house, watching for the right time. He probably got her Thought Bubbles on his cell phone. When she posted that she was going to Sinbad's, he'd headed straight there.

When her stomach stopped heaving, she went back to her room. There was so much yet to be done.

She signed out of Ella's account, and signed back in under her alias, Maxi Greer. A notification came up. She had twenty-five Friend requests. She went down the list, studying their faces and each of their profiles. Some of them she knew—they were Ella's friends from school. But others were strangers.

She carefully wrote down everything she could find about each person before accepting them as Friends. A chill went through her. The killer could be here, behind one of these facades, stalking her already. She typed into her Thought Bubble,

> I get really lonely being homeschooled. Nothing to do while my parents are at work. Hoping to make lots of friends here.

If that wasn't bait, she didn't know what was.

Her cell phone rang, startling her. She glanced at the Caller ID readout. It was her friend Laura, whom she hadn't talked to since the funeral. She couldn't talk to her now, either. Laura would want to know if there'd been any progress on Ella's case. She'd want to come over, hang out, talk. But Krista couldn't do it.

Besides, it was 7:00 a.m. No one should call her that early. Laura worked the night shift as a registered nurse, and sometimes lost track of time.

The phone stopped ringing. She went back to the computer, trying to decide whose life to pry into next.

Then her phone beeped. She'd gotten a text. She pulled it out of her purse. It was from Laura.

> I need to talk to u. It's about Ella's case.

Krista caught her breath. Maybe she'd heard something. She opened the phone and called Laura back.

Her friend answered quickly. "I knew you were avoiding me."

"It's kind of early."

"I know, I'm sorry." Laura lowered her voice to a whisper. "Listen, I'm at work at the hospital. I just wanted you to know there was another attack last night."

The words hit like a fist. Krista clutched her phone. "Who was it?"

"A college girl named Megan Quinn. The press hasn't gotten wind of it yet."

Krista felt sick again and headed for the bathroom. "Where did they find her body?"

"No, she's not dead. She escaped. She's here at the hospital."

Krista stopped in the bathroom, leaned against the cold tile. "Can she identify the person who attacked her?"

"I don't know. She's been beaten half to death. She is conscious, though. The police have been questioning her since she came in. I'd get fired if they knew I told you, but I thought you should know. It's really sad, because she's here all alone."

"Laura, I need to talk to her. I'm coming to the hospital."

"Krista, please don't. I'm telling you, I'll get fired."

"I won't tell them how I found out. But it could be the same person who killed Ella. She could help us find him."

There was a long pause. "All right, but the staff knows I know you. I had them all praying for you. If they see you, they'll know."

"I'll try to slip in without being noticed. What room is it?"

"Room 323. Krista, don't make me regret this. Wait an hour or so. I'm getting off soon, so I'll be gone."

Anger flared. "If we find Ella's killer, will you regret it?"

Another pause. "No, of course not."

She tried to breathe, telling herself to go easier on Laura. She was doing her a favor. "Thank you for telling me, Laura. I owe you one."

"You're welcome, girl. Call me when you feel like it."

Krista clicked off the phone and went to take a shower. She had promised to speak to the kids at Ella's high school this afternoon, so she needed to look decent. That would kill an hour and give her stomach time to calm. Then she would head to the hospital.

....

The hospital corridor was long and barren. The floor shone with an over-abundance of wax and smelled of antiseptic. It was too cold, and Krista shivered as she followed the maze to the elevators, then rode up to the third floor. She got off and looked for the numbers on the doors. Room 323 was on the opposite side, at the other end of the hall.

She'd worn her sunglasses and pulled her hair up into a ponytail, hoping she wouldn't catch anyone's eye. Her face had been on the local news quite a bit since Ella's disappearance. As she followed the numbers on the doors, she spotted Laura coming toward her. Her friend saw her, turned, and went the other way.

Krista pretended she hadn't seen her.

Another nurse was coming out of 323, so Krista paused at 321 and acted like she was going in. When the nurse passed, Krista went to 323. The door was slightly ajar. She knocked lightly, then pushed it open. A girl lay on the bed, her face scraped and swollen, her lip split, and her leg in a Velcro cast.

Krista brought her hand to her mouth. This could have been Ella, if only she'd been found in time.

The girl's swollen eyes were closed, as if she slept. A tray of untouched food sat beside her bed.

Krista stepped quietly into the room. There were no possessions out. The closet was open, and nothing hung there. She'd probably been brought here in an ambulance. How had she gotten away?

She went to the head of the bed, and the girl's eyes fluttered open. The white part of her right eye was bloody. "Could you get me some water, please?" She spoke as if it hurt, hardly moving her mouth.

"Of course." Krista put her purse down and found the

pitcher of water, poured her a cup. She brought it to Megan and helped her drink.

"Have my parents gotten here yet?"

Clearly, Megan assumed she was on the hospital staff. "I don't think so. Megan, I'm Krista Carmichael. I don't know if you've heard about my sister, Ella Carmichael ..."

Megan stared up at her. "The girl who was killed."

"Yes."

Megan's eyes filled with tears. "How did you know about me?"

Krista drew in a long breath. "A friend who works here told me. I hope you don't mind my coming. I just wanted to talk to you. The man who did this to you could be the same one who killed Ella."

Megan squeezed her eyes shut and nodded. "I haven't been able to identify him, so they can't catch him. I looked at tons of pictures, but he wasn't there." She tried to sit up. "Could you ... please let me use your phone? I need to call my roommate again. He has our address. Karen has to get out of there. I've been trying to call her all night, but last time they checked my blood pressure they moved the table. I can't reach the phone."

"Sure, of course." Krista handed Megan her cell phone and watched as Megan dialed. She could hear ringing, then finally voicemail picked up.

Megan hung up. "I've already left three messages. I'm really worried about her. I'm afraid she's in trouble. She hasn't picked up any of the times I've called. But she screens her calls and doesn't answer unless she knows the person. She wouldn't know the hospital number is me."

"Did you tell the police you were worried?"

"Yes. And they said they would go by and check on her. But I haven't heard anything. If she'd gotten my message, she would be here. What if he's already gotten to her?"

Krista frowned. "Did he say he would?"

"No, but he has my keys and my address. I got away, and he'd probably come after me at home. He wouldn't want me to talk. He'd kill me to keep me from identifying him. He could even come here. Anybody could walk in."

Krista shivered, but prickles of sweat broke out on her neck. "I'm sure she's okay. She probably got your voicemail and took off."

"No, she'd be here, with me. She didn't get it." She started to cry. "Where are my parents? I'm so scared." Megan reached for her covers, but they were tangled around one leg. Krista freed them and covered her.

"Where were they coming from?"

"New York. When I called them this morning they said they were taking the next flight here."

"I'm sure they'll be here soon. I'll stay with you until they come."

Megan met her eyes. "You will?"

"Yes. I'm supposed to speak at my sister's high school this afternoon, but if your parents don't get here by then, I'll cancel. And if anybody walks in here, I'll scream like a banshee."

"Thank you."

"You rest now, and I'll just sit here. Do you need another blanket?"

Megan nodded, and Krista looked around the room. A blanket lay folded on the recliner. She stretched it out over Megan.

But the girl couldn't rest. "I tried calling my other friends, but none of them picked up. They're probably asleep, not checking messages. Someone needs to check on Karen."

Krista patted her hand. "I can call my dad, get him to go check on her, if you want."

Megan's eyebrows lifted. "Her green Toyota would be there in the driveway in front of my door if she's home. My car will be there too. They're townhouses, so we park right in front of our door."

"All right, I'll call him."

A nurse pushed the door open and stepped inside. "Oh, you have a visitor."

Megan didn't give Krista up as an impostor.

The nurse came to the bed. "Aren't you going to eat?"

Megan looked at the food sitting on a tray beside the bed. "I don't think I can. Mouth's wired shut, and I can't reach it ..."

"I'll feed her," Krista said. "Leave it a little while longer."

The nurse looked pleased and left them.

Krista called her father, knowing she was waking him. She dreaded weighing him down with more pain. But he would want to know, and he'd want to help.

"Dad?"

"Yeah." He sounded groggy, and his voice held the same lifeless, dull quality that it had for the last three weeks. "What is it, Krista?"

Her eyes misted and her mouth shook. "Dad, last night another girl was attacked."

Silence, then, "Aw, no ..." His voice flattened to a whisper.

"She survived and escaped."

She heard his intake of breath, then, "Did they catch him?"

"No, not yet. I'm at the hospital with her now. Her name is Megan. She was ..." She hesitated, wondering how much to say in front of Megan. "She's been badly beaten."

He didn't speak, but she knew what state he was in. Her father had wept often since Ella's disappearance.

"Dad, I want to stay with her, but she's scared for her roommate. Her attacker has her keys and address. She's desperate for someone to go by there and see if Karen's all right. If her car's gone, maybe she got Megan's message and left. But if it's there ..." Her voice trailed off. "It's a green Toyota, and it would be in the parking space in front of their door, next to Megan's car."

There was a long pause. "All right, I'll go. What's the address?"

Krista got the address from Megan, and her father promised to call her when he got there. Krista clicked off the phone and turned to the food. "Now, what looks good to you?"

Megan looked down at the tray. "I don't think I can chew."

"All right. Then we'll start with the Jell-O."

fifteen

Another girl attacked. David absorbed the news like a poison, and it sickened him. But as life seemed to drain out of him, anger pumped adrenaline through his veins.

He pulled himself together, washed his face, and headed out to his car. He punched the address into his GPS and listened to the calm, unemotional voice telling him which way to drive.

His jaw ached as he chewed on the news. Another attack. It was too much.

If the killer was out there with his latest victim's house keys, he would be easy to trap. They should set up a stakeout of the girl's apartment and watch for the man to come. They should have a forensic artist at the hospital now, to draw a composite.

But the police had their own methods, ineffective though they might be. He couldn't trust them at all, not after they'd questioned him like a suspect a few days after Ella went missing. Cases like that mother who drove her sons into a lake, then claimed they were kidnapped, had made parents the first suspects in the disappearance of children.

Now he saw the police department as more of a nemesis than an ally. He couldn't forgive them for dragging their feet in searching for Ella in those first twenty-four hours. They hadn't even issued an Amber Alert until they finally saw the video from outside Sinbad's Convenience Store—and that was forty-eight hours later.

But it may not have mattered anyway. Ella had probably died within hours of her kidnapping.

This killer had to be stopped.

He reached the apartment complex, counted the buildings, and found Megan Quinn's townhouse. In the space in front, he saw the green Toyota, next to a white Hyundai. His stomach sank.

He double-parked behind those two cars and sat in his for a moment, staring at the door. His breath seemed trapped, his heart squeezed. Megan said Karen would be home if her car was there. Wanting to believe she was in there safe, oblivious to the danger, he got out of his car. David's limbs felt wooden as he started to the door. He knocked, but there was no answer. He banged more urgently. Maybe she was sleeping.

Or maybe Ella's murderer had come. Maybe he was in there now. David looked down at the doorknob. There was no way to tell if he'd used her key. He got a handkerchief out of his pocket, turned the knob.

It was unlocked. His heart jolted. And as he looked down at the knob, he saw a smear of blood on the casing.

Something had already happened.

The killer could still be there. He thought of bolting in, grabbing the man, and murdering him. But if he wasn't there—if the girl was dead—he'd taint the evidence that could lead the police to the pervert. His hands trembled as he pulled his cell phone out of his pocket. He dialed the number of the detective he'd been working with.

"Pensky."

"Detective, this is David Carmichael." David's pulse pounded in his temples.

"Hi, David. How are—?"

David cut him off. "You should have told me another girl had been attacked."

Silence. "David, we've been busy. We got the call in the middle of the night. We haven't had the chance—"

"My daughter Krista is with her."

Another pause. "With who?"

"The girl who was attacked last night. Megan." David scanned the windows of the apartment. The blinds were closed. "She asked me to come by Megan's apartment to check on her roommate. The door's unlocked, and there's blood on it. The girl's car is here."

"*Here?* You're there now?"

"Yes." He bent over, hand on his knee, trying to steady his breath. "I'm not leaving until you send somebody here to see if she's all right. Megan said the police told her you were doing that already. Why didn't you? Why didn't you send someone? Why didn't you watch for him?"

"We did. Her car wasn't there last night when we checked, so we posted a plain-clothes cop to watch her apartment."

"Well, where is he?" David yelled.

"He's in a tan Pontiac."

David scanned the cars, saw one that fit the description. He stalked toward it, and saw a man with his head back … sound asleep. With the heel of his hand, he struck the guy's window. The cop jumped.

"You idiot, you slept while a killer went into that apartment!"

The man opened his door. David grabbed his collar, pulled him out. "Get in there! She could be bleeding to death!"

He heard Pensky's voice in the phone. "Let me talk to him, David."

David thrust the phone at the useless cop, then turned away, both hands clutching his head. He heard sirens.

The groggy cop handed David his phone and headed for the door. "Calm down. She's probably just in there sleeping. You know how college kids are."

David looked at him. "So … what? You think she cut her hand on the way in? That maniac may be in there now."

As police cars descended on the place, David went back to his car and tried to stay out of the way.

He should call Krista back, tell her what he'd found. But why upset her and traumatize the girls further until he knew for sure?

Two cops went to the door, banged on it. Finally, pulling on gloves, they tested the knob. The door came open.

David leaned against his car, aching with hopelessness, as the cops went in, guns drawn. He waited for them to come back out, prayed that the girl wasn't there …

But moments ticked by too slowly, and they didn't come back. Instead, an ambulance arrived on the scene, no lights or sirens heralding its arrival.

She must be dead. David covered his mouth and wept. He watched, horrified, as they roped off the area with crime-scene tape.

Finally, Pensky pulled up. The detective got out and crossed the parking lot to David. "I guess you know by now."

David's face twisted, his lips compressed, and his forehead ached with the fresh wave of grief. He rubbed his mouth. "She's dead?"

"Yes. You were right. She wasn't home when we checked on her last night, but apparently the killer was waiting when she got home. I can tell you that the guy we stationed here will soon be looking for another job."

David turned and gave his car a savage kick, denting the fender. "What are you people doing? Why haven't you stopped this maniac?"

"David, we're working on it. This case will give us some trace evidence and DNA. Megan Quinn's case gave us even more, and she'll be able to identify the killer. We're making progress."

"But your progress comes from girls who are raped or dead. How many more?" He bent over again, staring at the pavement, trying to keep from imploding.

"David, I know this is hard. But I need for you to pull yourself together and go to the police department to make a formal statement about why you were here."

Not again. David's mouth fell open. "I told you why I came."

"We just need it in writing."

David breathed a disbelieving laugh. Being on the scene made him a person of interest. He might have known.

sixteen

The sudden ringing of Krista's phone made her spill the water she was helping Megan sip. She grabbed a napkin and dabbed at the wet spot on the girl's gown.

"Answer it," Megan said, pushing the cup away.

Krista checked the screen, clicked it on. "Dad?"

"Krista." Her dad's voice was shaky, hollow. "It's bad."

Krista reached out to steady herself on the bed table. "No, Dad," she whispered.

Megan stared at her. Krista heard his heavy breathing.

"The police ... they're in there."

Krista backed away from the bed, desperate to protect Megan from this news.

But Megan knew. Her face looked as if she'd just been beaten again. "She was there, wasn't she?"

Krista swallowed as that debilitating anger crushed

down her own sorrow. The muscles in her face grew tight, rigid.

"Karen!" Megan cried as she brought her hands to her face.

Krista pulled the girl into her arms and held her.

....

Megan's parents arrived at the hospital with swollen eyes and red noses from weeping at the horror that had intruded on their daughter's life. Krista left the hospital, assuring Megan that she would keep her informed about the search for the killer. When she got back to her car in the parking lot, she stared at the windshield. Rage pounded in her ears, and vengeance shivered through her body. Something had to be done.

She wondered what state her father was in after burying his own daughter, then discovering the murder of another. Already, he was falling apart. She had no comfort to offer him. But *she* would not crumble. She had to hold herself together long enough to do something that mattered.

With shaky hands, she called Ryan Adkins. His secretary did her usual avoidance routine. "I'm sorry, ma'am. Ryan's in a meeting. Is there anything I can tell him for you?"

"Tell him this is Krista Carmichael," she bit out through stiff lips. "Tell him a girl was brutally attacked and beaten last night. Tell him they found another murdered girl today. Tell him that makes three attacks connected to your company. That's what you can tell him for me!"

The secretary put her on hold, and Krista waited, tasting the bile in her throat. If he didn't come to the phone, she would go to GrapeVyne herself, find him in his meeting, and drag him out. She would throw a holy fit until everyone in that company listened.

After several minutes, he picked up. "Krista, this is Ryan."

"Another girl was murdered!" she yelled into the phone.

"Murdered? They called me this morning and told me she survived, that she was in the hospital."

"No, it's not her! Megan Quinn survived. It's her roommate."

"What?"

"This killer had Megan's keys and all her information, and he used them to go and finish the job he botched last night when he left Megan alive. He went to her apartment and didn't find Megan there, so he murdered her roommate." She wished she could see his face, because the silence on the phone told her nothing.

He cleared his throat. "Well, that's horrible."

"Is that all you have to say? Two girls are dead, another is beaten half to death, and a killer is still out there, using your community as a weapon. That would make you an accomplice."

"Krista, you're going too far—"

"You are responsible," she cried. "You've provided a haven for killers and online predators. You're so smart you came up with a billion-dollar company in your dorm room. Why don't you use some of those brains to figure out a way to catch this monster?"

"We're working on that now, Krista."

"Well, you're not working fast enough. How many other girls are going to die before you figure this out?"

"We've been talking to the police. They're on the case."

"The police didn't prevent this last murder, even though Megan told them she was worried about her roommate. My father had to go there and find her himself. My father, who'd just buried his own daughter, had to watch them roll another girl out on a gurney." She took in a wet breath. "Someone who was probably murdered by the same person who got Ella." Her voice was trembling, and she knew she was on the edge of an eruption that would make her seem hysterical. She tried to breathe.

Lowering her voice, she said, "Ryan, I'm appealing to you one more time. You seem like a decent person. You've got to do something about these Thought Bubbles." She wiped the tears from under her eyes. "You've created a trap for your clients to be stalked and destroyed, and if you can't find a way to stop these predators, then you need to shut your business down."

"I can't shut my business down, Krista. That wouldn't solve the problem. There would still be predators out there. They would just go to Facebook or MySpace or Twitter, or two dozen other places."

"I'm not asking you to do anything about the other ones. I'm only asking you to do something about yours."

"I'm doing what I can, Krista. I really am. I'm horrified by what happened to these girls. Just now I was in a meeting with my security team and with my legal counsel."

"You're going to *need* legal counsel," she snapped. "I'm going to file a lawsuit that will put your company out of business. I'll find every person who's gone missing connected to online communities, and we'll do a class action suit. I'll go before congressional committees and make them regulate what you guys do. I'll educate the public and make sure no sane parent will let their children go on these places ever again!"

"And how will you educate them, Krista? By using our communities? You used GrapeVyne to post your message to the killer. You used it to rally volunteers to search for Ella. I looked at your page, and you use it in your ministry for Bible studies. There are a lot of good things about GrapeVyne. It's not all evil."

"If you want to save the good, Ryan, then you need to do something about the bad."

His voice was maddeningly unruffled. "Well, I'm not shutting it down. Give me something realistic to do right now, and I will."

Krista tore a tissue out of a box on her console and wiped her nose. "There's a girl lying in the hospital right now who wants desperately to identify the killer. The police have given her all sorts of pictures and mug shots, but she hasn't been able to identify him yet. Maybe you could come to her room and show her pictures of her friends on Grape-Vync, and help her figure out if it could be any of them. Something she tells you might rattle something in that brain of yours. If you bring your own computer, you could probably dig into profiles of suspicious members. She says he was a middle-aged man with brown hair, about 220 pounds. He told her he'd been stalking her on GrapeVync."

"All right," he said. "Tell me which hospital. I'll go this afternoon."

She dropped her face into her hand. She supposed that would be all right. Megan's parents would want everything possible done to catch Megan's attacker.

"What's her condition?"

"Her jaw is broken and wired shut. She has torn ligaments in her knee, broken ribs, bruised kidneys. Both eyes are swollen, her lip is stitched, she has bruises that look like black ink. I don't think I have to tell you the rest of it."

Again, silence.

"He raped her and tried to bury her, too, Ryan. It's a miracle she got away. She's scared to death in there. She thinks he's going to come after her again."

"Then will you go with me? Since you already know her that might make things more comfortable for her."

His concern for Megan's comfort surprised her. She sighed. "I can't go until later this afternoon. I'm speaking at my sister's high school today. I plan to give them an earful."

"Why don't you give me a call when you're finished, and I'll meet you at the hospital?"

She hesitated a moment, wondering if she should tell him to go without her. But then she thought of Megan, devastated and upset. He was right. She would be afraid of a strange man in her room. Besides, she'd probably be dealing with police all morning and most of the afternoon. Yes, maybe he should wait for her. "All right," she said. "After I'm finished at the high school, I'll give you a call. Tell your secretary not to make me jump through hoops or threaten to bring down the company to get through to you."

She clicked off the phone and looked into the mirror, wiped her eyes. This had to be one of the worst days of her life. It went at the bottom of a list that kept growing. She was amassing quite a collection.

seventeen

Ryan hung up the phone and rubbed his face. Another girl dead. What was he going to do about this? Though he had to defend the company's image, he couldn't help feeling there was more that could be done.

Needing wisdom, he picked up the phone and called Henry Hearne, his mentor and one of the most influential members of his board of directors. "You got a minute to talk in person?" he asked.

"Sure, Kid. I'll be right over." Henry, one of the wealthiest men in the country, was the only one he knew who got away with calling him "Kid." Ryan took it as a term of endearment, since Henry had become a friend to him in so many ways.

A few minutes later, Henry knocked on his door, then stepped inside. Ryan motioned him to a chair. "Thanks for coming, Henry. I need some advice."

Henry took the chair across from Ryan's desk. Though he wore his usual suit and tie, he carried himself with comfort and an ease that made him more accessible than the "suits" who intimidated Ryan.

"You look like you're having a bad day," Henry said.

Ryan folded his hands under his chin. "It could be better."

"I worry about you, Kid. I don't think you're enjoying your role as CEO as much as you used to. Is the bureaucracy getting to you?"

Ryan smiled and shifted in his seat. None of the other board members would have asked him a thing like that. He was just expected to get along with them.

But Henry was different, and Ryan appreciated him. He was a humble man, who'd never paraded himself in front of the cameras like some of the other board members did. You'd never see him on talk shows or news commentaries, even though he had a wealth of knowledge about the economy and building businesses. He could put Donald Trump to shame. Henry owned a huge share of Willow Entertainment and ran its Internet division. He had been among the men who'd negotiated to buy Ryan's business and allowed him to stay on to run it. If not for Henry, he'd be one hundred million dollars poorer right now. And without the technology Henry had created at Willow Internet Division, GrapeVyne wouldn't be worth billions in advertising revenue.

"Sometimes I miss the good ole days, when it was just us computer nerds having fun."

Henry rubbed his chin, crossed his legs. "The company's going through growing pains now. It won't always be like this."

Ryan glanced at his monitor. "These murders are really getting to me. I got a call from the FBI this morning. Two more girls were attacked last night. One of them is dead."

Henry's eyebrows drew together. "Two more? Here in Houston?"

"Yes." Ryan leaned back in his chair. "And there are cases like it all across the country. Kids missing after agreeing to meet someone they friended online."

"All of them are connected to GrapeVyne?"

"Some, yes. I never bargained for this when I created the site. I just wanted it to be a fun place for people to hang out and communicate with their friends. I didn't think of predators scouring the sites for victims." He scratched his face and lowered his voice. "Henry, Ella Carmichael's sister keeps calling me and demanding that we make changes to the site. She considers me an accomplice to the killer. She's talking about a lawsuit."

"Well, that's ridiculous. This is not your fault, Kid. And it's not GrapeVyne's fault. Blaming us is like blaming Vint Cerf for creating the Internet. We're no more responsible for these attacks than he is."

"She suggested we remove Thought Bubbles from our system, since they encourage people to post too much information."

Henry chuckled. "If we took them down, the subscribers would just start Twittering. It wouldn't make anyone safer."

Ryan got up, looked out the window onto the street below. "But maybe some of her suggestions aren't out of line." He turned back to Henry. "What if we started reporting these cases on the advertising sidebar, so people could see how dangerous it is to post things that are too specific?"

"Do I need to remind you that without the ads on those sidebars we can't stay in business? We need all of that space."

"Then we need to figure out another place on the pages where we can put warnings, someplace where people will read them. Maybe we could send out a notice to everybody once a week with the latest missing persons. Kind of update them on what's going on. Sort of an online Amber Alert that would help locate missing persons, but also constantly remind them what could happen."

"So every time they log on, you want to hit them in the face with some dead kid who met his killer online?"

"No, not every time. Just once a week."

"Kids wouldn't read it."

"Then we send it to their parents."

"We don't ask them to provide their parents' information if they're fourteen or above."

"Well, maybe we should, Henry. Maybe that's something we can change."

Henry laughed. "And that will help our business, how?"

"Well, it might not help our business, but it could save lives."

Henry got up and came around the desk, set his hands on Ryan's shoulders. "We've got to let the police handle this, Ryan. The more entangled you get in this situation, the guiltier we'll look. You won't be able to stop and say this has gone too far. If you take any responsibility at all for what happened to these girls, you might as well take all of it."

Ryan sank back down. "If these attacks just hadn't happened right here in Houston."

Henry slid his hands into his pockets, jangled his change. "You said two girls were dead. What happened to the third?"

"She's in the hospital."

"Is she conscious?"

"Yes, I think so."

"And what's the prognosis?"

"Well, I guess she's going to survive, but she was beaten pretty badly."

He paced across the office, staring at the carpet. "Has she been able to identify the killer?"

"No, not yet."

Henry rubbed his face, then fixed his eyes back on Ryan. "Maybe when they find the guy it'll be clear that this had nothing to do with us. Girls who are irresponsible with information on the Internet might be irresponsible in other ways. She could have gotten involved with the wrong guy. It could be anything. We don't necessarily know that it had anything to do with GrapeVyne."

"She said that the killer *told* her he'd been following her on GrapeVyne."

"Ryan, I'm warning you, you need to stay out of this. If the press calls, avoid them."

"What if they corner me? What if I have to talk?"

"Then take as little responsibility as possible. Tell them that your security team is doing all it can to provide protection for our clients, but that ultimately it's the responsibility of the members. Then wash your hands of it."

"I'm not sure I can." Ryan didn't want to tell him that he'd agreed to go to the hospital that afternoon or that Krista was going with him. He knew what Henry would say. "Thank you for your advice, Henry. I appreciate it. I always value your wisdom."

Henry went to the door. "Think of the company, Kid. Hundreds of jobs depend on you doing the right thing."

He closed the door, and Ryan dropped back into his chair. Hundreds of jobs might depend on him, but hundreds of lives might also. There must be some way to provide a little more safety for their clients.

He had a team that had helped build this community and was able to capture the imaginations of millions of people. Surely they were creative enough to put security measures into place to ensure that this kind of thing didn't happen anymore. All it would require was educating the public. But how could they do that, when people rarely read their Terms of Service anymore and skipped right past any notices that GrapeVyne sent out? Nobody was interested in what they had to say.

He didn't like the idea that Krista, as an individual, was doing more than his entire company to make online communities safer—speaking at a school this afternoon, after learning of Megan Quinn and her roommate. As upset as she'd been when she called, he couldn't imagine how she'd hold together to give a speech.

Then again, he'd seen her strength.

Where had she said she was speaking? Maybe he needed to attend. Her small voice had the power to do great damage to his company. But somehow, he couldn't think of her as the enemy.

He got online and went to Ella's GrapeVyne site, found the name of her school.

Then he packed his laptop in his briefcase. He'd show up at the school, wearing sunglasses and a ski cap, blending into the crowd so that he could listen to Krista. If he was careful, no one would notice him. He could still look like a high school kid if he tried. He'd had virtually the same wardrobe since his high school days, after all.

He got his jacket, shrugged it on, and told his secretary he'd be out for the afternoon.

eighteen

Ryan looked like anything but a student as he pulled his Jaguar into the high school's parking lot, behind the bus he'd followed from the Vo-tech a few blocks away. The car had caught the attention of the students at the back of the bus. But if he could distance himself from his car, he might be able to blend in. He pulled his gray ski cap over his ears, and shoved on his sunglasses. Then he ambled up the sidewalk as students stepped off the bus in front of him.

He followed the last of the students into the building, blending in like one of them. A teacher stood in the school corridor, directing traffic.

"Into the auditorium, people. Quiet as you go in."

The students ignored the teacher's admonishment to be quiet as they followed the others pouring in. Ryan went in and took a seat in the back row.

As the auditorium filled up with chattering kids, he saw Krista sitting on the front row next to the principal. She looked pale and small, and as she turned to talk to the principal, he saw dark circles under her red eyes. But her chin was high and determined.

He watched as teachers monitored the place, keeping order among their students, but the low chatter seemed disrespectful. He wondered if they knew that Ella's sister was the speaker and that they were here for such a serious matter.

When everyone had taken a seat, the principal went on stage and spoke into the microphone. "I guess you all know we're here today to remember Ella Carmichael, who was a dear friend to so many of you and whose death impacted our lives greatly. I've asked her sister to speak to you today, and I hope you'll pay attention to her, because she has something to say that you need to hear. This is Ella's sister, Krista Carmichael. Krista, come on up."

There was a smattering of applause as Krista took the stage. She hadn't dressed up for the occasion. She wasn't here to impress anyone. She stood in a pair of jeans and a cream-colored sweater, her unadorned blonde hair long and straight.

Krista took the microphone. "Thank you, Mr. Trenton." She looked down at the floor, collecting herself.

Even from where he sat, Ryan could see how hard this was for her.

"First, I'd like to thank you all for helping so much when Ella was missing. A lot of you came and volunteered to help look for her, and for that I'll be eternally grateful. As you know, she was found, and her death tells a story that's important for us to hear. Ella's life had a purpose, even though it was short." Her voice broke. She cleared her throat, looked down, and went on.

"And if Ella's death can save your life, then I'll believe that even that had a purpose."

Ryan watched as she crossed the stage to a cart that held a laptop computer. A PowerPoint slide projected Ella's GrapeVyne page onto the screen behind Krista. Krista pointed out all the places where Ella had given information to her killer. Her voice was flat and emotionless as she went through each of the Thought Bubbles and pictures, moments in Ella's life recorded for all to see. The school was so quiet, you could hear a whisper.

Krista put the microphone close to her mouth and stepped to the edge of the stage. A shadow fell over her as she moved out of the stage lights. "Guys, what I'm trying to say is that the killer is still out there. He's reading your profiles, listening in on your GrapeVyne Thought Bubbles, your Facebook status updates, your Tweets. Last night a girl from Rice University was attacked, and just like Ella, her Thought Bubbles led the killer right to where she was. She escaped and is in the hospital now, but after she escaped, the killer went to her house and murdered her roommate."

A gasp rose from the crowd, and Ryan saw faces turning to each other as they whispered. Some of the girls began crying.

"I was with her when she got the news about her roommate." She stopped, and Ryan looked across the auditorium. No one was looking down at their phones, sending their own Thought Bubbles through cyberspace. They were all transfixed on Krista.

"He's bloodthirsty," she said into the microphone, just above a whisper. "And you could be next. Don't think that just because you post things only to your friends that you're safe. You all know that you've accepted people as Friends who you've never met, that you've looked on someone's profile when they asked to Friend you and thought, 'Hey, that person looks cool.' You don't know who's behind that cool picture. It could be the latest up-and-coming rock star, or it could be somebody's killer. And I realize I'm scaring you to death. But if that's what it takes to make you think about what you post online, then I've succeeded today. And Ella's death will not have been in vain."

She charged them with going home and changing their profiles, erasing anything on their online sites that would give a predator information, deleting any Friends they didn't know personally. Ryan sat in the back row, realizing how much damage she could do to his company if she spoke publicly more often, or if she contacted the media. Part of him rooted for her and hoped she succeeded; the other part dreaded the trouble her success would cause him with his board of directors.

When she finished, Ryan stayed in his seat as the students ambled out. He'd never seen a high school assembly break up with such thoughtful silence. Many of the students wiped tears from their faces or patted each others' backs as they exited the room. No one here had escaped the impact of Ella Carmichael's death.

He got up and walked against the flow of people down to the front row where Krista stood. She was shutting down the computer as she spoke quietly to the principal. As he went toward her, Ryan took his hat off and kept his face down, and waited on the side of the auditorium until the principal walked away.

The moment Krista was alone, Ryan approached her. "Good job," he said.

It took her a moment to recognize him out of context. "Were you here the whole time?"

"In the back."

Her eyes narrowed suspiciously. "Why did you come?"

"I just wanted to listen."

"Well, you heard." She closed the laptop. "And hopefully all the students will go home and make some changes."

"Hopefully," Ryan said.

"But there are only six hundred students here. Grape-Vyne could reach several million at once."

He hit his cap against his leg. "You have to understand, Krista. I don't own the company anymore."

She breathed a laugh and bent over to put the laptop in its case. "Give me a break."

"Seriously, I'm not the one who's calling the shots."

"Get real. I've read about you. You've got a hundred million dollars sitting in the bank and a seven-figure annual salary to keep working there, but you're not in control? Every employee there works for you."

"But I have a board of directors I have to answer to. You have to understand that if profits fall, I'm going to be out. There are clauses in my contract that make me accountable to them."

"Is that why you slunk in here on the sly? So no one would recognize you? Are you embarrassed to be seen here? You afraid they'll fire you?"

"I didn't want to distract anyone from you."

"I would have gladly given you the microphone."

"Okay," he admitted, "I've been cautioned not to get the company entangled with this. We're not responsible, and my being here could be misinterpreted."

She zipped up her briefcase with a jerk. "You are responsible. You're just as responsible as any business who invites kids onto their premises. If a fire broke out and children were killed, they would be sued. Well, get a clue. A fire has broken out, and people are dying." She grabbed her purse off her seat, slung the strap over her shoulder, and started for the door.

"Krista."

She stopped and look back. "What?"

"I thought we were going to the hospital."

Her face was still pink. "I figured you had some excuse not to go. Don't want your board of directors mad at you, do you?"

"I said I would go, and I will."

She looked like he'd ripped her sails. "All right. We'll go now. I'll drive."

He had to smile. She wanted the upper hand, and he supposed she had earned it. He followed behind her as she made her way out of the building.

nineteen

The local media had gotten wind of Megan's attack and Karen Anders' murder by the time Ryan and Krista arrived at the hospital. They clustered outside the main entrance with their cameras cued up and their reporters waiting for word about the person they were now calling a serial killer.

Though Ryan knew no one was watching for him, he feared the reporters might recognize him if he and Krista went in that entrance. In fact, Krista just might cause her own stir.

"Pull around, and we'll go in through the ER entrance," he said.

Krista didn't argue as she drove to the other entrance and found a parking space.

Ryan carried his briefcase with his laptop and followed

Krista into the hospital and down the long hall. Her shoulders were stiff, guarded. He wondered what she was like when she smiled. He didn't suppose she'd done that in quite a while.

As they approached Room 323, Ryan dreaded the encounter. This was out of his comfort zone, something he never would have done if guilt didn't plague him. When friends from work were hospitalized, he never went to see them. Didn't everyone hate being visited when they felt their worst?

Krista knocked. A voice called for them to come in, and she pushed the door open and stepped inside. Tentatively, Ryan followed her in, and saw what he assumed were Megan's parents, sitting on the vinyl sofa next to the window. On the bed lay a girl who looked lucky to be alive.

"Krista," the girl said.

Krista crossed the room and bent down to hug her. "How is she doing?" she asked Megan's parents.

"She's okay," her mother said. "It's been a rough day."

Ryan stepped further into the room. Krista turned back to him. "Megan, ... Mr. and Mrs. Quinn, this is Ryan Adkins."

They gave no indication that they recognized the name. "He's the President and CEO of GrapeVyne Corporation."

Megan's parents still didn't bat an eye, and she realized they didn't know what that was. Megan tried to sit up. "The guy used GrapeVyne to get to me," she said through her locked jaw. "The man ... he's on GrapeVyne somewhere. He told me. The FBI sent a composite artist, but my description wasn't good enough. The picture wasn't right. It didn't look enough like him. We can't use it at all."

"Don't beat yourself up," her father said. "It was dark and you were traumatized."

"But I saw him clearly at the airport. I know I'd recognize him if I saw him. I just get confused when we break it down into eyes and nose and mouth ..."

"That's why I'm here," Ryan said. "Maybe I can help you identify him. I'm really sorry about what happened to you."He set his briefcase down on a chair, pulled his laptop out. "I pulled out the Friends that you and Ella Carmichael have in common. There are about twenty-five."

"Really?" Megan asked. "I don't even know anybody in high school here."

"But you had 1500 Friends."

Her parents gave Megan an astonished look. "Fifteen hundred people?" her mother asked. "You posted your thoughts for fifteen hundred strangers?"

Megan shook her head. "I know you've talked to me about giving out information to strangers, but Mom, it was such a great way to make friends in college. And a great way to stay in touch with old friends. I didn't know ..."

She did know, Ryan thought. Her parents had clearly warned her. "Ella had a lot of Friends too—1143 of them. And since there are only six hundred people at her high school, she couldn't possibly have known most of her online friends. A lot of them were probably complete strangers."

"I shouldn't have Friended anyone I didn't know," Megan said. "I wish I could take it back."

"Well, we can start with where we are," Ryan said. He set the laptop on her bed where she could see the screen. "Do you know any of these twenty-five people personally?"

She went down the list. "I know Michael and Greg. Susan ..."

He deleted everyone she mentioned, which left nineteen people she'd never met. "Krista, come here and tell me if you recognize any of these as being real people that Ella knew."

Krista came over and looked at the list. She was able

to identify four people as Ella's personal friends. That left fifteen suspicious profiles, most of them girls.

"This gives us a starting point," Ryan said. "I'll turn these names over to the FBI, and their cyber crimes unit can trace these people back to their original source. If anyone is not who she says she is, hopefully they'll be able to tell."

Krista stared at him. "Can't you tell right now?"

"All I can do is look at their profiles. It's against our Terms of Service for people to set up aliases, but people do it all the time. And that makes it tricky to track down their real identity."

Megan's father stood up. "How long do you think it'll take for the cyber crimes unit to trace these people back?"

"I don't know," Ryan said. "I don't know how many people will be working on it or how much time they're devoting to it."

"My daughter's attacker is still out there," he bit out. "He killed her roommate. He could come after her again."

"They haven't posted a guard?"

"No, we've asked for one all day, but nothing's been done."

Krista turned to him. "You have influence, Ryan."

He frowned. "What?"

"You could call the FBI or the police or whoever, and get them to station a guard outside Megan's room. This is life or death. She's not safe."

He looked at the girl with the bloody eye, at her father, her mother. Krista was right. They did need to guard her. "Okay, I'll make a phone call right now." He would pay someone himself if he had to.

It took about two minutes for Ryan to tell his secretary what he wanted done. When he snapped his phone shut,

Krista turned back to Megan's mother. "Is someone staying with her tonight? Because I'd be glad to."

"One of us will." Megan's mother patted the bag next to her. "I have a gun, and I'll use it in a heartbeat."

Megan closed her eyes, her face twisting. Krista shook her head. "It's a dangerous world we live in. And it's getting more dangerous all the time."

By the time they came out of the hospital, word had gotten out that Ryan Adkins was there. Reporters surrounded the door they'd gone in, and flashed pictures and shouted questions as they came out.

"Ryan, why are you here?"

"Is GrapeVyne responsible for the murders?"

"Do you know the girl who was attacked?"

Ryan muttered "No comment" as he and Krista pushed through the crowd to her car. By the time they got it unlocked, one reporter had realized who Krista was.

"Miss Carmichael, do you think the same person who killed your sister is involved in the latest attacks?"

Krista got in and closed the door. As Ryan slipped in, he said, "Go! Let's get out of here."

"How? They're blocking me!"

"Just pull out slowly. They'll have to move."

Krista pulled out, and the crowd grudgingly parted. She put the car into Drive and inched forward.

"Keep going," Ryan said. "Just move. They'll get it."

She finally got through them and drove to the exit. "They'll follow us."

He watched in the rear window as the reporters ran across the parking lot toward their cars. He turned back around and searched for an escape. There was a strip mall up ahead. "Pull in there and go behind the buildings. They'll race right past, and then we can head back to my car."

She did as he suggested and took a hard right, pulling behind the stores. Hopefully none of the reporters had gotten to their cars in time to see her turn off the road.

She cut off the engine, and they both sat motionless. Krista finally broke the silence. "That was crazy."

"Tell me about it." He looked back. No one had followed. "It worked. Let's just sit here a minute until they all have time to pass." He drew in a deep breath. "My board of directors isn't going to like it. *I* don't like it. I never should have come."

"You did the right thing, Ryan."

"It'll be all over cable news before I can get back to the office."

"It's a good thing. It shows that GrapeVyne cares."

"Yeah, well, my board members may not see it that way." He leaned his head back on the headrest and closed his eyes. He didn't want to think about it, so he racked his brain for something to talk to her about that didn't involve the murder. "So what do you do for a living?"

She glanced at him as though the question surprised her. "Why?"

"Just wondered. I don't know much about you."

"I work with at-risk teen girls, at a rec center called Eagle's Wings."

He opened his eyes and frowned. "Eagle's Wings? Where'd that come from?"

"From the Bible — Isaiah 40:31. It says, 'But those who hope in the Lord will renew their strength. They will soar on wings like eagles; they will run and not grow weary, they will walk and not be faint.' The girls we minister to need strength. We get them off the streets, help them get their GEDs, teach them Bible studies, train them with life skills, and counsel them."

That explained the Bible studies on her GrapeVyne page.

He could have guessed she worked in a cause-driven job. "So who pays you?"

"We're supported by several local churches and individual donations."

"Not much money in that, huh?"

Krista shook her head, clearly irritated at his question. "Everyone's not motivated by money, Ryan."

He took the blow. "I read your GrapeVyne page. You were valedictorian in both high school and college. You could have gotten some big corporate job, but you chose to work for a nonprofit?"

"That's where I'm needed."

"So where is this place?"

"It's on Kickrow Street."

"Really? That's a pretty bad area."

"Exactly. That's where our girls live."

"But ... don't you feel like you're in danger coming and going every day?"

She stared at a spot on her windshield. "My dad was totally against it when I took the job. He worried himself sick. But I convinced him that God was calling me there, so he finally let it go. It's ironic that I wasn't the one who was stalked and murdered. He never thought it would happen to Ella."

Her gaze fixed on something outside the window, and he felt her melancholy growing heavier. "Have you been back to work since her funeral?"

She nodded. "I was there Tuesday. I warned the girls about GrapeVyne."

Tuesday? She was even tougher than he thought.

"When we painted the front room of the center, I painted scripture along the top of the wall. The first thing you see when you come in the building is, 'Be strong and courageous,' from the book of Joshua. The girls who come there, they need that courage and strength. They're all in danger every day of their lives." Her voice cracked. She cleared her throat. "I try to teach them how to put on the armor of God to protect themselves. But I didn't protect Ella."

He looked at her. "Krista, you can't seriously be blaming yourself."

She didn't answer, and for a moment he thought she was going to shut down. She'd probably never meant to get so personal with him. But he was glad for the glimpse into her heart.

"Really, Krista," he said softly. "How could it be your fault?"

The corners of her mouth trembled. "It was my job. I've been helping raise her since she was born. My mom died after complications from having her when I was eleven. My dad ... he was so changed by Mom's death ... he couldn't really connect with either of us that well for a while. I kind of took over, like her surrogate mother."

"Tough duty for an eleven-year-old. But even your mother couldn't have protected Ella from this guy."

She clutched the steering wheel, her knuckles white. "Why didn't I teach her the dangers of online predators? I had her password." Her voice lowered to a whisper. "I was so busy working with the girls in our ministry that I neglected my own sister!"

He touched her arm. "Krista, it wasn't neglect. You couldn't be there for her twenty-four/seven."

"If I had just watched her Internet activity, she'd be alive." Tears welled in her eyes. "But ... maybe I can save another girl. Someone else who's making herself prey for this guy. Maybe I can catch him and stop him."

Something in her tone told him she had a plan. Was she going to go looking for this guy? "Krista, it's fine to be strong and courageous. But don't let your guts lead you into danger yourself."

She looked at him then with those intense eyes. "That's what real love is all about. Putting yourself on the line."

"For people you don't know?"

"I don't have to know them to care what happens to them." Sighing, she turned the ignition. "The coast is probably clear by now."

"Yeah," he said.

She was quiet as she pulled out into traffic and headed back to the school, where Ryan's car was parked. As he turned her words over in his mind, he told himself he was reading too much into them. She hadn't said she was going to do anything stupid. She was a rational person, after all.

By the time they reached the school, Ryan had convinced himself that Krista's plan was to speak at more schools about the dangers of online communities.

As she pulled up next to his car, Krista looked over at him. "Thank you for coming. I really appreciate it."

He sat motionless for a moment, not wanting to get out. "I know what you think of me."

Her chuckle had no glee behind it. "Oh yeah? What do I think?"

"That I'm some corporate pig who's just trying to make a buck."

She didn't answer.

"But the truth is, I was just a computer nerd, fooling around with an idea, and it got blown all out of proportion."

"Poor you."

Man, she was tough. "I'm not complaining," he said. "I just don't like being painted with that brush of yours. When I watched you get up and talk to those kids today, I was amazed. You had them in the palm of your hand. They were riveted."

"They knew Ella," she said. "She was well-liked. Her death hurt all of them."

"But it was more than that," he said. "You're a good speaker. I'm guessing that you make a big impact on all the girls you work with."

That didn't seem to give her any pleasure. "Thank you."

"I'm just saying that you have determination and a passion that comes out in your speaking. If you went on TV and did interviews ..."

"I don't want to go on TV and talk about Ella."

"Then would you consider just coming to talk to my board of directors?" The words were out before he could recall them.

She snapped a look at him. "Are you serious?"

"Yes. I don't think it would hurt anything for them to hear from you directly. In fact, it might be a good thing. I can't promise you that the changes will be made, but it could at least give them the perspective that I've gotten from listening to you."

Her face softened. "I would really appreciate that opportunity."

Their eyes locked, and he fought the urge to push a stray strand of hair out of her eyes. "You remind me of the way I used to be," he said.

Again, she whispered a laugh. "Why do you say that?"

"Confidence, passion ... feelings I used to have."

"Used to? You seem pretty confident to me."

He shrugged. "Things have changed a lot since I started in my dorm room. I was happier sitting in a twelve-by-fourteen room with a bunch of computers and a few friends, trying to fill a need, than I've ever been running a major corporation. But again, I can't complain."

"It sounds a little like complaining."

"No, not at all. I'm happy to be where I am. Who would have expected a kid like me to make this much money? I was raised by a single mom who worked two jobs. I only went to MIT because I got a full ride."

"Willow's offer must've blown you away."

"It did. I bought my mom a new house. Helped her retire."

She almost smiled. "That's nice."

"Yeah, it was kind of fun. She always did everything for everyone else. No one ever did much for her. She was the casserole queen at church. When someone died or was sick, she was the first one over with her casserole and a hug." He paused and lowered his voice. "But then she met Louis, her new husband, and he started milking me for as much money as I'd give them."

"Really? Your mom let him do that?"

He wished he had some water; suddenly his mouth was dry. Why had he taken the conversation here?

"She was lonely and she loved him."

"What about your dad?"

"They're divorced." He hoped she caught the period on the end of that sentence. He opened his door and started to get out.

"You grew up in church?" she asked, stopping him.

He smiled. So that was what impressed her. "That's right. Every time the doors opened."

"Do you still go?"

"No, haven't been in years."

Her disappointment was clear, and he wished he had a better answer. "Did you stop believing?"

He wondered why the question made him so uncomfortable. "Not really. I still believe in God."

"You just don't think he's worthy of worship?" The words came softly, just above a whisper. Not accusing.

"To tell you the truth, I don't give it much thought anymore. Church isn't what it should be."

"What do you think it should be?"

"I don't know. Honest, authentic, not just a list of don'ts."

"My church is honest and authentic. You should come with me sometime."

He smiled and checked her eyes. Was she serious? The thought of going anywhere with her energized him. "I'd like that."

"Really?"

"Sure, why not?"

"Because I'm the enemy, according to your board of directors. One of those people you're not supposed to get mixed up with."

He knew she was right, but if he had this chance to spend more time with her, he wasn't going to let it pass. "They can't keep me from going to church."

"Okay. You can go with me sometime. Meanwhile, I'll be waiting to hear back from you about talking to your board of directors."

He nodded, wondering if he should have even mentioned it. He might talk himself out of it before it actually happened. He got out of the car, leaned back in. "About Megan, I'm going to keep working on this. I really want the killer to be found. I want you to know that GrapeVyne will do everything we can to help the FBI find him."

"Thank you." She reached in her purse and pulled out a business card, handed it to him. "Just in case you find out anything ..."

He took the card. "All right, then we'll be in touch." He took a last look at her, wishing he could stay a little longer. Finally, he got into his car.

twenty

K rista's house was dark when she got home, but her father's car sat in the garage. She stepped into the house, went into the living room where he usually sat watching the news. He wasn't there. She turned on the light, chasing away the dark shadows that hung like specters over the place, and walked into the hallway.

"Dad?" she called.

"In here." She heard his voice coming from Ella's room, and she stepped into the doorway and saw him sitting in the dark on Ella's bed, his legs crossed beneath him, his back leaning against the wall. How many times had she seen her sister sitting like that on the bed, watching *The Hills* on television and talking to her friends on her laptop?

She turned on the lamp. Her dad's face came into view. His eyes were red, bloodshot. "Dad, are you all right?"

His lips were tight, and his tongue seemed to rub something on his teeth. "He'll kill more of them," he said in a hoarse voice. "It's not over. He's kindled his bloodlust now. It's going to get even worse."

She went to the bed and sat down next to him, touched his knee. "Dad, I'm so sorry I sent you to that apartment. I never would've done it if I'd really thought—"

"The cop fell asleep," he cut in. "She warned them. And the guy who was supposed to be watching out for her ... fell asleep." He rubbed his mouth. "Have they notified Karen's parents yet?"

"I don't know. I'm sure they probably have."

His eyes settled on some distant target, and she knew he was imagining the phone call those parents had gotten.

"I spoke at the high school this afternoon," she said, hoping to change the subject. "I think it went well. I'm hoping that some of the kids will listen."

"The killer could be one of them. It could be anybody. A kid ... a teacher."

"Megan says it was a middle-aged man, not a young man, if he's the same one who killed Ella."

He locked into her eyes. "Middle-aged? Really? I thought it was ... one of her friends." His eyes filled with tears again, and he raised his hand to rub the stubble on his jaw. "I thought it was Tim Moore."

"I met Tim at the funeral," she said. "I never thought it was him." She wondered how long he'd been sitting here like this. The despair in his eyes was severe ... She'd never seen him like this. But he'd never had a child murdered before.

"What has this world come to?" he choked out. "I don't want to live in a world like this."

The thought of her father committing suicide had occurred to her more than once. "Dad, I need you. Please don't think like that."

"Everything is so meaningless. What we've built ... our family ... where's the hope?"

Krista racked her brain for some fragment of what he needed. "Today when I was speaking to the high school, Ryan Adkins was there."

"Who is Ryan Adkins?"

"He's the CEO of GrapeVyne Corporation. It's a big victory to have him there, Dad. It means he's listening to me, that he cares. *That's* hope."

"He doesn't care," he sneered. "He's the one who created this whole system that makes young girls spill their guts to any stranger who's watching. He probably just came so he could figure out how much damage you were going to do to his company."

"Actually, it's more than that. He went with me to see Megan, and he helped her identify a few people on her Grape-Vync list who could possibly be the culprit. They probably have fake identities, of course, but it's possible that this is a start. He's telling the FBI. Dad, if this brings about changes in GrapeVyne and saves other lives, then maybe Ella's death does have a purpose. Maybe it's so we would get out there and do something about it. Educate the public. Maybe God has given us a forum here."

"A forum?" He said the word as though it sickened him. "I never asked for a forum. I never wanted to be famous for having lost a child. First God took my wife, and now he's taken my child. If you can find a purpose in that with your precious 'forum,' then you're welcome to it. I don't want anything to do with it."

Her dad had been the one to teach her about purpose and meaning. Though he hadn't ever done Bible studies in their home, he did always get them to church. And when they asked him questions, he answered with wisdom and insight, from a perspective of God's kingdom. It shook her to know that his faith was waning, that doubts were crowding over him.

"Maybe it is just *my* forum. If I can really help people and protect lives, then I want to try. Ryan even said that I could come and speak to the board of directors of Grape-Vyne. That's a huge opportunity, because it could make them take notice and really make some changes."

"They won't listen to you," he said. "They're all about profits."

"I don't think Ryan really is. He seems like a nice guy. Somebody like us."

He got up and walked from the room, his shoulders hunched and eyes on the floor. "Waste your time if you want to."

Krista stayed on Ella's bed, drowning in the wake of his despair. "Ella, what's happening to us?" she whispered. She knew her sister couldn't hear. She was up in heaven with their mother, sitting at the feet of Jesus, thrilled to be there, with no more sadness and no more heartache. She wouldn't want to come home if she could.

Krista walked out into the hall and looked toward her father's bedroom. He'd gone into the dark again, and closed the door behind him. She imagined him sitting on the edge of the bed, staring into darkness. Was he suicidal? Had it gotten that bad? Had her stupid decision to send him over to Megan's apartment been more than he could take?

She checked the cabinet in the bathroom where they kept their prescription drugs, went through each bottle and made sure there was nothing with which he could do himself harm. They didn't have any guns in the house. He'd always been an avid pacifist.

She went into the kitchen and looked around. Her father

probably hadn't eaten any more than she had in the last few days. She couldn't remember the last time she'd choked down a meal, and her clothes were looser than they'd been three weeks ago.

That was something she could do for him. Make him a meal.

She opened the refrigerator, stared at the contents. She needed to go to the grocery store. It was almost empty. But she found some cold cuts and lettuce that had not yet spoiled. She made a sandwich, found some chips in the pantry, poured a glass of iced tea, and took it back to her father.

"Dad?" she asked at the door. There was no answer, so she opened it, looked inside. He wasn't on the bed. She turned on the light and saw him across the room, sitting in a rocking chair staring into the dark.

"Daddy, I want you to eat something. I made you a sandwich."

"I can't eat, Krista."

She took it to him anyway, set it on the table next to him. "Dad, I need for you to eat. Can you do it for me?"

He drew in a deep breath, let it out in a long sigh. "You aren't eating either."

"I will. I promise I'll eat if you will. Ella wouldn't want her death to do us both in. This is a horrible time, and I don't know how we're going to get through it, but I need you to live. Ella is happy. She's with Mom, and she's in a place she wouldn't want to come home from. Whatever happened to her, I have to believe it's all out of her memory now. There are no more tears in heaven."

He seemed to shake out of his reverie, and she saw his eyes fill with the image of what she had just described.

"Please, Daddy. Take a bite."

He picked up the sandwich, brought it to his mouth and

ate. She knew how it tasted to him. He might as well be eating cardboard. He chewed slowly, deliberately. "Eat the whole thing, even if you don't feel like it. Please?"

"You need to let me be, Krista," he muttered.

She got up. "Dad, I'm just trying to save what's left of my family. I can't lose anyone else."

She watched him force himself to take another bite, saw the slow, methodical chewing. "There's iced tea in the glass. I'll get you more if you want."

"Thank you, sweetie. Now you go eat too."

She left the room, and as she rounded the corner into the living room, she realized he'd turned the light back off. Why was he drawn to the darkness now? Did he think somehow he would find Ella there? Ella was in the light, not in dark shadows. But they each had to cope with their grief in their own way.

She went to her computer, turned it on, and pulled up Maxi Greer's GrapeVyne page. She had her own way of dealing with her grief. Luring the killer would bring resolution to both of their pain. No matter what it cost her, she would make him pay.

twenty-one

The clothes Megan had worn into the hospital weren't fit to be worn out. They were soaked with blood and mud, and they'd been shredded as nurses had cut them from her body. Her broken jaw was wired, so she couldn't move it, and tape and bandages covered cuts and lacerations. Her right leg was in a brace that kept her from moving her injured knee.

Her face was swollen beyond recognition, and some of her bruises had turned black, as though her flesh was dying and rotting off. The doctors assured her it was just pooled blood, and the bruises would fade in the next week or two.

They'd given her a wheelchair for the ride to her parents' rental van, and her mother walked behind her, carrying crutches that she would use to get around at home.

Home. She couldn't go back to her apartment, not to

live. Karen's blood was probably still on that regal bed she'd bought when they moved in. Her parents had money, and they'd given her a credit card to outfit her room and the living room. Karen had found an opulent, carved wooden headboard that cost $5,000, the kind of bed you'd keep for fifty years, then pass on to your grandchild. The mattress was top-of-the-line. Megan imagined it soaked in blood now.

Had Karen ever seen the man's face? Did she even know what hit her?

Of course she did. He got his thrills from the things he did before the murder. She was certain he'd tormented Karen first, the way he'd tormented Megan. Surely he'd realized it wasn't her, Megan, as he'd bludgeoned Karen to death. Had his anger at Megan's escape cost Karen her life?

Megan supposed he was committed to murder the moment he crossed the threshold. He'd probably waited hours, then gone to the apartment to see if Megan had somehow made it home. He'd found Karen asleep in her bed, her Bible on her bed table.

You good Christian girls ... so innocent ... so naive.

He had come determined to kill someone. Now Karen's death wouldn't satisfy him. He'd have to come back for the girl who could identify him.

"Honey, are you all right?"

Her mother had been weepy since she'd arrived from New York. The attack on her daughter may as well have been an attack on her. She hadn't slept since Megan called them with the news. She'd sat by Megan's side every day, every moment, refusing to shower or walk downstairs to the cafeteria. "I'm okay," she said, but it was a lie. As the nurse rolled her through the automatic double doors to the outside, Megan's heart raced. Her lungs grew heavy, tight, and she thought they would explode.

Panic. She was a sitting duck, visible to anyone who had her in his sights.

Her dad was waiting in the red minivan with the Hertz sticker. If the killer was watching, it would be too easy to follow. Why had he gotten a red one?

She couldn't breathe.

Her dad got out and opened the side door. "Come on, honey, let's get you in."

They moved the foot rests to the side, coaxed her to her good leg. She stood, trembling. Her head swirled and her vision strobed from black to bright. When the dizziness faded, she looked beyond the car to the parking lot, and the hill beyond. Was he there, waiting for her?

Another car pulled up behind her dad's, and she jumped and almost fell. But a woman sat behind the wheel.

"Come on, honey, put your arm around my neck." Her dad helped her to the car and she slid in. "Do you want to lie down?"

Yes, that would keep her out of sight. "Guess so," she said. Her mother ran around the car and opened the opposite door, put her pillow in, and eased her down. On the other side, her father took another pillow from the cart with the few things she'd accumulated while in the hospital, and propped her leg.

They loaded the things on the cart into the van, then closed the doors. Her mother sat in one of the seats in front of Megan, as her father got into the driver's seat. Megan closed her eyes and prayed that God would protect them.

The ride was silent, except for her mother's sniffing.

"I need to go to my apartment and get my things," Megan said.

"No, not now," her mother said. "Your father will go and pack everything you have. Don't worry."

"Where will he put it? I don't have another place to live." The words brought the sorrow back. So much of her life was changing.

Her mother turned in her seat and looked back at Megan. "Honey, we want you to come home. You need to be with us to recover."

"Mom, we've talked about this."

"Just lay out this semester and you can finish in the fall."

"I can't," she said. "I have a job lined up. I'm starting it in June. They expect me to have my degree by then."

"But school starts in a couple of days. You're not in any shape to get around campus."

"I can't let him take everything away from me. He's done enough. I still have a future. A plan. I can't change it now."

"Honey, there'll be other jobs."

"I want this one." The editing job at a New York publisher was her dream job. She'd spent last summer interning at HarperCollins, and they'd offered her the permanent job in Editorial on her last day. She'd looked forward to it since then. She couldn't wait to finish school and start working.

"You could transfer to a school closer to home."

"No, Mom. Most colleges don't take transfer credits unless you have at least two years' worth of courses left to take. I only have one semester left."

Her mother's protests fell silent. "We'll talk about it later."

Megan lay on the car seat, staring at the cloth ceiling. "I need to call Karen's parents."

"You can do that when we get settled in the hotel."

"I want to go to her memorial service tonight."

Her mother turned around again. "Are you sure, honey?"

"Yes, absolutely sure. She would have been there for me."

As she said those words, she closed her eyes and struggled to hold back the tears overtaking her. Her battle wasn't over. She knew it had just begun.

twenty-two

Karen Anders' memorial service was held on the quad at Rice University, because there wasn't a church, funeral home, or other venue big enough to accommodate the thousands of students who wanted to come. Megan got there fifteen minutes before the service and agreed to let her parents push her in a wheelchair. Without it she'd be standing for most of the service.

Her friends were waiting on the curb, and they all rallied around the car as she got out.

When she was settled in the wheelchair, her friend Brennie came toward her, her face over-bright, as if she hoped her fake smile would lighten Megan's mood. Each day since she learned of the attack, Brennie had spent hours at the hospital, full of chatter to distract Megan. But now and then her grief spilled out.

She leaned over and hugged Megan. "I love you, girl. We're gonna get through this."

Megan wasn't so sure. "Are Karen's parents here?"

"Yes, they want to see you. They're at the front. I'll take you to them."

Before they moved, other friends gave her quiet hugs, pats on the shoulder, tearful smiles. Her ex-boyfriend, who'd moved on to a dance major, was misty-eyed. "I'm praying for you, Meg. You're gonna bounce back. You're a strong person."

She wanted to scream. Brennie took the wheelchair from Megan's mother and pushed it through the crowd. As people stared at her and gasped, Megan felt a rising sense of shame. They all knew what had happened to her, that she'd been violated ...

Would anyone ever look at her the same? As she rolled past, her mother and father beside her, some reached out to give her a reassuring touch. Others whispered to their friends.

She scanned the faces as she cut through the crowd. Was her attacker here? Did he dare come here, when he knew she could identify him? But it was night, and she wasn't likely to see him if he blended into the crowd.

The closed coffin lay on the podium. Megan was grateful that she wouldn't have to view Karen's injuries. Did she look as battered as Megan? Was her face smashed? Her jaw broken? Had he snapped bones before he raped and murdered her?

Karen's parents stood on the grass in front of the podium, accepting hugs and condolences from the line of people waiting to speak to them. She saw the strain on their pale faces, the looks of anguish. Like her, they probably wanted to run away before this final ceremony was held.

Brennie pushed her to the front of the line, and Karen's parents saw them coming. Extracting themselves from those wanting to speak to them, they bent down and clung to her. "Oh, Megan," Karen's mother said. "Look what he did to you."

"I'm okay," she said. "I'll recover. But I'm so sorry ... about Karen. I tried to warn her. I called over and over."

"We know you did," Karen's father whispered in her ear. "We heard all your frantic messages. He just got to her too soon."

The guitar music on the stage began, signaling that the funeral was about to begin. The candles they'd all been given as they arrived were lit, and a soft glow painted the faces of the mourners.

Karen and Megan's pastor preached the service, and told about Karen's sweet heart in ministering to the poor by working at the local soup kitchen once a month. She'd also spent summers as a counselor at a camp for those with cerebral palsy. He told of how she'd dreamed of being a missionary, and how she'd led four people to Christ on her last mission trip to Mexico.

Megan wondered if he'd been told that the killer targeted Christians. Had Karen gotten a martyr's reward when she entered the gates of heaven?

Pastor Mike looked down at Megan and the students standing around her. "Megan, I know from talking to you that you have guilt feelings about this senseless, unbelievable tragedy. But Karen wouldn't want you to suffer in that way. She wouldn't want you to give that man the satisfaction of your self-torment. This was not your fault."

Megan squeezed her eyes closed, shunning comfort.

"Mr. and Mrs. Anders, what Karen would want is for you to know that she's in a place more beautiful and miraculous than anything we could imagine on earth. And in heaven, time doesn't pass like it does here. Let her have her joy, and be assured that before she knows it, she'll be with her family and friends again."

The group of friends who did everything together held hands in a grief-stricken chain as they stood around the wheelchair, and Megan's own parents looked like they might fall apart. As the sermon finished and the praise band led them in a praise chorus, Megan stayed silent. She couldn't open her mouth wide enough to sing, and besides, she didn't have a song in her. She was tired ... exhausted ... and in pain that racked through every nerve of her body.

But she would go to the burial ceremony no matter what it cost her. She would be there for Karen now, even if she wasn't there for her before.

twenty-three

The candlelight memorial service for Karen Anders was underway when David got to Rice University. He pulled into the parking lot adjacent to the quad, and saw what looked like thousands of students assembled there. He got out of his car, slid his hands into his pockets, and walked toward the crowd.

A friend of Karen was on the stage telling stories about her, and kids wiped their eyes and hugged each other.

David didn't hear the words. He hadn't come here to listen. He'd come because this perverted killer was the type who fed on the suffering he caused. He would have come here and pretended to care, watched the faces of other potential victims, stalked more prey.

David's gaze touched on one face after another, searching for someone who looked out of place.

He saw several people his own age, their faces illuminated by the candles they held. Megan said he was in his
forties ... brown hair ... 220 pounds ... five-ten or eleven.
David scanned the crowd, looking for anyone who fit that
description.

And then he saw him ... a man standing on the outskirts
of the crowd, not holding a candle. His back was to David,
so he couldn't see the man's face. He stood with his hands
in his jacket pockets, as though the service didn't move him.

David moved closer to him, and in the glow of the security light overhead, he saw the writing on his jacket.

Emerson High School.

Ella's school!

David's heart stumbled as he moved closer. The man's
face came into view. It was Ralph Krebbs, Ella's history
teacher, who also went to their church. He was a deacon
and Sunday school teacher, and the basketball coach of the
girls' church league. He had brown hair, looked to be about
five-eleven ... probably around 220 pounds.

Instant hatred registered in David's chest, locking in his
certainty that he was the one. Of course. Why hadn't he seen
it before? He wasn't just some nice guy who cared about the
spiritual lives of his students and players. No, he was a pervert, a stalker. He was capable of horrible things.

Though it was forty degrees, David broke out in a sweat.

Someone got on the stage with a guitar and sang the
chorus of "The Anchor Holds." As candles flickered and
tears glistened, David knew what he had to do.

....

When the service broke up, David watched as the teacher
spoke to a few students. Several girls came up to Krebbs
with hugs. As he watched, David clamped his teeth so tight

that his jaw ached. He fought the urge to run up to them and warn the girls to get away from him, that he might be a hardened and cold-blooded killer, and that if they weren't careful, one of them could be his next victim.

As Krebbs started back to his car, David followed at a distance. He saw him get into a blue F-150 pickup, in a different parking lot than David had parked in. As Krebbs started his truck, David hurried back to his own car. He pulled out in traffic, desperately trying to see the F-150, but he'd lost him.

He wiped the sweat on his forehead with his sleeve and called information. "Houston, Texas," he said to the automated voice. "Ralph Krebbs."

He waited as a human came on and helped him figure out which Ralph Krebbs it was. When he was pretty sure he'd gotten the right number—one with the same prefix he had at home—he got the address.

It was only a few blocks from his house, and two blocks from Sinbad's, where Ella was last seen.

It had to be him. Why hadn't he thought of it before?

He found his way to the right street, and drove slowly down it, looking at mailboxes and counting down to Krebbs' house. What did he know about the man? He was single, middle-aged, no children of his own. Put on a nice-guy act at church, had everybody fooled. Even David had been fooled.

He saw the house then, and there was the blue pickup sitting in the carport. He must have just gotten home.

David pulled his car to the curb outside the house and sat there for a moment, staring toward the lit windows, wondering if Krebbs was online now, stalking his next unsuspecting victim.

David thought of just calling the police, but what would he tell them? That Krebbs looked suspicious at the service?

That he fit the profile? That he had access to these young girls? That they might have trusted him?

No, they'd blow it off and say there was no evidence. But David didn't have time for a nice clean case, while Krebbs murdered more young girls.

But he didn't have a weapon. All he had were his bare hands. Though it felt like enough, he knew Krebbs was bigger than he was. If Krebbs overpowered him, this opportunity to expose him would be wasted. He wasn't afraid for himself, but he couldn't risk Krebbs getting away with any evidence.

Instead of killing him, he'd go in his house like an unannounced guest and find the evidence he needed.

It was time to act.

He got out of his car and crossed the grass. Biting his lip, he reached the front door. Blood pumped into his fingers, strength and danger into his hands.

He knocked on the door.

He heard the sound of a TV, heard footsteps as Krebbs crossed the room. He heard the bolt being turned, the door creaking open.

Krebbs looked out at him and smiled. "David ..."

David didn't recognize his own voice. "I need to talk to you," he said.

twenty-four

Krebbs stepped back from the door, inviting David in. "Of course we can talk. I was just thinking about you."

As he closed the door, David's molars ground. "Oh, yeah?"

"Yes. I was at that girl's funeral at Rice."

"Karen," David said. "Her name is Karen."

"Right." Krebbs gestured for him to sit on the couch, but David kept standing. "Her poor parents. I thought of you and Krista, what you must be going through."

It almost looked authentic. David looked around the room for anything that could confirm his suspicions. But Krebbs was a neat freak. Nothing lay out of place.

"David, I heard about a grief support group at a Presbyterian church—I can't remember which one, but I can find out if you think you'd be interested."

David rubbed his stubbled jaw. "I don't know if I'm ready for that."

"Okay, I understand. When you're ready ..."

David forced himself to look at the man. "I've just been trying to create a time line. I wondered, when was the last time you saw Ella?"

Krebbs' gaze darted away. "Had to be at church, the Sunday before she disappeared."

David saw the computer on the desk in the living room. The screen saver flashed different personal photographs every few seconds. He watched as the girls' basketball team filled the screen. Slowly, he stepped toward it.

"My Sunday school lesson that day was about how Satan roams around looking for someone to devour ..."

The screen saver picture changed, and he saw Krebbs standing with his arm around Ella. She was in her basketball jersey, a trusting smile on her face.

Fury erupted in his chest. Setting his chin, David reached out and moved the mouse. A GrapeVyne page sprang to life, Karen Anders' face in the upper corner. His mouth fell open.

"David, that picture was taken at our last game."

David turned and lunged. Krebbs fell as David got his hands around his throat. Krebbs fought him off, clawing his neck to loosen David's grip.

"You killed her, didn't you, you slimy piece of garbage!"

Krebbs' voice was strained and shredded. "No, David! Stop!"

He was bigger than David, stronger, and he managed to flip David over and break his grip. David grabbed his hair, and kneed his groin, pulled him to his side, and was on top of him again.

"She trusted you," he spat. "You betrayed her and raped her."

He couldn't get his hands around Krebbs' neck again, so he grabbed his red face. Veins bulged out.

Krebbs kept his chin pressed to his chest. "I didn't do it, David!" He hit David, threw him off, and slid across the floor to a table by the door. He got a drawer open as David threw himself at him again.

Krebbs pulled out a gun and flipped around, slid away from him. "Get back, David."

David stopped, his breath coming in gasps.

"I don't want to hurt you."

David looked at the gun. He had failed again. "Just go ahead and shoot," he said. "Just kill me too."

Krebbs got to his feet, holding the gun aimed at David's chest. Sweat covered his face, and his breath was heavy. "David, I understand why you'd want me dead if I killed Ella. But I didn't. I *didn't*."

"I saw you at the service tonight."

"Yes, I was there. I just wanted to show my support for the family. And some of her friends came from our youth group. I wanted to be there for them. I could never hurt Ella, David. Never. The week she disappeared I was out of town, in Washington, DC, getting the Teacher of the Year award." He reached for a framed newspaper article on the wall, thrust it at David. "That's me in the third row with all those other teachers."

David took the picture, looked at the date.

"And a few nights ago, when those two girls were attacked, I had two basketball games that night. At least a hundred people saw me there. You can check. Yes, I have Ella's picture. She was a great kid. I want to remember her. And everybody in Houston has gone to Karen's GrapeVyne page today."

David felt the life draining out of him. He sat back on the floor, set his hands on his knees, and lowered his head.

Could it be that he was wrong? The alibi looked convincing ...

Krebbs sat down on the floor facing David, still holding the gun. His face twisted, and he began to cry. "David, I'm so sorry she's dead. Please believe me."

David covered his face. What had he done? He'd come in here ready to commit murder. He'd been so sure.

He was losing it. And now he was in real trouble. "Go ahead and call the police," David said.

Krebbs shook his head. "I don't want to do that."

"Why? I would have killed you if I could. I tried."

He lowered the gun. "Nobody has to know, David."

David wiped his face and looked at Krebbs. He knew him to be a good man. He worked hard for the church, for the school, for the kids. He'd been a good influence, a help in raising Ella and Krista.

How could he ever think he was capable of murder?

Krebbs put the gun down and got up, held out his hand. David took it, and Krebbs pulled him to his feet.

"I'm sorry," David managed to say.

"It's okay, man. I would have done the same thing."

"I thought ..."

"I know."

David pulled in a long, ragged breath. Wiping his face again on his sleeve, he went to the door, opened it.

"David, next time you suspect someone, call the police. Don't just go in swinging. Somebody might kill you."

David closed the door and stepped back into the night. He hated who he had become.

And more than he ever had before, he just wanted to die.

twenty-five

The friends and trusted employees in Ryan's inner circle hated a conference room setting, so he'd designed a special room that inspired their creativity. It looked more like a playroom than a conference room.

The place had a bank of computers around the walls for war-room type work, when they all needed to be online together. But instead of a table in the center of the room, there were couches and chaise lounge chairs. A cappuccino maker and theatre-style popcorn popper sat on the counter, and in most of their meetings, someone brought in a pizza or donuts to snack on while they worked.

To offset all the calories consumed in this building, Ryan had installed a gym on the first floor, where they could burn them off.

He'd brought no food today, but he hoped they'd still give him their best.

Bridgit, a chubby thirty-year-old computer analyst, was wearing sweatpants and a wrinkled T-shirt that looked like it had been slept in. He pictured her getting up this morning and forgetting to shower or brush her teeth. She was focused, and her single-mindedness always benefitted GrapeVyne.

Deuce, Shaffer, and Eli were all programmers who hated to be pulled away from their cluttered desks. Ryan hoped he could engage them in this new project so they wouldn't sulk.

Ian came in with Andrea and Alexis, twins with off-the-chart IQs. He'd met them in college, and they were among his first hires. He could always depend on them.

Ian had finally showered, and his hair actually looked clean, though Ryan doubted he'd run a brush through it in days. He had that glazed look that told Ryan he'd been deep in the middle of something on his computer, and probably hadn't even looked away in hours.

They came in and took their various seats around the room, some lying down with their feet on the arm of a sofa, others plopping in front of the computers.

"Everybody's here," Ryan said. "I appreciate you all coming."

"Nothing to eat?" Deuce asked.

"No, not right now. This is serious, guys. I need to have a brainstorming session."

That made some of them perk up. They loved brainstorming.

Ryan sat on the pool table, and with his legs swinging, said, "Guys, I'm sure you've all heard about the murders."

"What murders?" Andrea asked.

"Ella Carmichael and Karen Anders."

"Who are they?" Alexis asked.

Ryan sighed.

"They're the girls who were killed by an online predator who found them through their Thought Bubbles," Eli said, scratching his shaved head. "What planet have you been on?"

"I've been busy," Alexis said. "Besides, I don't watch the news. It's too depressing."

"Obviously."

Ryan went back over what had happened to both of the dead girls, as well as Megan's attack. "I was thinking that maybe we could get a little more proactive in figuring out who the killer is. Maybe we could use the Data-Gather program to isolate who the killer could be."

"That program's only for advertising," Ian said. "Besides, none of us works with it. All that data is gathered on the Willow side."

"I don't even know what it is," Shaffer said. "What are we talking about?"

Ryan slid off the table and went to the computer he had hooked up to the projector. The computer desktop came up on the big screen.

"Data-Gather is a program someone at Willow designed so that the advertising department could gather information about our clients and target them in their ads."

"Target them how?" Andrea asked.

Ian was getting irritated. "Andrea, stop proving that geniuses have no common sense."

Eli threw a paper wad at Ian. "They don't pay her for common sense. See Andrea, advertisers don't want to waste their money advertising maternity clothes to men. They don't want to advertise wrinkle cream to teens. So we use the program to spy on our subscribers."

"Okay, I got it," Andrea said.

"No, not spy," Ryan said. "We just gather a few basic facts they post in their profiles, like their age, their gender, their region of the country, the kind of music they like ... stuff like that."

"And that's legal?" Andrea asked.

"Perfectly. It's being done all across the Internet. Advertisers love it, because they get a lot more bang for their buck."

"So you called us here to explain the Data-Gather program?" Bridgit asked, looking at her watch.

"No. I wanted to brainstorm about how we could use that software to help identify who the predators are on GrapeVyne."

"You mean, like, have it flag all those who look at porn?" Deuce asked.

"That would be one way. Maybe it could flag them if they look at porn and have underage girls as their Grape-Vyne Friends, or if they go to the pages of people outside their age group. We could also tweak it to monitor whose pages they're viewing."

"Sounds a little like Big Brother," Alexis said. "Creeps me out."

"Maybe we should *be* Big Brother, not in the Orwellian sense, but in the sense that we're protecting our younger siblings."

"So you want us to brainstorm search criteria for the Data-Gather program, to make it find predators?" Ian asked.

"Yes. We get the computer to do the work for us."

"But who's going to follow up with the people who are flagged? What if we find potential predators? What do we do with them?" Bridgit asked. "Do we turn them over to the police? Doesn't that kind of cross the line of privacy laws? Doesn't it equate to illegal searches?"

"We'll get the attorneys in on this eventually, to make sure we don't violate any laws. But meanwhile, I just want you guys working on the new search strings. I know you're all really busy, but this needs to be done ASAP. I don't want any more girls to die."

In seconds they were all at the computers, pulling up ideas and hammering out solutions.

He knew they'd conquer this before the day was out.

twenty-six

The "Welcome Home, Megan" sign on the door of the Weiss College dorm lifted Megan's spirits somewhat. She'd been assigned to that dorm when she'd come to Rice University as a freshman, and though she'd moved off-campus, she would be considered part of the Weiss College family until she graduated. Since she dared not go back to the apartment where Karen was murdered, Brennie had invited her to room with her. Brennie's former roommate had flunked out the semester before, and they hadn't assigned her a new one yet.

Megan felt she would be safer in the dorm than she was in an apartment. It had more security, and people couldn't come and go unless they had a key or checked in at the front desk.

The girls who'd turned out to welcome her hugged her

with teary eyes and condolences. Megan would rather have come in unnoticed. She didn't want to talk, didn't want to answer questions, didn't want to have to comfort those who were torn up over her plight ... and Karen's death.

Her apartment was still a crime scene, so her father was only allowed to go in for a moment, while the detective was there, to get some of her clothes and personal items. It didn't take long to move those few items into the dorm.

The girls helped her, then left her alone to say good-bye to her parents.

As soon as they were alone, her mother burst into tears. "You don't belong here, honey. You need to come home. I can't stand the thought of leaving you here."

"I'll be okay, Mom." But the way she spoke with her wired jaw belied her words.

"You need to heal. Getting around campus with that knee is going to be a major ordeal. And you're the only witness. He might come after you—"

Megan knew that was true. She expected him every moment of the day and dreamed about him at night. "I won't go out alone, ever," she said. "I promise, Mom. I'm not going to take chances. I'm scared too."

Her father's face seemed etched with sorrow. "I checked," he said, "and you can withdraw with a partial refund up until February 19. If you decide you can't handle it, honey, you call us, and you can fly right home."

"I know."

"Even if you decide after that date. We'll forfeit the money."

She pulled them both into a hug, and they all wept. Then finally, they let her go.

She said good-bye to them, then lay on her new, unfamiliar bed, staring at the ceiling. Classes started the day after tomorrow. She needed to run some errands, needed to buy a new phone. But she felt so weak, so tired, and pain still racked through her. How would she manage?

After a while, Brennie came back in and sat on the edge of Megan's bed. "Okay, so what do you need to get done before classes start?"

"I need to get a new cell phone."

"Okay, let's go."

Megan sat up. "You don't have to—"

"Megan, I love you, and I'm all yours today."

"But you've done enough, letting me move in when you finally had the chance to have your own room."

"I hate living alone. And I hate not being able to check on you when I'm not here. So let's go get that phone."

....

Since Megan hadn't posted her phone number on her GrapeVyne site, she thought it would be safe for her to activate her new phone with the same number she'd had before. Since she didn't have her SIM card, she'd have to enter her phone numbers again.

But as soon as the clerk turned it on, she heard a chime. The clerk handed it to her. "You must have gotten these texts after you lost your phone."

Megan took the phone and saw a series of texts from her friends. Karen's was prominent.

> Megan, where are u? I thought you'd b here by now.

Then:

> I'm going out. Call me when you're home.

Brennie snatched the phone. "Don't read these. It's not healthy."

Megan grabbed it back. "Don't erase them!" She scanned through them, reading each one, chronicling her friend's attempts to reach her while Megan had been fighting for her life. Finally, she came to the last text, dated yesterday.

U can't hide from me. I'll kill you next time.

Megan dropped the phone as though it had burned her. "What is it?" Brennie asked, stooping to pick it up. "The text. It's from him." "Him?" Brennie picked up the phone, read the text. Breath whooshed out of her, as if she'd been kicked in the gut. "Megan, we have to call the police."

....

As soon as Krista got the call from Megan, she met her at the police station and sat with her at the police detective's desk. They'd brought Megan several more books of mug shots to review, and still she hadn't been able to find the man who'd attacked her. Krista wished she could help her, but only Megan knew what he looked like. She wondered if Megan was in any shape to remember details about the killer. Maybe she just hadn't seen him clearly. Maybe she couldn't remember.

"I see him so vividly in my dreams," Megan said. "I'll never forget that face. He didn't look like someone who could do something like that. He looked normal. Nice. I wouldn't have gone with him if he'd looked evil." She closed the book of mug shots. "Why isn't he here?"

"Maybe he's never been charged with a crime before."

"That's the only people in these pictures?" she asked. "People who've been arrested before?"

"I think so."

The detective who'd been out of the room for some time

came back in. "I have good news," he said. "The text came from a pay-as-you-go phone registered under a bogus name. We pinged it, and we have it located. If this dude has it with him, we just might be close to catching him."

Krista squeezed Megan's hand. "Are you going to pick him up?"

"I just dispatched some men to go there. If you don't mind hanging around for a minute, Megan, we might need you to identify him."

He went out of the room, and Megan began to sweat.

Krista touched her shoulder. "Are you okay?"

"Yeah. I just ... I'm afraid to see him."

"I don't think they'll make you stand face-to-face with him. They'll probably have you look at a line-up. That's what they do on TV. You can see them, but they can't see you."

Megan was trembling, her thin emotional cord frayed. Krista's own heart raced with anticipation and dread. "Let's pray, Megan. They have to catch him."

....

They were still praying when the detective came back in. They both looked up. "Did they catch him?" Megan asked.

He sighed. "We got the phone, but not him. We found it in a Dumpster."

Krista closed her eyes, and Megan dropped her head down on the table. "Oh, no."

"Where was the Dumpster?" Krista asked.

"It was on Willow Court, near the GrapeVyne Corporation building."

Megan brought her head up. "GrapeVyne?"

Krista frowned. "Wait a minute. Are you saying that the killer, knowing Megan would reactivate her phone, bought a go-phone and texted her this message, then tossed it in the GrapeVyne Dumpster?"

"That seems to be the case."

"Well, do you think it's someone who works there?"

"He'd have to be stupid to dispose of it near where he works. He'd know we could locate it."

"But maybe he *doesn't* know. Maybe he thought a go-phone was so anonymous that it couldn't be traced to him."

"We're considering every possibility. But it's more likely that he's playing with us, reminding us that GrapeVyne was his tool for finding you. There aren't any residential homes on that street. It's only businesses, and GrapeVyne and Willow Entertainment take up two city blocks. The Dumpster was between the two buildings."

Krista and Megan looked at each other, unsatisfied. Krista didn't know which scenario to believe. But it couldn't be a coincidence.

twenty-seven

I t was found at GrapeVyne? When?"
"Saturday."

Ryan held the phone to his ear and stepped to the glass
wall that separated his office from his employees. "No way,"
he told the FBI agent. "Nobody here would have done anything like that."

"It may not be one of your employees. But just in case,
we need to know who in that company viewed Ella's or
Megan's pages prior to their attacks."

Ryan frowned. "I don't have any way to find that out.
Not without going to each person's individual computer and
looking at their browsing history."

"Then maybe that's necessary. We can send some people
from our cyber crimes task force to help us figure this out.
We can do it after hours."

"But even if you find someone, that doesn't mean that person is guilty. My employees are all over our members' pages. Someone might have gone to their pages for some other reason."

"It's a starting place. We'd like to do it tonight."

He sighed. "Well, I have no objections, but I do have employees here at night. Some of my workers don't ever go home."

"Then we need you to shut it down for tonight. Tell them they *have* to go home."

He didn't like the sound of that. "I can't do that without clearing it with my board of directors."

"You don't have any authority to make decisions on your own?"

"Well, yes. Some. But this is a pretty big deal."

"We need secrecy, Ryan. If we tell everyone what we're doing, there's no point in doing it. We don't want to give people the chance to clean up their caches."

He finally agreed, knowing he was going to catch a lot of flack for it. Before he made the announcement, he decided to ask Ian's advice on what to tell the workers. He hurried across the floor to his friend's desk. As he approached him, he saw Megan's face on Ian's computer screen.

"Whatcha doing?"

Ian jumped. "Man, you scared me." He turned back to his monitor and minimized his screen so the picture would go away. "Nothing. I was just looking at her page, trying to get a clue."

Ryan sat down on Ian's cluttered desk.

"I've been working on the Data-Gather code," Ian said. "I called Willow and asked for their software, but they were reluctant to give it. No worries, though. I hacked into their computer and got it on my own."

Ryan winced. "You did what? You can't do that! I could have called Henry Hearne and asked him."

"That's no fun. You can still ask him, but we've gotten a head start. And just in case he says no, we'll still have it."

Ryan didn't like the sound of that.

"Bridgit's been working hard to make the modifications in the search strings. Maybe if we stay until the wee hours, we'll get it done."

"Not tonight," Ryan said. "I need to close us down tonight."

Ian rubbed his eyes. "What for?"

"The FBI asked me to. I'm not sure why, but they need to do some investigating in here tonight."

"Here? In our offices?"

"That's right. Seems the killer texted Megan, threatening her. They pinged the phone and found it in a Dumpster outside our offices."

Ian's face changed. "No way. Are you kidding me?"

"That's what they said."

"So ... what? They're going to search GrapeVyne?"

"I don't really know what they're going to do," he lied. "They just want to come in, and they've asked me to shut it down. I need to come up with a story to tell the employees. Something that makes sense."

Ian stared at his own reflection in his screen. "Tell them we're shutting down for some computer maintenance."

"Will that fly, when they're the ones who do the maintenance?"

"Oh, right. No, it probably won't." He snapped his fingers. "Tell them we have a leak in some of the water lines, and you have to get a construction crew in."

"Yes, that would work."

"Some of them can work from home anyway."

Ryan hadn't thought of that. Most of them worked on their laptops from home. How would the FBI search those computers?

This was just too complicated.

But somehow, he'd have to figure it out.

twenty-eight

Since the FBI didn't want Ryan announcing that they were coming that night to spy on his employees' computers, he could do nothing about them taking their laptops home. But that still left all of the desktop computers in the building, including those used on the customer service floors.

He let the cyber crimes agents in and paced the floor as they studied each computer's cache, to see who had viewed Megan's or Ella's pages before their attacks. Because they were also working on his own computer, he lay on the couch in the Rumpus Room and tried to sleep while they worked. But sleep wouldn't come.

Whose phone had sent Megan that text? Could it be someone here at GrapeVyne? Could he be working with an evil serial killer?

It couldn't be any of his engineers. But maybe it was someone he didn't know well. Someone from customer service. He hoped the agents found what they were looking for.

When they'd finally narrowed it down to sixteen computers that had viewed Megan's or Ella's pages in the days prior to their attacks, they enlisted Ryan's help. He went from one computer to another with an agent named Levin, looking to see how the page was viewed, and what business that employee might have had there.

He sat down at Sharon Crain's computer. "Sharon's one of my photo screeners. So she could have legitimately hit both girls' pages if they posted any photos."

"Megan posted one just minutes before her kidnapping," Agent Levin said. "Ella posted one the morning of her disappearance. So what does Sharon do here?"

Ryan showed them. "We try to filter out porn. So her job is to delete pictures that are pornographic. I only have women doing this, since the men might get hung up on it."

"Makes sense."

He pulled up a screen with a hundred thumbnail snapshots. "These are some of the pictures that were uploaded to our site today. Sharon would scan these pretty quickly, deleting anything that catches her attention." He skimmed the page, found a picture that wasn't appropriate, pointed it out.

"So technically, Sharon wouldn't have necessarily gone to Megan's page. She just would have looked at the photos Megan uploaded, and that would register as a hit on her page."

"Right," Levin said.

"She may not have even done more than glance at it. Moving at the pace she does, she would move right past it."

"Okay, she's fine. We're looking for a man, anyway."

They moved on to the next six on the list, who were also women who did the same task.

The next person on the list was someone in customer service. They pulled his computer up, and Ryan did a search to see how he'd used the girls' pages. "Okay," he said. "This guy checks for spam operations. Whenever a member adds too many Friends in one day, he goes to their sites to make sure they're not just hitting people with spam."

"What kind of client would do that?"

"Bands, for instance, or authors, or any other commercial enterprise that's using our site to advertise. There are parameters they have to abide by according to our Terms of Service."

"Can you tell if either of the girls did that on the day he viewed their pages?"

Ryan went deep into their program and pulled up a spreadsheet. "Yep. Megan added thirty-five new Friends three days before her attack, the same day this guy viewed her page. Perfectly legit."

"All right, let's move on."

They went through everyone else on the list, and in every case, there was a reason the employee was drawn to Megan's or Ella's pages.

By the time they were finished, it was 4:00 a.m. Ryan felt the stress in his neck and down his back.

"So that covers every computer except for the laptops that went home last night?" Levin asked.

"Right. Those and the computers at Willow," Ryan said.

"Wait. Willow has access to GrapeVyne members?"

"Technically, yeah. They handle the advertising data, so they have servers with information about our members."

"Then we'll need to examine their computers too."

Ryan shrugged. "Guys, I don't have any access to Willow.

I'm not even allowed to go through their building without security. They're extra tight over there."

"Then who do we need to contact?"

"One of the executives at Willow. John Stanley, Henry Hearne, or the big guy himself, Marvin Bainbridge."

Levin sighed and looked at his watch. "Well, we're probably not likely to get anyone on the phone tonight. If we have to go through those guys, we'll have to have a subpoena and search warrant. By the time we get all that, the killer could have deleted all his information."

It only then occurred to Ryan that he should have demanded a search warrant too. But that wouldn't help them find the killer any faster. He'd wanted to help in any way he could. "Good luck with that, guys."

"Maybe you could put in a word, get them to invite us to do the same thing over there."

"They don't listen to me," Ryan said. "They have their own agenda, and they're pretty tough to convince of anything. I'm the stepchild of the whole company. They can't ignore me completely, though, because of how much money GrapeVyne makes the company."

By the time the agents left, Ryan was wiped out. He locked up behind them, got a change of clothes out of one of the file cabinets in his office, and went to take a shower. When he'd gotten dressed, he stretched out on the couch again and tried to get a couple of hours' sleep before his people began arriving for work.

twenty-nine

At 5:00 a.m., Krista was still at her computer. So far, her alter ego, Maxi Greer, had twenty-eight people who'd agreed to be her Friends, and twelve more had initiated friendship. She focused on those twelve, certain that the killer might be among them.

But she couldn't appear too anxious. She had to play it slow, to keep his interest and not raise any suspicion.

She wrote:

> Guess I should go get an hour or so of sleep. I can't sleep late this morning.

A boy named Sammy answered her.

> Why not? You're homeschooled, aren't you?

Quickly, she checked his profile. He was from Houston, in the same area as she. She wrote:

Yes, but my mom makes me get up early to do
school before she goes to work. She'll kill me if
she finds out I've been on here all night.

····

What time do you get up?

····

Six. She goes to work at ten.

····

So you only study for four hours?

····

Yes, it's a pretty intense four hours.

····

What do you do for the rest of the day?

This was the kind of question a predator might ask. Getting her schedule would be at the top of his priorities. She
swallowed.

Hang out by myself and watch TV.

Her face burned as she waited for a reply.

Sounds like fun.

As she touched the keyboard, her fingers trembled.

You should come over sometime and hang out.

Again, a long pause.

I have school.

····

So come after school.

She waited, certain that she'd found the man who murdered Ella. But he was gone too long. Where was he? Had
he signed off?

She'd almost given up, when his answer flashed onto the screen.

> I can't go to a stranger's house. You could be
> an axe murderer for all I know. Hahaha.

The wind was knocked from her sails and confusion overtook her. Could he be exactly who he said he was? A sixteen-year-old kid talking to a girl on the computer?

Was *she* the predator?

Another line flashed up.

> And you shouldn't be inviting strange guys over.
> Don't you know about those girls who were
> murdered?

Her throat almost closed.

> Sorry. You're right. I'm stupid like that sometimes.
> ....
> It's okay. It was just me. But next time, it might
> be someone crazy. I have to get some sleep
> now. Talk to you soon, okay?

He signed off and she sat back in her chair, wondering if this was the killer's modus operandi, to build trust in his victim. Or was this just some kid who really thought she was stupid?

How could she know? She realized she was sweating and wiped her forehead on her sleeve. She really did need some sleep.

Before signing off, she sent out a Thought Bubble:

> Going to bed so my mom will think I slept, so
> I can get up and study and sit by myself. Like
> every other day.

She hoped the killer's antennae went up at the sound of her loneliness. Maybe, if Sammy wasn't the one, the real killer would contact her tomorrow.

Or was he too smart to interact with her? Maybe he was just listening. Some of the people who'd Friended her hadn't talked to her at all. He could be biding his time, gathering information from all the other conversations she was having, putting things together.

Soon enough, she'd have the chance to draw him out. Soon enough, she would see her sister's murderer face-to-face.

thirty

Brennie was a good friend. On the first day of classes, she drove Megan to the Liberal Arts building and let her out at the curb. Though Megan had learned to get around fine with the crutches, walking all the way across campus was a little too difficult, especially with a backpack on her back. After class, her friend Jennifer, who didn't have class until the afternoon, would pick her up and deliver her back to the dorm.

Staying around other people at all times would keep the killer from coming for her. At least, that was what she hoped. But he was bold and hungry, and didn't think like a sane person.

She limped into her class and took a seat at the back of the room. A couple of people spoke softly to her as she passed. Others just regarded her with sad eyes. Some ignored her altogether, as if they feared embarrassing her.

She emptied her backpack and laid her books on her desk, then slipped into it. One of the girls who'd spoken when she came in got up and came to her. "Do you need something to prop your foot on? I could run get you a chair."

Already she could feel her leg swelling under the brace. Propping it up would help. "If you don't mind," she said. "I don't want you to be late."

"No problem, I have plenty of time." The girl rushed out and came back in with a folding chair.

She set it up sideways, then lifted Megan's leg and carefully placed it on the chair.

"Better?"

"Much. Thanks. I really appreciate it."

The girl went back to her seat as the rest of the class filed in. Finally, the professor came in. Megan had had her before and knew how tough she was. The only way to pass her class was to take copious notes, then spend hours going over them. She tried to focus as the woman began.

Ten minutes in, she found herself watching the door, almost expecting the killer to step into the doorway with an AK-47 and mow down the entire class, just to make sure Megan died. Her heart raced, her chest felt tight again. Her vision went from bright to black, then back again.

"Miss Quinn? Are you all right?"

She blinked. "Yes. I'm fine."

"You looked like you were about to faint."

She decided to make a joke of it. "My skin looks really white against the black of my bruises."

Nervous chuckles rippled over the room.

"Let me know if you need anything," the professor said.

Compassion from this, the most hardened of her professors? She felt that shame again. She hated pity.

She tried to tune back into the lecture, but couldn't focus. Her gaze drifted across the room. Several students had their cell phones on their desks, carefully hidden behind the people in front of them, texting. Some of them were probably Tweeting or doing Facebook, or filling in Thought Bubbles on GrapeVyne. She felt that panic again, and she wanted to fly out of her seat and beg everyone to stop telling the world where they were at every moment of the day. She wanted to beg them not to mention that she was in this room. She wanted to tell them that their lives were like vapor, and that they could evaporate as quickly as Karen's life had. That evil lurked in cyberspace, and may be lurking in the halls of academia.

But she stayed quiet, trying to write down what her lecturer said. By the end of the class, perspiration dripped from her face. She tried to control her breathing, in ... deep breath ... out ... long breath.

When they were dismissed, she found herself afraid to step outside the room. But she had to. Everyone was leaving. She couldn't be found here alone. She got up and loaded her books back in, slipped on her backpack, and put her crutches under her arms. When she went through the building's glass doors, she saw Jennifer waiting in her car. As she went toward it, she looked from side to side for a brown-haired man who personified evil.

She didn't see him anywhere. But she knew he was around, somewhere, waiting for the right time.

thirty-one

Ryan wished he could skip the Tuesday board meeting, because he knew what was coming. Reports of his visit to the hospital last week hadn't just come and gone—for the past week the *Houston Chronicle* had had daily editorials about GrapeVyne's responsibility in the murders. He'd already had lengthy conversations with each of the board members, but none of them was satisfied. And if they'd found out that the FBI had swarmed the place last night, and that he'd allowed them in without a warrant ... well, it would only get worse. So as soon as the meeting was scheduled, he'd invited Krista to speak to them. Maybe hearing her plea for changes would make them listen to his ideas for change.

Fighting the fatigue in his bones, he headed down the stairs. When he got to the second-floor landing, he saw down to the first floor, where Krista waited nervously in the lobby. She had her laptop open on her knees, probably going over her PowerPoint presentation.

She looked as tired as he. Maybe they should have done this another day.

As he hit the first floor, he crossed the lobby to Krista. "You ready for this?"

She closed her laptop and stood up. "I don't know. I'll do my best."

He met her red eyes, noted the shadows under them. "You okay?"

"Just tired. I didn't get much sleep."

"Yeah, me either. We can do it another day if you want to."

She shook her head. "No, it's important. I want to do it now."

"Okay, then let's do it. We meet next door, in the Willow Internet Division. Come on with me. You'll have to wait downstairs until I can let the board know you're coming. I'll call you up when it's time. That place ... they have more security than we have, so you have to stay in the lobby until I get them to come down and get you."

"What's all the security about?" she asked as they went out and crossed the lawn to Willow.

"Industrial spies," he said. "A lot of companies would love to get some of our code and check out our technology. And then there are hackers, who could get in and mess up accounts. Willow has a lot of interests, and way more equipment and computers and companies than we do."

He said good-bye to her in the Willow lobby, then went with a security guard onto the elevator.

His hands were clammy as he got to the conference room and pulled the door open. The board members were around the table already, sipping coffee. Newspapers were strewn across the table.

They all looked up at him. No one was smiling.

"Hello, gentlemen." He set his briefcase down, pulled out his laptop, and took his seat at the table. "I see you've been reading the papers."

Henry Hearne sat with arms crossed over his chest. The other board members had looks of restrained anger on their faces. The silence was deafening.

Ryan hated this. The whole reason he'd started a business in college was so he wouldn't have bosses to answer to. Now he had a roomful of them.

"Look, I know you guys are upset. Who knew the chatter about my hospital visit would go on this long? But I think one sure way to put it to rest is to help locate this killer."

"Kid, do you have any idea how you've made us look?" Henry asked, his chin set.

"I hope I made us look like we have compassion for the victims, and concern for finding this madman."

"Are you blind?" John Stanley bit out. "The news isn't touting our *compassion*. They're making us look like a shopping center for predators."

"I know what they're saying, but I plan to do a few interviews explaining the new security measures we're going to implement and letting people know that we're as concerned as they are about what's going on."

"No, absolutely not." Henry sat straighter and pointed at him. "You will not do any interviews. You will stay out of the public eye until this blows over."

Ryan looked at the man who'd been his mentor. Was he really forbidding him? "Henry, I represent GrapeVyne. I created it. No one cares more about it than I do. We can do the right thing without hurting revenue."

John Stanley coughed into his hand, cleared his throat. "What security measures are you referring to, Ryan? Because I don't recall agreeing to any new measures."

Ryan thought of going over his ideas, but these men were in no mood for that. Maybe Krista could soften them up. "If we could just pause this discussion for a little while, I have someone here who'd like to weigh in. I've asked Krista Carmichael to come speak to us today, so that you can see from her perspective what needs to be done."

Henry hit the table. "I'm not interested in her perspective! How dare you invite her here without clearing it with us first? You are not in control here, Ryan! You are an employee of this company!"

"Henry, I'm asking you to hear her out. Her sister's dead! She deserves twenty minutes of our time. Then we'll discuss it."

Henry looked at John Stanley, then at the others. Turning his palms up and muttering, "Unbelievable," he sat back hard in his chair.

Ryan knew this was not a good idea, but he couldn't leave Krista sitting down in the lobby. It would be too embarrassing to tell her that he didn't have enough clout, as CEO of GrapeVyne, to make the board members listen to her. He hoped they'd put their anger on ice until she was finished.

Ryan called security and asked them to escort Krista to the conference room. When she came in, he moved his chair to the side and plugged her computer into the projector. He introduced her, but the board members couldn't have been colder.

That clearly made her nervous. Her voice was shaky as she started her plea for changes, but after the first moment or so, that passion he'd heard as she'd spoken to the high school kids returned. He watched the closed faces of his board members as she spoke, and tried to keep her going with encouraging looks.

When she was finished, he thanked her and escorted her out. He knew the men were slashing him with their tongues, lambasting him behind his back. When he returned to the conference room, they did it to his face.

"Ryan, we're busy men. The next time you want to parade a victim in front of us, why don't you ask us if we'd like to hear it?"

"It's pertinent to what's going on," he said. "Did you hear anything she said?"

Henry cut in. "We heard plenty, Kid."

"And you still don't want to make changes?"

"There's no need. We haven't done anything wrong."

Ryan couldn't leave it at that. "All right. What if I told you that the killer is still taunting Megan Quinn? That the moment she bought a new cell phone, she saw a text from him? And when police pinged the number the text came from, they found the phone ... in our Dumpster."

Everyone gaped at him.

"What are you saying, Ryan?" Henry asked.

"I'm saying that the killer could very well be someone who works here."

"That's absurd!"

"Is it? The people who work in these buildings have access to a lot of information. They wouldn't have to be accepted as Friends. They could get on anyone's account, anytime, and gather all the information they need. And whether you accept that or not doesn't matter. The FBI is looking into it."

John rubbed his face. "This is getting worse and worse. Has this cell phone business gotten out to the press?"

"Not yet. But it's just a matter of time. That's another reason we need to make these changes. Even if we implement a Band-Aid fix, it would make us look like we were trying to do the right thing. In fact, let's get crazy and actually *do* the right thing. Henry, I'd like for you to give us the software for Willow's Data-Gather program. My team would like to take that software and modify it with some new search strings that might help us locate the killer."

Henry looked as if he'd just been asked to sacrifice one of his children. "Absolutely not. That software isn't for anyone's eyes but those in my employ who've been given clearance for it."

"But we're your employees too. We can be trusted. I'd only give access to my people at the top tier of GrapeVyne, and they know what they're doing."

Henry passed a do-you-believe-this look to his colleagues. "We're already gathering all the data we need. Tell me what you want, and we'll get you that information ourselves."

Ryan didn't like it. If he did it that way, anyone on Willow's staff could leave out the info they didn't want him to have. No, he'd feel better if his own people were doing it. He leaned back in his chair. "Why won't you trust us with it?"

"Because if one of your people ever leaves GrapeVyne, they'll take that information with them. I don't want them to have it. It's proprietary information ..."

"That information technically belongs to the individual GrapeVyne members, not Willow. Besides, my employees won't leave GrapeVyne if we keep them happy here. And even if they did, these are people with integrity. They're not going to pirate that software. In fact, they could probably build their own, and it would be even better than what you've got. But that would take time. I want this done immediately, and you already have it."

Hearne set his jaw. "Not going to happen. Sorry, Kid."

He could see in the man's face that he wasn't going to change his mind, so he let up. It was probably a good thing, after all, that Ian had hacked into their computers and had already gotten the software. Henry underestimated the power of Ryan's team.

He changed gears back to PR. "Can you at least look at this from a marketing standpoint? We could be the company that cares. We could make other social networks look like they don't care. It could actually drive business to our community. And again, I'm willing to do interviews setting the record straight. But first I have to have something to tell them. Changes we're making. We need to decide on what to do, and fast."

"I say we implement a study to see how much revenue will be lost with each suggested change. Then we can decide," John said.

Ryan sighed. "All right, I'll get it started immediately. But I hope you understand that timing is of the essence. The sooner we act, the sooner we can stop these predators from going after our customers. These Houston murders have got to stop, and we might be the ones to stop them. Don't you want to be heroes?"

His board members only stared at him.

thirty-two

Ryan went back to the GrapeVyne building, dropped his notes in his office, then headed across the Rumpus Room to Ian. Ian's eyes were bloodshot and glazed as he stared at the numbers going across his screen.

"How's it going?" Ryan asked, pulling up a chair.

"Pretty good," Ian said without looking up. "I'm checking Bridgit's work to make sure this will work before we run it on the system."

"Yeah, about that. Henry said we couldn't have the software. He preferred that we tell them what we need, and they'll give us the information."

"It'll take those morons months to get it done, whereas I'm almost finished."

"But we're forbidden to use their software. I only told you to hack it so we could get a jump on it. But now that they've said no—"

Ian laughed as he typed in some commands. "I love that word, *forbidden*. Just makes me tremble." He looked up. "You're not going to make me stop this, are you?"

Ryan studied the numbers on the screen. Yes, it looked like their work had been successful. The information they got here could make a real difference in the investigation. He couldn't pull them off it now. It could be a matter of life and death. "No, not after you've come this far. All I can tell you is, don't get caught."

Ian sighed. "I can't make that promise. Someone at Willow's already onto me. I got an instant message from him a few minutes ago."

Ryan's heart jolted. "From who?"

"Guy named Jeff Hall. He's an engineer over there. He asked me who I was and how I'd logged into their server."

Ryan groaned. "What did you say?"

"Nothing. I didn't answer him."

"He'll figure out it's you. He'll tell Henry." Ryan tried to think. "Well, don't answer. Maybe it'll blow over."

But as he headed back to his desk, he knew that wouldn't happen. Jeff Hall would surely tell his superiors about the breach of security. Unless Ryan intervened, word would definitely get back to Henry Hearne. He supposed he could get Ian to plead ignorance and say that he misunderstood Ryan's instructions. That he thought he had gotten clearance to use that software.

He paced his office, thinking through possibilities. Maybe he needed to walk over to Willow, find the engineer who'd IM'd Ian, and try to do some damage control. Maybe he could convince him that Ian wasn't up to anything sinister. That he'd just overstepped his bounds in the interest of finding the killer.

Yes, that could work.

He ran down the stairs and out, crossed to the Willow building again. The guard at the security desk was on the phone and didn't see him. Ryan slipped into the stairwell and took the stairs up two at a time. Most of the engineers were on the top two floors, so he bypassed the first four. When he reached the fifth floor, he opened the door to the floor and stepped out of the stairwell. The temperature had changed. The floor was warmer—almost hot. There were no people in sight here, but dozens of huge computer servers that collected and sorted data. Though GrapeVyne was a company that always needed more servers, Willow had at least ten times as many as they had.

How could that be?

Fearful that he'd get caught here before he was able to talk to Jeff Hall, Ryan headed up one more floor. He came out of the stairwell and saw another roomful of computers, then a floor full of offices.

He stepped into the first one. An Asian lady was busy, bent over her desk.

"Excuse me."

She looked up.

"Could you tell me where I can find Jeff Hall?"

She pointed to her left. "Third office." She looked him over. "Are you allowed in here?"

"Sure," he said. "I work here."

She waved him on, and Ryan headed to Hall's office. The door was open a crack, so he knocked on the casing and waited.

"Come in."

He stepped inside the office. "Jeff?"

The engineer looked nothing like the ones who worked at GrapeVyne. He was wearing a tucked-in button-down shirt and tie, khaki pants, and a Willow Entertainment badge. His hair was moussed and glistened like crude oil under the florescent bulbs. He shot Ryan a surprised look. "How did you get in here?"

"I'm Ryan Adkins, from next door."

"I know who you are. You don't have clearance to be on this floor."

The hostility surprised him. "Look, I just wanted to tell you something. One of my engineers just got an IM from you."

"Yes. It's Ian Lombardi, isn't it?"

Ryan didn't want to confirm that. "I just wanted to talk to you about what's going on over there."

Jeff got up, closed the door, and motioned for Ryan to sit. "I'm listening."

"Three women have been attacked here in Houston, and their predator apparently found at least two of them through GrapeVyne. Two of them are dead, and one is still living, but she fears for her life. We want to help find him before he strikes again. So I told my engineers that I was going to talk to Henry Hearne about getting clearance to use your Data-Gather software, to modify the search strings so that we could narrow down possible predators."

"And Mr. Hearne said no."

"Well, yes. But by the time I could get back and tell my people that, they'd found a way to get the software and had already started working on it."

"They don't have clearance!" Jeff said. "They can't just hack into our system!"

"They jumped the gun, that's all."

"They should be in prison."

Ryan gave a disgusted grunt. "No, they shouldn't. The predator should be. They did it so we could find him. The girl who survived her attack, she can identify the killer. He's going to try to shut her up before she does. We have to find him before that happens." He noticed a wedding ring on Jeff's finger and a picture of a bride on his desk. "What if your wife is next? What if he's stalking her through her GrapeVyne page right now, and he shows up and surprises her? What if he does to her what was done to those girls?"

"I don't let my wife on GrapeVyne."

Ryan laughed, but decided to let that ride. "My engineers want to stop this insanity. They were overzealous, but they were trying to do the right thing."

"Are you asking me not to report this security breach?"

"I'm asking you to think like a human and not like a corporate puppet." He knew the moment he'd said it, he shouldn't have.

"You're a bigger puppet than I am, Mr. CEO. You sold yourself to Willow for a hundred million. But don't think they have to keep you on if they begin to feel our company is threatened."

Was that jealousy in his tone? Trying not to provoke him, Ryan softened his voice. "Look, this was not like some breach that threatens Willow's secrets. We're all under the same umbrella, right? My guys can be trusted with secrecy. I'll just tell them to bag the project and not do it again. There's no need to report this to anyone."

Jeff just stared at him, a muscle in his jaw popping.

"This dude is going to kill more people," Ryan tried again. "We feel a real tension over there about that. We're trying to save lives. That's all, man."

Jeff got to his feet, opened the door, dismissing him. "I'll think about it."

That was all he was going to get for now. "No harm done, right?" Ryan stepped out of the room.

"And for the future, you're only allowed on the third

floor, where the conference room is. You're not allowed on the fourth, fifth, or sixth floors at all. Nobody is. Only those who've been carefully screened are allowed up here."

Ryan couldn't believe this guy. "You know I'm not a spy. I'm the CEO of one of Willow's major holdings."

"I don't care who you are." He escorted Ryan to the elevator and watched as he got on.

"I appreciate your giving me a few minutes," Ryan said, reaching out to shake Jeff's hand as he got on.

Jeff didn't shake. He just stood there, giving him a steely-eyed stare, as the doors slowly closed.

thirty-three

Krista was spent when she left the Willow building and got back to her car. She locked the door and sat there for a moment, seeing the faces of those men again. They'd looked angry when she went in, and she wasn't sure anything she'd said had gotten through to them.

She felt barren, ineffective.

Fatigue clawed at her spine and the muscles of her neck and back, but she didn't want to take time to sleep. She needed to go somewhere where she could make a difference.

She drove to the teen center. The street that she'd always breezed past before looked worse today ... eerie ... evil. She saw a couple of men smoking in front of a mechanic's shop, watching her as she drove by. At the pawn shop, a man stood at a car, leaned in, talking.

Her heart tripped as she pulled into the parking lot next

to the Eagle's Wings center. Carla's van was here, and so was her husband's. She saw two girls walking toward the place. They lifted their hands in a wave.

She got out, locked her car, and hurried inside. The place was full of activity. Christian music played overhead, and several girls sat at the computers, their GrapeVyne pages up. She tried to smile as she went in and spoke to each of them. But her gaze caught on those pages. For a moment she stood behind them, watching what they typed.

Some of them were on her own page, exchanging comments with other girls who were discussing her Bible studies.

"Krista, look at this!"

She turned and looked through the door into the next room, where they had three sewing machines set up. A girl named Flo was wearing the outfit she'd been working on, modeling it like she walked the runway.

"Flo, did you finish it?"

"All by myself. Miss Carla helped a little ..."

"Hardly at all," Carla said. "She did this whole thing alone. Look at the detail, Krista. Flo, you have a gift. I could see you working in fashion design. It's so unique, and so you."

The girl who'd been quiet and shy for the first month she'd come to the center giggled as she regarded her image in the mirror. "I could wear this to my auntie's wedding."

"You should," Krista said. "It really is pretty. I wish I could sew, but about all I can do is hem pants and sew on buttons."

"This even has a zipper," Flo bragged.

This was what their work here was all about. Flo saw herself differently now. She was someone with talent, someone who was beautiful ... someone with worth.

If only they could keep her here, locked away, and never

let her go back into her drug-infested neighborhood. They couldn't do that, of course, but maybe they could help her find her own way out of it.

Flo went to change out of her outfit, and Carla turned to Krista and lowered her voice. "Honey, you didn't have to come in today. Gus is here, helping. You look really tired."

"I was just up late."

Carla got tears in her eyes. "Have the police got any leads?"

Krista blew out a deep breath. "No, I don't think so. If they do, they're not telling us."

"How's your dad?"

Krista wanted to lie and say he was fine, but he needed prayer. "He's just ... horrible. So depressed. I don't know how much more he can take. It would do him a lot of good if they found the killer."

"It would do you a lot of good too. And the rest of us." Carla walked to the window, looked up the street. "I sometimes wonder if it's someone around here. But Ella didn't come here that much."

"No, Dad would have had a fit."

"But it still could be, you know. Somebody who's hot because we don't let men in the club. Or someone who watches. There are always men standing outside ..."

"Megan described him. She said he was white and clean-cut, in his forties, with brown hair." She looked over Carla's shoulder toward the mechanic's shop across the street. The men were of all races, but the white ones she saw didn't fit the killer's description.

"What are you ladies lookin' at?" Gus's deep voice shook the room.

Carla looked over her shoulder. "Nothing. Just looking to see who's watching us."

Gus came over and gave Krista a hug. "You okay, darlin'?"

"Yeah, I'm fine. Thanks, Gus."

The burly man looked at his wife. "I switched out that light fixture. It's workin' good now."

"What would we do without you?" She kissed his scruffy cheek and ruffled his hair.

"Listen, ladies. We got that shotgun in the office. I want you to use it if you need to. And Krista, if I were you, I'd get a gun to keep with you."

"I know. I've been thinking that myself. How do you do it? Don't you have to apply for a license or something?"

"No, you just walk into a gun store and they'll give you the paperwork."

"Isn't there a waiting period?"

"Not in this state. You buy it and walk out with it the same day, after you register it. The clerk at the store will call the registration in."

She swallowed. "So I could literally have one today? Would I be able to carry it in my car, or do I have to have some special permit?"

"You have to have a concealed weapon permit if you carry it in your purse," Carla said. "But that takes months to get. If you just carry it in your car, you don't need anything extra."

It was a good idea.

She hung around the place for a little longer, then slipped out and headed for Bass Pro Shop. If she was going to bait Ella's killer, she was going to need a weapon.

thirty-four

When the board of directors called another meeting that afternoon, Ryan knew he'd have some explaining to do. As he arrived at the meeting, he realized it had been going on for some time without him. The men who drove his company looked somber and angry as he took his place at the end of the table. "What's this meeting about?"

Marvin Bainbridge leaned on the table. "Ryan, we've been discussing the things that have gone on in the company the last few days, and as you know, we're very concerned."

Ryan nodded. "As I am."

Henry Hearne's lips had stiffened into thin, hard lines. "Ryan, we understand that you violated Willow's security in at least three ways."

"I can explain," he said. "I'd told my staff that I was going to ask for permission to run your Data-Gather program—"

"We told you no. Ian Lombardi hacked into our system and stole our software."

"Come on, guys. It wasn't stealing."

"And then you violated security again, by going onto the upper floors without an escort."

"That was no big deal. I just wanted to talk to Jeff Hall to tell him why my staff—"

"Ryan, we've been told you let the FBI into the building without a warrant."

Ryan froze. "Okay, look ..."

"We're not really interested in any more of your explanations," John Stanley cut in sharply. He looked at his colleagues. "Why don't we just cut to the chase, gentlemen?"

Marvin drew in a deep breath and folded his hands. "Ryan, we made some decisions today. First, we are terminating Ian Lombardi's employment."

Ryan sprang up. "Come on, guys. He's my most valuable asset. I can't do half of what I do without him. He's impossible to replace."

"Oh, we'll replace him, all right."

Ryan couldn't stand for this. "Don't I get any say in this?"

"No, you don't."

He couldn't believe this. He looked around the room, searching for one pair of eyes that still had some reason left. When he saw only glaring accusation, he decided to play his trump card.

"Look, guys. If he goes, I go."

"That brings us to our next decision," Henry said.

"What? You're firing me?"

"Ryan, your contract with us states that you have the job unless or until we make the decision that it's no longer in Willow's best interest to keep you."

"But I built this company! I'm the driving force behind it! Not you. Ian and I are the heart of GrapeVyne ... the brains. You'll be killing it without us."

"There are plenty of employees who still know how to keep GrapeVyne running, and we have access to many well-qualified design and computer engineers. We'll have you both replaced within the next few days."

Ryan's mouth hung open. "You're serious?"

"We no longer need your services."

Stunned, Ryan gaped at them. "I wouldn't have sold GrapeVyne to you if you hadn't agreed to keep me and my staff on board! That was the deal!"

"We feel that your latest decisions are costing this company its reputation, and you've behaved more like a rival than a coworker. We own the company and we can do with it as we please. We've decided that you are no longer needed here," Henry said.

John's voice was lower. "We've called security to come and escort you off the premises. You'll have an hour to pack up your personal items. They'll help you. We'll expect you to turn in your laptop and phone and your appropriate keys."

Ryan just stared. This was really happening. "Couldn't you have given me a warning?"

"We did. We told you to stop getting entangled with Krista Carmichael, to stop apologizing for our company, to stop all of this, but you wouldn't listen. We see this as our only option."

Ryan looked from one board member to the next, and his eyes settled on Henry Hearne, the man he'd trusted. "Henry? Did you vote for this?"

Henry's eyes were cold. "We have a responsibility to our employees and to our stockholders, Kid."

Ryan picked up his laptop, shoved it into his briefcase.

Threats raced through his mind. "Fine. Then I'll have time to do more interviews. I'll be free to go on every talk show."

"Are you threatening us?" Henry asked.

Ryan dropped his hands. "No, I'm just telling you, the changes I wanted to make in this company were for the good of it, and doing the right thing is still important to me, even if I'm unemployed."

"Then you need to consult an attorney to review your contract commitments — namely, the noncompete agreement, the nondisclosure clauses, and the industrial secrecy clauses regarding anything having to do with Willow or GrapeVyne. If you talk to the press, we will sue you for every penny you've ever made with us, and then some."

Ryan clicked his briefcase shut, then stormed to the door. When he opened it, two bulky GrapeVyne security guys he'd hired himself were waiting there for him.

Ryan looked up at them. "Jose … Andy …"

They both looked apologetic, and under his breath, Jose whispered, "Sorry, boss."

They walked him across to the GrapeVyne building. Silently, they rode the elevator up to the top floor. When they got off, he saw the crowd around Ian's desk. His staff looked stunned, and some of the women were crying.

He crossed the Rumpus Room floor. "Ian, I'm so sorry."

Ian gave him a doleful look. "It's not your fault, man. They're lunatics, is what they are. Without us, this business wouldn't even exist."

Ryan looked down at his feet. "They're deluded into believing they can run it better."

"They'll run it, that's for sure. Right into the ground."

As Jose and Andy stood by and watched, Ryan filled three small boxes with his personal items. He didn't have the heart to get anything else out of his office. He supposed whoever occupied it next could have his things if they wanted them. Otherwise, they could pack them up and send them to him.

"We'll need your laptop," Jose said.

Ryan thought of trying to talk them out of taking it, since it had all of his code for GrapeVyne, as well as other startup ideas he'd had. But he knew better. Instead, he said, "Give me a minute to delete some personal files."

Since he'd always been good to the security guys, they gave him the time. He quickly typed in the command to erase all the computer's data. He waited as the computer deleted everything.

Andy checked his watch. "Time's almost up, Ryan. We've got to walk you out."

"Just a few more minutes." He glanced out his glass wall, saw Ian at his desk doing the same thing. They'd always thought alike.

Jose came around his desk, saw what he was doing. "I don't think you're supposed to do that."

"I'm not doing anything to hurt the company," Ryan said, "but I have a lot of coding on there that isn't owned by GrapeVyne. They were ideas I was playing with, and I don't want GrapeVyne to have them if I'm not on staff, so I'm deleting them."

"But the GrapeVyne files—"

"Bridgit has everything that belongs to GrapeVyne."

Jose sighed, but he didn't push it any farther.

Ryan handed a box to each guard and started for the door, but then thought better of it. Going back to his desk, he picked up his phone and dialed the number that would give him intercom access across the offices. "Hi everybody, this is Ryan," he said, and through the glass wall he could see everybody on his floor turning to look at him. "Willow has just given Ian and me pink slips. I just wanted to tell you what an honor and privilege it's been to work with all of you. You're the greatest team anybody could ever have, and you guys are responsible for making this company a success." His voice broke, and he cleared his throat. "I'm sorry my part in it has to end this way, but that's how it goes. But I wanted to say good-bye. I consider you all friends. Stay in touch."

His mouth was shaking as he retrieved the remaining box and backed out of the office.

"One more thing," Andy said.

Ryan turned back.

"Your Blackberry."

Great. He'd forgotten they'd want that. He reached into his pocket, pulled it out and quickly did a hard reset, erasing everything on it. Then he tossed it to Andy. Now what would he do? His Blackberry was like a third arm. He didn't even have a land-line at home. He'd have to go directly to the phone company and buy another one.

Unbelievable.

Ian was headed his way as he pressed the elevator button. Suddenly, applause erupted from those in the Rumpus Room. He turned and saw that all the employees were standing and clapping from their desks. Many of them were crying.

He and Ian offered sad waves, then shifting his box, Ryan got on the elevator. Ian stepped on behind him, and their four security guards squeezed on with them.

"Ain't over, man," Ian said.

Ryan didn't want to hear Ian's bluster. It *felt* over. He leaned back against the wall as he took his last elevator ride down. Then he stepped out to the parking garage ... an unemployed man. The brainchild he'd developed was no longer his.

thirty-five

Krista had never expected to wind up in a Bass Pro Shop. She pushed through the turnstile at the front of the store, then stood just inside, looking around at the rustic decor and the merchandise that was as foreign to her as an unknown language.

"Can I help you find anything?" the elderly man at the turnstile asked.

"Guns." The breathiness in her voice embarrassed her. "Where are the guns?"

"Upstairs. Hunting."

She headed for the stairs. Why did she feel like she was doing something wrong? She'd never planned to own a gun, never wanted to. The thought of all that could go wrong made her heart thud. Things like ... forgetting it was loaded and having it go off. Or firing it for target practice, and having it jam and explode in her hand. What if someone broke in and stole it?

She got to the top of the stairs and looked around. The room was appropriately dark, with rustic walls and low lights. Why did men love having the lights dim? Her father had always loved closing the blinds and watching TV in the dark, while she and her sister loved the light pouring in.

Now she kept the blinds closed too. The killer had snuffed the sunshine out of their home. That was why she needed a gun.

She cut through the hunting clothes and found the area with the rifles and shotguns lined up on the wall. A glass-front counter stood in front of it, with handguns on the glass shelves. She approached it and looked inside, saw dozens of firearms in various shapes, sizes, and prices.

A salesman approached her. "Help you, ma'am?"

"Yes." She adjusted her purse on her shoulder, then set her hands on the counter. "I'm looking for a pistol. A small one that I could handle. Maybe like this one." She pointed to one in the glass case.

"So ... you want an automatic or a revolver?"

Had he pegged her for an impostor? An ignorant pacifist masquerading as an NRA member? "Oh ... sorry. Why don't you tell me the difference?"

He pulled out a handgun and showed her the cylinder with the holes. So they still had those? She thought they were only in old western movies. He put that one back, and pulled out one with a label that said "Automatic." He removed the clip and showed her how it was loaded.

"I see." She stared down at the glass, looking around. "What do you recommend?"

"You're a beginner," he said, without a trace of humor in his eyes. Either he'd been trained not to laugh at newbies, or it was no big deal. "Do you want it for self-defense and target practice?"

No, she thought, *I want it for hunting down my sister's killer.* She cleared her throat. "Yes."

"Some of these have a lot of kick and might not be comfortable for you."

I don't care if it's comfortable, she thought. *All I need is one shot.*

"Clips sometimes jam, unless you clean the gun after you use them. I'd recommend a revolver for you. You're pretty small." He pulled another one out. "This is a popular model for women. It's not very powerful, only a .22, but it's good for self-defense."

She took it, hoping he didn't see the tremor in her hands. It was a little heavier than she expected. But somewhere she'd read that a gun was more stable if it was heavier. She looked at the price. It wouldn't put her savings account into overdraft. She studied the gun, didn't even know what to ask. "It says 'LR.' What does that mean?"

"Long range. And it's a six-inch barrel, for more accuracy. Its weight might help you take better aim. And this one here is a double-action. You don't have to cock it. You just pull the trigger."

That had to be good, didn't it? She looked around at the others in the case, glanced at the case next to it, read the tags. There were .357s, .38 Specials, .44 Magnums. She'd heard all those numbers before, but didn't know what they represented. It overwhelmed her, and she wasn't in the mood for being overwhelmed.

Quickly, she made a decision. "Okay, I'll take this one." She handed it back to him.

"All right. I'll get the paperwork for you to fill out."

Dread sank through her. He brought her papers, and

she filled in the blanks. As he called the registration in, she paced in front of the counter. What would the state police know about her? Would they have notations next to her Social Security number, reminding them that her sister was murdered? Would they guess how she planned to use it? What if they turned her down?

But the sales clerk came back and boxed up the gun, shoving the finished paperwork in. Relief flooded through her.

When she finished the purchase, he walked her out, as store policy dictated. She supposed he had to make sure she didn't snap the bullets in and fire like a maniac.

As if she knew how.

She hoped she could find a firing range, and someone to teach her what in the world she was doing.

When she got home, she went into the quiet house, feeling a bit more empowered as she set her box on the table. Her father wasn't home, so she sat down and took the gun out of the box. There was a red lock on it, but the salesman had shown her how to remove it. She found the key, took it off.

Her hands were still trembling as she slipped her hand around the grip, her finger in front of the trigger. What had she been thinking? Why would the clerk sell her something so big?

She pushed the slide with her thumb, making the cylinder pop out. She made sure it wasn't loaded, then popped it back in. Lifting the gun, she aimed at the wall and squeezed the trigger ... and squeezed ... and squeezed.

"You've got to be kidding me." She couldn't pull the trigger. There was too much resistance. She gripped the gun with both hands and squeezed with two fingers. It still resisted, but finally it clicked, pinching her finger.

This was no good. How had she bought a gun she could barely shoot?

She would have to take it back. She rifled through the bag with the box of .22 bullets, and found the receipt.

All Gun Sales Are Final

Great. She sat back in her chair, wondering if a burst of adrenaline would help her shoot if the time came. Target practice would be miserable. Her fingers just weren't strong enough.

She should have gone to the gym more often.

The thought of finger-calisthenics pulled her thoughts to a halt, and she smiled. She was an idiot. A complete idiot. She started to laugh—soft, breezy laughter, then it turned into hysterical laughter that lost its way in her head, making her fold over the table and lay her forehead against the wood. Tears rose up in her eyes, as gales of hilarity seized her.

Finally, she rounded over the rise of her laughter and slid the slope back down. When the laughter died, her face was wet.

All humor drained from her heart as she stared at the gun. She was stuck with it, and she couldn't afford another one. It would have to do. She'd practice, and build up the strength in her fingers. She wondered if they had mini barbells made especially for fingers. Somehow, she didn't find that thought amusing anymore.

She put the gun back in its box, not sure what else to do with it. Gathering the bag with her boxes of ammunition, she took them into her room and hid them on a shelf in her closet. Her dad would be scared to death to know she had a gun, as if she were an eight-year-old girl breaking into the gun cabinet.

Maybe he was right.

But even knowing how hard it was to shoot, she hoped the gun would give any attacker pause. He wouldn't know she was a limp-fingered beginner. Maybe it would serve its purpose whether she ever fired it or not.

thirty-six

Ian followed Ryan to the Apple Store, and they stood side by side as they ordered new laptops and iPhones. As they waited for their orders, Ian unloaded.

"There's something not right about this whole thing, man."

"No, it isn't right. It's downright wrong."

"I don't mean in a moral sense. I mean in the sense that something smells in Denmark."

The reference to Hamlet didn't quite click. "What do you mean?"

"Do you realize how much information that Data-Gather program is collecting? It's not just advertising stuff, man. It's schedules, likes and dislikes, habits, connections, of every person on our site. It's like they're looking into people's homes. Only not into their homes. Into their heads. It's scary."

"But that's no surprise. We knew they were doing this for advertisers."

"The advertisers need to know what time people go to work? What time they get home? What political affiliations they have? What banks they use? What their kids' names are? *Pictures* of their kids?"

"Data-Gather collects all that?"

"Yeah, man. They have search strings for all that stuff." A clerk came near them with a customer, showing her the latest notebook computer. Ian lowered his voice. "I don't think this is just about advertising. I think it's something else. If this is legal, it's sure not ethical. And firing me isn't going to get me off their scent."

"Ian, if you hack in again, they'll know," Ryan whispered. "They'll have you arrested."

"Not if I do it right."

"What do you think you're gonna find?"

Ian shrugged. "I don't know. Maybe where all this information is really going. What it's really gonna be used for. Man, we need to get together and figure this out. I'm telling you, something stinketh."

"Then let's do it, Hamlet. My house or thine?"

"How 'bout yours? My garbage is probably festering."

Armed with their new equipment, they went by Ian's house to get his backup drive, then headed to Ryan's house.

Though Ryan had the resources to buy much bigger digs when he'd moved to Houston, he'd bought a 1500-square-foot home in a subdivision. The realtor, who'd hoped for a huge commission, had asked him for a wish list for the house of his dreams. At twenty-three, he really didn't have a dream for a house, so his list included a bedroom, a toilet that flushed, and a microwave oven.

She did better than that, but he rejected all of the mansions before going in. Finally, she humored him with a new house in a neighborhood close to work. He'd walked through it once before deciding to buy it.

The place was still not furnished, except for his living room and bedroom. The dining room and other two bedrooms sat empty. But he was doing better than Ian, who'd bought one of those mansions but still slept on a mattress on his bedroom floor.

When they unloaded their new laptops, they transferred their files from their backup drives. Because Ian was a backup fanatic, he had backups of his backups. He'd even backed up the code he'd gotten from Willow's computer on a small external drive he'd kept in his briefcase. While their computers worked on transferring their files, they sent out emails to all of their contacts, letting them know their new phone numbers.

When they finished with that, Ian showed Ryan the code and search strings he'd gotten from Willow's computers. His friend was right. The amount of data they were gathering about GrapeVyne clients was unwarranted, even for advertising purposes. If something illegal was going on, it might explain their reaction to the breach.

"Do you think they acquired GrapeVyne to help them collect all that data about millions of people?" Ian asked.

Ryan couldn't believe that was true. "They acquired us because we were worth a lot, and they knew the sky was the limit."

"I don't know. There we were, this break-even company, and they swooped in with millions of dollars. For what? Our business model wasn't that profitable."

"They saw our potential. And we've fulfilled it. We've made them a good profit for the last few years, and our membership is growing by twenty-five thousand people a day."

Ian looked at Ryan. "So tell me again what you saw when you went over there?"

Ryan leaned back and messed up his hair. "An entire floor of servers."

"So why would they need that? They need it because they're collecting all this data on millions and millions of people. Don't you get it?"

"No, not really."

"Well, just imagine what all that information in the hands of the wrong group could do. It could be given to terrorists, rogue nations, political groups ..."

"Where do you get this stuff?"

"I'm telling you, it doesn't take a brain surgeon to figure out that this is too much. They fired us over it, Ryan. They weren't just mad because I overstepped my bounds. They fired us because we were getting too close to the truth."

Ryan tried to process that. "So what if that's it? What can we do about it?"

"I'm going to start by finding out everything I can about the board members. What their interests are, where they invest their money, political affiliations, other companies they have interest in."

"Ian, please don't be reckless. Don't hack into any accounts—"

The doorbell rang. What now? Ryan went to the door, looked out through the peephole. Krista Carmichael stood there.

He turned back, saw the laundry on his couch, the shoes on the floor, books and papers everywhere.

"Hold on a minute!" he called as he ran back and scooped up the laundry. "Get your shoes, man. It's Krista."

Ian slipped his feet back into his shoes. "What is up with you?"

"I don't want her to think I'm a pig. She's never been here before." He ran into his bedroom and dropped the clothes on his bed. There wasn't time to clean off his coffee table or straighten papers.

He tried to steady his breathing and opened the door. "Krista!"

She looked distraught. "Ryan, I'm so sorry. I just heard on the news you were fired."

"It's on the news?" He motioned her in, then turned on his TV. FOX News had a crawl about him at the bottom of the screen. "Good grief." He turned to Ian. "Look at this."

Ian shook his head. "You didn't think this would go unnoticed, did you?"

"It's my fault, isn't it?" Krista asked.

"No, it's not your fault. Krista, this is Ian."

"You were fired too," she said in greeting. "This is horrible. If you hadn't had me come and talk to the board of directors, they wouldn't have gotten so mad. I never meant for you to lose your jobs. That's the last thing I wanted."

"I appreciate that," Ryan said, "but that's not really the reason we were fired."

"What are you going to do?"

"We're still trying to regroup," he said. "It's not like either of us will go hungry. But since they're reporting this on cable news, I'm going to be getting interview requests. I just sent the media an email with my updated contact info, and I should be hearing from them soon. The problem is, I've been threatened with a hefty lawsuit if I talk to the press about GrapeVyne or Willow, so I can't. But you can."

She frowned. "What?"

"You can go to the interviews with me. I'll say a few things about Internet safety and then turn it over to you. You can say the things I'm legally not allowed to say."

Ian chuckled. "Way to get revenge. I like it."

Ryan sighed. "I'm not out for revenge. I just want to make a difference. If I have contract prohibitions, then we have to find another way to alert the public." He looked at her. "What do you say?"

She frowned. "I don't know. Television makes me nervous."

"Krista, people need to hear from you right now. Between the two of us we could really raise awareness. Isn't that what you've wanted?"

She thought about that for a minute, dropped her head down, and looked at her feet. Her silky hair fell over her face, and he fought the urge to sweep it back behind her ear.

"What program would we go on?"

He shrugged. "Take your pick. Probably got my choice here."

"When?"

"Tomorrow?" he asked. "That would give us enough time to decide what we want to say. We could send those statistics you have ahead for them to put on the screen while we're talking."

He saw the conflict on her face, the wheels turning behind her eyes. "I guess I can't really say no, can I? It's what I've wanted. To educate the public. You'd give me a forum that I would never have by myself."

"So I'll get the forum, and you'll give them the one-two punch."

Ian cleared his throat. "Are you gonna tell the press what Willow's doing?"

"I don't know. I have to think about it." Ryan gave Krista a self-conscious glance. "So let's get together tonight and prep for the interviews."

Ian looked up from his computer, grinning. Ryan wanted to kill him.

"I can't," she said. "I have church tonight."

"On Wednesday night?"

"Yes, it's our mid-week service. I need to go."

"You can't skip just this once?"

She shook her head. "I don't like to miss. Some of the girls at the teen center come, and I need to be there. It's only an hour. You could come with me, though, and we could work on the interview afterward."

Again, Ian shot him a look. Ryan ignored him this time. "Yeah, I can come with you. It's been a long time since I've done church, but I guess it's like riding a bicycle."

"What about you, Ian?" Krista said. "Why don't you come too?"

Ian shook his head. "Can't. I'm Jewish."

Ryan grunted. "You are not Jewish! You're Italian."

Ian grinned. "I was thinking of converting."

Krista smiled. "Okay, maybe another time. Ryan, do you want me to pick you up?"

"How about I pick *you* up?"

She looked troubled. "I don't know. I don't really want to show up for church in a Jaguar. It would call a lot of attention to us."

He laughed. "You're disparaging my car? Ian, did you hear that? She's disparaging my car."

Ian grinned. "I knew I liked her."

Her laugh was like music. "So it starts at six. Why don't you come to my house at five thirty, and we'll go in my car?"

"Okay, I'll be there."

She started back to the door. "Shalom, Ian."

Ian laughed as she closed the door behind her. "She's a doll. You better not blow this date."

"It's not a date. It's church."

"Church with *her*. It's a date, man."

"It's not a date." Ryan went to the window and looked out at Krista as she pulled out of the driveway. "She probably sees me as a project. Her latest mission field. Once she gets me in church, she won't give me the time of day."

"Do you hear yourself? You're a millionaire, and you're worried that this girl won't like you. Don't you know we both got better looking the minute we started depositing those checks? She's probably giddy."

"She's not like that. You heard her. She doesn't even want to be seen in my car."

Ian chuckled. "Anyway ... wish I had some hot chick to get my mind off my unemployment. If you don't think of her that way, mind if I ask her out?"

"You'd have to give up your dream of converting to Judaism."

"Can do. So that's a yes?"

"No," Ryan said. "That's a no."

Ian grinned like a fifth-grader as he went back to his computer. "I don't blame you, man."

Ryan wondered what they wore to mid-week services these days. The last thing he wanted to do was embarrass his date.

thirty-seven

David's hands were shaking as he sat over coffee with Megan Quinn in Rice Coffeehouse, on the university campus. Upbeat pop music played over the sound system, and the voices of students around them were out of sync with his dark mood.

Megan seemed nervous and kept looking around, probably searching for the man who'd attacked her. Her face looked terrible, purple bruises attesting to how close she'd come to death. Her crutches leaned against her booth, and she kept her hand on one of them, as if to use it as a weapon if she needed it. David could see that her torture hadn't yet ended.

"The police haven't found the guy yet," he said. "And that's just not acceptable. He's still out there, and we have to stop him."

"I agree," Megan said. "But what can we do?"

"I'm going to find him myself. So I need as clear a description as you gave the police. Every detail you can think of. I know you said he was about five foot ten and had dark hair. But I need more. When you first saw him, before you were afraid of him, what did you see? What made you trust him?"

She sighed, and veins in her forehead bulged, as if the very act of thinking about him caused her blood pressure to spike. "He didn't look like a killer. He looked like a clean-cut, decent person when I first saw him. He had on a long raincoat. His smile seemed ... pleasant."

"Did you notice the color of his eyes?"

"No, it was kind of dark."

"So his hair. You said it was brown. Dark brown, light brown ... ?"

"Dark."

"Did you see the color of his shirt?"

She frowned. "How will that help you find him?"

"If he's someone I know, I might recognize the shirt. Maybe if it was someone Ella knew, that's why she got in his car."

"Oh." She looked off into the distance. "I think his shirt was white."

That wasn't helpful. He tried something else. "What about his face? Did he have bags under his eyes? Dark circles?"

"I couldn't see that clearly," she said.

"Was his nose big or small?"

"Long," she said. "His lips were kind of thick."

An immediate image popped into his mind. Ron Luzzo at his church had thick lips and a long nose. He was about five-ten and had brown hair.

Ron Luzzo. He was an insurance salesman. He'd watched Ella grow up and had running jokes with her, hugs and high fives. Could he have been her killer?

"What kind of accent did he have? Was it Texan?"

"A little, but not heavy. His voice was deep. Authoritative."

He wasn't sure if Ron Luzzo had that kind of voice, but then, he didn't have a young girl's perspective.

"I know someone that could be," he said. "I'll try to get a picture of him and show it to you."

She looked hopeful. "You can send it to my phone."

"All right." He would see him at church tonight. If he sent it to her from his phone, he could have an answer from her right away. If it was him, he'd make sure the man didn't get away. He'd inflict instant justice.

He took Megan back to her dorm, dropped her off at the door, and watched her crutch her way in. For a moment he sat there, wondering how many bones in Ella's body had been broken before he'd thrown her into her grave. How many stitches would she have needed if they'd patched her back up?

His mouth went dry, and he couldn't swallow.

Did he almost have her killer? His stomach roiled as he started his car. Instead of going home, he went to Ron's insurance agency and parked at the business next door, facing the man's building. He located Ron's blue Mercedes in the parking lot and kept his eye on it. Soon the workday would end, and Ron would come out. When he did, he would follow him. Ron would probably go straight to church, since it was Wednesday.

It was the first time in his life David thought of his church's sanctuary as a place where evil lurked. But tonight it did. And he was going to expel it if it was the last thing he did.

He didn't want to make another mistake like he had with Krebbs. He had to take it easy, make sure. But if he did ... and if Luzzo was the one who'd murdered Ella ... then David would kill him.

And then he'd kill himself.

thirty-eight

David got to church early that night and sat on the back row of the small sanctuary. Ron would be there. He never missed.

He tapped his foot, nervous about seeing him. As people came in and slid into the pews, several of them spoke to him. David nodded but said little, not wanting pity or condolences, and certainly not interested in small talk. A few of the women came over and hugged him, but thankfully most of them left him alone.

He saw Ron walk in on the other side of the sanctuary just as the music was starting. He took a seat with his wife, who was already there, midway up. As they stood to sing their first worship song, David went down the empty back row, to the other side of the auditorium, and took his seat where he could photograph Ron with his phone when church was over and Ron came out.

The praise chorus swelled over the church, setting the mood and tone for tonight's worship. But David couldn't worship. Instead, he kept his eyes on the back of Ron Luzzo's brown hair.

Someone slipped into the pew at the other end of his row, and he glanced over. Krista and a man were coming to sit with him.

Krista moved close to him. "Dad," she whispered, "this is Ryan Adkins, of GrapeVyne."

"GrapeVyne?" David asked, shooting him a look. "What is *he* doing here?"

"Be nice," she said.

Ryan reached around her to shake his hand. David reluctantly shook it.

As Krista sang with the others, David stood stiff, wondering what in the world she was doing bringing that Grape-Vyne tycoon to church? Sure, he probably needed it, given the evil his company was doing. But why did he have to come with Krista?

He glanced at Adkins again, wondering if he was up to something. Was he taking advantage of Krista while she was vulnerable? What did he want with her, this boy millionaire who'd created the network that cost Ella her life?

David's eyes strayed back to Ron Luzzo. He'd bent over to pick up his three-year-old grandchild. He watched the man kiss the little girl's cheek. As he saw Ron's profile, he looked for scratches or cuts that would indicate he'd been in a fight. There was nothing, but of course there wouldn't be. He'd had weeks to heal. But as Ron's hand came up to sweep his granddaughter's hair out of her eyes, David saw a scar on the back of his hand.

Murderous hatred erupted inside David. He wanted to kill him, right here, right now. It would be justifiable homicide.

But no, he couldn't attack again. He had to control himself ... and think. He needed a picture of him to email to Megan. She could confirm it, and then he could decide what to do.

He felt Krista shift beside him, and he glanced at his firstborn. Tears welled in her eyes as she sang praises to God. No, he couldn't follow his gut and attack Ron here, and turn her place of worship into a house of blood. Why take that from her too?

He'd do it somewhere else.

His temples throbbed as he sat through the sermon, counting minutes until he could capture Ron Luzzo's image and send it to Megan.

••••

Krista felt the warmth of Ryan's arm next to hers. He was singing the hymn without looking at the book, and he had a nice voice, deep and on pitch. She wouldn't have expected that of him.

She struggled with the tears in her eyes as she forced herself to sing the words.

"A mighty fortress is our God, a bulwark never failing ..."

She sang the words as though she believed them, as though she could find shelter and protection and peace in that fortress, as though nothing bad could ever happen under the watch-care of her Lord. But something terrible *had* happened. That fortress hadn't protected Ella. It hadn't protected their mother. It wasn't comforting her dad. How could she sing these words as if she believed them?

But she couldn't let go of her faith, could she? Not when her whole life centered around it. Her job was all about that. She taught others to trust in that fortress. She had memorized and taught large blocks of scripture, reminding the girls daily of God's holy protection.

Where were you, God, when Ella was screaming?

But she kept singing, holding back the tears, doing all the right things at all the right times, keeping that facade of faith and courage, inspiring others to be what she was not.

Ryan touched her hand. She looked at him, and he whispered, "Are you okay?"

She nodded and kept singing. As they hit the second verse, he sang louder, as if the Holy Spirit reminded him where he belonged.

She couldn't let him know of her doubts and her failures in faith, not when he was responding. She couldn't let anyone know. She was supposed to be a model Christian, a role model for young, at-risk girls. What kind of role model would she be if they knew how angry she was? If they knew her rage? If they knew the questions burning through her chest ... demanding answers.

Relief washed over her when the song came to an end. She sat down and focused on pulling back her tears.

....

When finally the service was over, David put his phone in camera mode and held it out in front of him, waiting to snap the picture.

Krista noticed. "Dad, are you all right?"

He watched Ron as he leaned over to talk to his granddaughter again, then kissed his daughter's cheek. Ron turned back to say something to his wife, and they both laughed.

David looked at Ron's other hand. There were two more scars, on two of his fingers.

"Dad?"

He looked at Krista, irritated. "What?"

"I said we'd see you at home. Ryan is coming over because we're going on the *Today Show* tomorrow morning ..."

Ron was coming out of his pew, falling in behind the others exiting the room. He spoke to someone in front of him. More laughter.

"Dad?"

"Later, Krista."

She stared at him for a moment, then gave up and went the other way out of the pew.

Several people spoke to David as they passed, but he didn't answer. As Ron came toward him, he focused the phone on his face. When he was close enough to get a clear picture, he snapped it, then flipped his phone shut.

As Ron approached David, his cheeky smile faded, and a serious look came to his eyes as he reached out to shake his hand. "Good to see you back, David. I've been praying for you."

David didn't take his hand. Instead, he turned and went the other way. He walked out to his car without responding to anyone, got in, and scanned the parking lot for Ron's Mercedes. As he waited for Ron to come out of the church, he emailed the picture to Megan.

Sweat beads broke out on David's lip as Ron got into his car. David started his car and waited for Ron to pull out of his space. He pulled out of his own and followed, with three cars between them. After a couple of miles, Ron pulled in at a McDonald's. His wife pulled in next to him, and they both went in.

David parked near them and watched. If he heard from Megan before Ron came back out, he'd have the opportunity then to do what he needed to do.

Suddenly, his phone chimed, and he looked down to see a text from Megan.

That's not him. Sorry, Mr. Carmichael.

The wind whooshed out of him. He wrote back,

Are you sure?

She returned,

Yes. Positive.

As his eyes filled with angry tears, he saw Ron coming out with his wife and a bag of food. Ron kissed his wife as he got into his car.

David leaned his head back against his headrest. He could have killed him, the wrong man. Again. He was losing it. Dropping his face into the circle of his arms, he wept.

It wasn't him. It wasn't him.

So who was it? Why couldn't the police find him?

Was Ella's killer going to get away with that vile, vicious act? Was he going to kill more girls?

David had never wanted to die more than he did at that moment. But he had to find the killer first. He might be the next victim's only hope.

thirty-nine

Krista was quiet on the drive back to her house.
"Church was nice," Ryan said. "It's been a long time."

She forced a smile. "I love my church."

"Maybe I'll go again sometime."

She wondered if she should encourage him to keep coming with her. He clearly needed church, but being there with him made her feel too close to him, and that wasn't good. The last thing she needed was to get involved with someone who didn't share her Christian goals or passions. "Why'd you quit going in the first place?"

He shrugged. "I don't know. I guess when I went to college, I stayed up too late, couldn't get up in the morning. Just never tried."

"Didn't you miss it? Didn't you want to worship?"

"Sometimes, when I thought about it. But mostly I didn't think about it. It's pretty typical of college kids, I guess, when your parents aren't there to make you go. Did you live at home during college?"

The question made her bristle. "Yes, but that's not why I kept going. I went because I believed. Because I needed that renewal each week. I needed the fellowship. I wanted to show God my honor and gratitude." She knew her words weren't winsome. Her tone wouldn't make him say, "I want what she has." Instead it was biting. "And just for the record, I lived at home during college because I was helping raise my little sister. She needed me."

Her voice choked off, and she felt Ryan's soft eyes on her.

"I didn't mean that there was anything wrong with you living at home. I knew why you did."

She couldn't speak. As she drove, she fought back the tears that had ambushed her in church, those tears that she didn't want to cry in front of him.

"Those girls who were there," he said, "the ones from your ministry. They sure look up to you."

Again, she didn't know what to say. Several of the girls had stopped her on the way out, and she'd introduced them to Ryan. Her mind strayed back to the traitorous thoughts she'd had in church. If those girls knew her thoughts, they wouldn't look up to her anymore. They would see her as someone like them, someone who was wrestling with God, someone who could barely hold herself together.

They would see that the woman who constantly told them to be strong and courageous was, herself, weak and cowardly. They'd know that she feared constantly for her own life and the lives of others.

"Do a lot of them come to church?"

She cleared her tight throat. "Carla brings whoever shows up at the center before she leaves for church. Sometimes there's a handful; sometimes they fill a whole van."

"That's nice, that you help people all day long. That's what it's all about, isn't it?"

She couldn't imagine what was going through his mind. "What *what's* all about?"

"Life. Christianity, I guess."

As she stopped at a red light, she met his eyes. "Yes, that's what it's all about. Helping others. Giving them what you have to give."

She didn't know how much she had left to give. If she couldn't give them hope ... if she couldn't offer them security ...

"Maybe it's time for me to step out and start helping people too," he said softly. "Meeting you ... going to church ... it felt good. When I was growing up in youth group, going to Christian camps, I thought I'd help people. I thought I'd care more."

"It's not too late," she said.

"No, I guess it isn't."

····

Ryan was quiet as she drove the rest of the way to her house, where he'd left his car. He couldn't explain the feelings that had been revived in him as he'd sat in that church, singing those songs, listening to the old familiar scriptures that his mother had taught him as a kid.

Krista was so much more than a first glance would indicate. Her devotion to God and to needy people was real, and her work made his look like play. She was willing to get her hands dirty. Maybe he should be more willing too.

But the grief behind her eyes got to him. He'd seen how

uncomfortable she seemed in church, how tears burst into her eyes, then vanished without falling. He'd seen how the songs had made her face harder and her shoulders stiffer. He'd seen the complicated dynamics between her and her dad, how she was invisible to him ... or close to it.

It wasn't the right time to get involved with her. But he didn't think he could help himself. He liked being with her, even when she gently brooded, even when she wasn't talking. Her very presence was like a tug on his soul, back into step with the God he'd abandoned.

But there was something uncomfortable and unsafe about that. Something that stirred fear in his heart. If he went back to his Christian roots, started back to church, worshipped God, what would be required of him? Did he even want to make the commitment to God, only to abandon it again?

He honestly didn't know.

Maybe it was just his firing and this point of uncertainty in his life that were giving him thoughts like this. Maybe it was his desire to be with Krista. Or maybe he was just homesick for God.

When they got back to her house, he got out and stood in the driveway. "Thanks for inviting me."

"Sure. Anytime." She paused. "So come on in, and we can go over some things for the interview."

Ian would have punched the air with victory at an invitation inside, but Ryan knew she was strictly business. He followed her in the back door, into the kitchen. As he walked in, Ryan looked around. The eat-in kitchen looked like it had recently been a happy place. Though the Carmichaels clearly didn't have money falling off trees for granite countertops and upscale backsplashes, the place was clean and had feminine touches that he assumed were Krista's.

Family pictures adorned the walls, some of her mother,

some of Ella, and the room had the potential for a happy yellow glow.

"Maybe you should go over my notes," she said, "and help me figure out what I need to say and what to leave out."

"You don't need notes. I want you to talk from your heart about what happened to Ella."

She sighed. "I'm just a little nervous."

"You? The woman who stormed into my building demanding to see me? The woman who had no qualms about calling me a predator?"

She smiled. He really liked it when she did. "I can do things like that. But with the camera and the lights and the famous person interviewing me ... that's all a little different."

"You'll be great. Just pretend you're standing in front of thousands of young people, because you will be. Only it'll be millions. We're on the first hour of the *Today Show* tomorrow, so kids will see it before they go to school. More importantly, parents will see it."

She felt a little sick. "How long are they giving us?"

"Eight minutes."

"Eight minutes? That isn't much time."

"It's an eternity in morning talk show time. It just means we need to be tight. I'll answer questions about my firing, being as vague as possible, and then I'll throw it to you and give you the bulk of the time."

She just looked at him, clearly surprised that he wouldn't try to keep the spotlight on himself.

"We have to be at the affiliate studio by six-thirty, and they'll link us to New York. So I'll pick you up at five-forty-five. It'll still be a little dark, so you don't have to worry about being seen in my car."

Again, a weak smile. "Okay, I'll be ready."

"So let's practice," he said. "I'll be Matt Lauer, and you be you."

"I'd rather be Matt."

He winked at her. "Trust me, you're good at you."

Her cheeks blushed pink, which endeared her to him even more.

They practiced the interview until she was confident that she could handle it. Her dad came home as Ryan was getting ready to leave. Feeling awkward at the man's clear disdain for him, he tried to shake his hand. "Hi, Mr. Carmichael."

Her father looked at Ryan like he didn't belong there, then shot a scathing look to Krista.

"Dad, Ryan came in with me so we could get ready for our interview on the *Today Show* tomorrow."

David wasn't appeased by the explanation. Without a word, he pushed on through the house.

Ryan glanced at Krista. "Am I not supposed to be in here?"

She shook her head. "No, it's fine. I'm twenty-five years old. He's just ... not himself."

She didn't have to finish the explanation. Ryan knew what she meant. The man was having trouble coping with life, now that his youngest child's life had been taken. He couldn't say he blamed him.

He thanked her again for taking him with her to church, then said good-bye. But when he got into his Jaguar, he sat for a moment before turning the ignition, and prayed an awkward prayer for Krista and her dad. He couldn't remember the last time he'd prayed. It had been a long time. But the pain in that house was palpable, and they needed God's help.

And the more he thought about it, the more he realized that *he* needed God's help too.

forty

When Ryan got home, Ian was right where he'd left him. He sat on the sofa, laptop on his knees, staring intently at the screen. "Back already? So how was your date?"

Ryan kicked off his shoes and grabbed his own laptop. "I told you, it wasn't a date."

"Okay. So how was church?"

"Pretty good, actually." He looked at Ian's screen, saw a picture of Marvin Bainbridge, who held the controlling interest in Willow Entertainment. "You haven't broken any laws from my server, have you?"

"No, I've just been doing research, which we probably should have done before you sold the company."

"I did do research. I knew who those guys were, who the company was. But I was this little peon with a big idea, and they were waving money like they had it to burn."

"You didn't do the right kind of research. I'm not talking about their professional lives and all the PR they've released about themselves. I'm talking about their personal lives."

Ryan groaned. "You're not hacking into their personal computers, are you? Please tell me you're not."

"No, but dude, there's some stuff here you need to see."

"What?"

Ian typed something in, and a picture of Henry Hearne came up. "Bainbridge and the others look pretty straight and narrow, but Henry ..."

Ryan narrowed his eyes. "What about him?"

"I found some speeches he made back in the seventies. He was a pretty radical guy back then, a member of this weird political party called the Forward Party. In one of the speeches he talked about controlling the masses by using technology to gather information about them."

"Controlling the masses? For what purpose?"

"To advance their political agenda. I'm still trying to figure out exactly what they wanted. But the point is, he's the one who created the Data-Gather program. It looks like this is all part of the plan. And GrapeVyne was the perfect tool. Millions of people willing to give personal details about their lives."

"So are you implying that the whole board of directors is in on this?"

"I don't know. I've only connected Hearne to this so far, but I'm looking at Bainbridge now. They may have believed GrapeVyne was a treasure trove when they bought it, or they might have had other intentions."

Ryan shook his head. "I don't know. It seems like a stretch. Just because Henry made some speeches forty years ago ..."

"Ryan, we got fired today. They may have given you some song and dance about your making the company look bad, but this was about me hacking into Data-Gather.

That's too close to the nerve center of their operations, and they wanted us out so we couldn't get any closer."

Ryan read the article, then shook his head. "Well, if it's true, we can't prove it."

"I'm not finished yet."

Ryan didn't know whether to believe it, but he was too tired to follow Ian's conspiracy theory. "Look, I don't know if this is right or not. But right now, I just need to get some sleep. I'm going on the *Today Show* in the morning, really early."

"Are you telling me to go home?"

"You can stay here if you want. I'm just saying I don't much care whether the board members are on some political bandwagon or not. It has nothing to do with me."

"But what if they're doing something illegal? What if this is all some sinister plot—"

"Ian ..."

"What if you just told the FBI about it and let them sort it out? What if we gave them the info I found on the search strings—"

"One thing at a time, okay? I'm seriously maxed out here."

"Okay, never mind. I'll just keep gathering my own data. Don't worry about it."

Ryan couldn't help worrying. "So you're staying here tonight?"

"I might go home when I'm finished."

"Okay, lock up. I'm going to bed."

He barely had the energy to undress. As he fell into bed, he knew that Ian would still be here when he got up.

forty-one

After Ryan had gone, Krista found her dad in his room, sitting in his rocking chair beside his bed. The bed hadn't been made up in weeks—not since Ella had gone missing. A pile of clothes lay on a club chair in the corner—probably everything he'd worn since that horrible day. She should have noticed it sooner, she thought. She should have washed his clothes.

A lone lamp was on, and dust motes floated around it. The room smelled stale.

"Dad? Are you all right?"

He didn't look at her. "Of course I am. Stop asking me that."

"But you seemed upset that Ryan was here."

"He doesn't have any business here. He runs the company that contributed to Ella's death. Why should I treat him like an honored guest?"

She sat down on the corner of the bed, facing him. "He got fired today, probably for helping me. He let me talk to the board members about changes to their site, and the next thing I knew, they fired him. I never meant for him to make such a sacrifice to help me, but he did."

Her father didn't answer.

"Did you hear me tonight when I told you we're going on the *Today Show* tomorrow?"

"I heard you. You're going to become quite a celebrity."

That felt like a slap across her face. "I don't want to be a celebrity, Dad. I just want to save lives."

He looked at her then, and his eyes softened. "Are you seeing him?"

The question surprised her. "No, we're just friends. Even that's a surprise to me, because I didn't think I was going to like him. But he's just an ordinary guy, like us."

"He's not like us. He makes millions of dollars a year."

"Made."

"Somehow I think he'll survive losing his job."

"So you don't like him because he's rich?"

"I don't like him because he created a portal for the worst kind of evil."

"He didn't mean for it to be. And he's trying to change it. Going on the *Today Show* will stir up a lot of trouble for him, but he's willing to do it to keep any more girls from giving out the kind of information that leads predators to them."

He didn't answer. He just stared straight ahead. She wondered where he'd gone.

"Dad? Are you going to watch?"

"I might go back to work tomorrow. I have to do it sometime."

"But we're on in the first hour, before work."

He sighed. "Guess I will, then."

She went over to him and kissed him on the cheek, then hugged him. He put his arms around her, but they lacked strength or warmth.

She missed her father.

"You'd better go to bed if you have to get up that early," he said.

She straightened, aware that he was trying to get rid of her. "Yeah, you're right. Hope I can sleep."

When she went to bed, she lay awake into the wee hours, going over and over what she would say in the morning, and praying that her words could make a difference and protect the thousands who would hear her.

She prayed for Ryan, that the worship service tonight had impacted him in an eternal way, and that God would help him with his troubles.

And then she prayed that God would forgive her for the thoughts she'd let slink into her consciousness tonight. She prayed he would take them away and restore her faith in him. But the more she wished them gone, the more they plagued her.

How could God know the number of hairs on Ella's head, but not stop this crazed killer from abducting her on the street?

How could a family who served God be ripped apart by such tragic events?

How could a trusting young girl be molested that way?

How could a perverted monster still be free to roam the streets looking for someone to devour?

She finally gave up sleeping and turned on her laptop. Sitting at her desk, she opened her real GrapeVyne page, the one where she posted her Bible studies for the girls at the center. She had email from two of them. They were turning in their assignments. She checked their answers, saw that they really had understood what they'd read. They were learning to get sustenance from God's Word. Learning that their security was in Him.

It wasn't false security ... was it?

Certain that her thoughts were pushing toward blasphemy, she banished them from her mind, signed out, then signed back in under her fake name. Maxi's page came up, and she saw that she had five emails. They were all from the same person—a boy named Steven, who claimed he was seventeen.

As she opened his first email, a shiver went down her spine. A real kid would have communicated with her by commenting on her Vyne, out in the open, where others could view his quips. This one was doing it out of the public eye, in her private Inbox.

> Don't tell me a girl as hot as you doesn't have friends. I'm here if you ever need to talk. I'm a good listener.

She clicked on the second email. It said simply,

> Hello? Are you there?

"Yes," she whispered aloud. "I'm right here." She clicked on his third email, biting her lip.

> Maxi. I love that name. I don't know anyone else with that name. It's one of a kind, like you. I love your sense of humor on your Vyne. Most people I know are pretty boring, so I put a high premium on girls who make me laugh. I'm feeling very insecure that you haven't written me back. What gives?

A high premium? That wasn't something a kid would say. It sounded like something a man *pretending* to be a kid would say.

She clicked on Steven's face, and his profile came up. It said he was born in October, was a junior in high school, played guitar in a band, and also played soccer. He listed Cold Play as his favorite musical group, *Big Brother* as his favorite TV show. The high school he'd listed was only twenty miles away. She clicked on his photos and saw an album with pictures of him with his band, pictures with girls, pictures with friends and family.

If the killer had designed this profile, he'd done a good job of making himself look real. But she knew he could have stolen those pictures from anyone's site. As long as no one who knew the real boy saw them, the killer could get away with it. That would be another reason to email her privately, instead of commenting publicly on her Vyne.

She replied,

> Sorry, I've been busy today and didn't see your email. I had to go to a science fair for home-schoolers. I didn't win, but oh well. It's okay because I'm not that into the whole bacteria thing. (I'd tell you about my project, but it's pretty sick.)
>
> I looked at your profile and love that you're in a band. What kind of music do you play?
>
> We should get together sometime. We don't live that far apart.
>
> Maxi

She drew in a ragged breath, set her laptop on her bed,

and hugged her knees, wondering if he'd be up this late, scavenging the Internet for his next victim.

What was she doing? This was crazy. She was setting herself up for disaster. Her father could have another trag-edy on his hands.

But it wouldn't be as tragic as Ella's death was. Ella was the one her father adored.

But nothing was going to happen. She had a gun, and as long as she could get both forefingers around the trigger, she could use it. She wouldn't hesitate to do that to defend herself ... and to catch him.

She heard a chime and looked back at the computer. Steven had written back.

> I'd love to meet you. Just say the word. I'd even
> skip school to see you.

Muscles rigid, she typed,

> Let me think about it. I'm pretty busy for the
> next couple of days, but I can probably spare
> an hour sometime.

She sent it, then closed out of the program. Her heart raced. Maybe she should just contact the police with his name.

And tell them what? That she'd created a fake persona, and some kid had taken the bait? That he'd done what any kid might do?

No, it wouldn't raise any red flags for them. But it did for her. She could take care of it herself.

She went back to bed, stared at the ceiling, trying to imagine how it would play out. She would set up a meeting time ... a place. She would see who showed up and lingered, see if he was a middle-aged man or a seventeen-year-old kid. She would try to get a picture.

Sleep never came, but morning did. She finally got up, and saw that her dad's bedroom lamp was on. She went to his doorway, saw him asleep in his chair, still fully dressed. She went in and touched his shoulder. "Dad?"

He stirred and looked up at her.

"Why don't you get in bed? You don't have to get up for another hour or so."

He moved to the bed and lay down on top of the covers, his back to her. She went to his closet, got out a blanket, and laid it over him. Then, kissing his cheek, she went to get ready for her interview.

forty-two

Krista sat in front of her makeup mirror, staring at her reflection, hardly recognizing herself. She had dark circles like bruises under her eyes, and lines were etched from her nose to her mouth. She was aging too fast.

She didn't even know how to do makeup for television, but she needed to look her best. People would listen if they thought she looked nice. She put on her base a little thicker than usual, smudged a light retoucher under her eyes. It helped a little. When she finished, she went to her closet. Standing in front of it, she tried to imagine what would look best on television. Should she wear a pattern or a solid?

Why hadn't she figured this out last night?

She pulled out a black dress with a scooped neck and long sleeves. Ella had been with her when she bought it. She had insisted she buy a cute belt to go with it. She slipped the dress on and found the belt.

Ella had good taste.

Who would have thought she'd wear the dress and belt Ella picked out, to talk about her murder on national television?

That sick feeling returned to the pit of her stomach.

She checked her watch. It was almost time for Ryan to be here. She went into her living room and sat in front of the window, watching for headlights through the sheers. A yellow streetlight lit the area just in front of their house.

Somewhere out there, a killer lurked.

Her head began to ache, and she wondered if she would make it through the interview. When she saw headlights turn into the driveway, she stood up and drew in a deep breath and told herself she could do this. It would be over in a little while.

....

Ryan thought Krista looked lovely as she walked out to his car. He considered getting out and opening her door for her, the way his mother taught him, but nobody did that anymore, and he didn't want to look too anxious. Still, if anyone deserved that kind of attention, she did.

She got into the Jaguar, closed the door. "Hi."

"Morning," he said.

She tried to smile. "Feels like the middle of the night."

"Did you sleep?"

"Not one wink."

"Me either. Well, you look nice, anyway," he said.

As he backed out of her driveway, she folded her arms as if she were cold. He turned on the heater.

"I'm pretty nervous," she said.

"You'll be great. Just pretend you're standing in front of those kids you spoke to the other day. And this can't be worse than talking to my board of directors."

"Yeah, but look what happened with that." She sighed and got comfortable in the plush leather seat. "Besides, that was easy, because I was angry at everyone at GrapeVyne."

"Then get angry again, if it helps you. People will listen to you because of what happened."

She looked out the window as he headed for the highway that would take them to the part of town where the NBC affiliate was. There were few cars on the dark road, but an occasional pair of headlights passed them. He glanced in his rearview mirror. A pair of headlights behind him was blinding him. He moved the mirror so the reflection wouldn't be so bright.

He pulled onto the interstate, his Jaguar swallowing up the road.

"If I get too shaky or lose my train of thought, you'll jump in and help me?"

"As much as I can without saying anything myself about GrapeVyne and Willow."

"Have you talked to a lawyer about this?" she asked. "Are you sure that your being there isn't enough to get you sued?"

"Nope. But if I'm the one giving you access, I'm going to do it, whatever happens."

He looked in his rearview mirror again. The headlights were too close. "Wish this truck would stop tailgating me. It's six in the morning and the road's wide open, and he has to sit on my tail."

She glanced out the back window. "Maybe it's a teenager. I tried to teach Ella to drive, and she always wanted to hug the car in front of us." She turned back around. "So you didn't sleep last night?"

He shook his head. "Not much. Ian was there all night on the trail of some big conspiracy theory."

"He didn't go home at all?"

"No, but that's no surprise. He used to stay at work for days on end, which is the reason I made sure we had showers in our new building. He's single-mindedly focused on whatever he's working on. That's why he's so valuable. I think part of it may be that he doesn't like to be alone. He grew up in a family with ten kids, so he always had roommates. Never had any privacy, so he's not really into that."

"Does it bother you when he stays at your house all night?"

"No, I like having him around. It's like the old days, when we shared a twelve-by-fourteen-foot dorm room. Good times." He glanced in the mirror again. The headlights reflecting off his rearview mirror lit up his face.

"So what's the conspiracy?"

He hesitated, not sure he should mention it. "Before we were fired, we saw some things on Willow's servers that worried us. Things that weren't supposed to be there."

"What kind of things?"

He didn't answer right away.

"That's okay, you don't have to tell me."

"It's just that ... I'm not sure that we really know what's going on yet. But Ian thinks Willow is gathering way more data about our GrapeVyne clients than we thought. Things that aren't just for targeting advertising. Things that they're collecting ... for other reasons."

"That sounds pretty scary."

"Yeah, it is. So he's been up all night trying to figure out who's in on it and what they could be using it for."

"I knew it," she said. "People are putting way too much information on the Internet, and there's not really any such thing as true security, is there?"

"No, actually, there's not. Databases are only as secure

as the people who control them. And even with the best developers and engineers and designers, with every change to a site come security breaches. But we don't have the whole picture yet."

"If they have something to hide, they're not going to like your going on TV, are they?"

"No, they'll be mad as hornets. I may only get one shot at this before they try to shut me up." He slammed his steering wheel. "That truck is getting on my nerves."

She turned again, saw that the truck was still riding way too close to their bumper. Ryan had sped up to eighty, and the truck kept up. Finally, it changed lanes and sped up. "He's going around you."

Ryan slowed down to let them go by. But the truck got even with him and stayed there. He slowed even more, and so did the truck. "What is he doing?"

Moonlight glistened on the truck's window, and he saw it coming down. Ryan touched his brakes.

Thunder cracked ... his windshield shattered. No, not thunder ... gunfire.

Krista screamed.

Someone was trying to kill them!

"Get down!" Ryan cried.

Krista bent double, covering her head. Ryan's car spun as another bullet knocked out the backseat's side window.

He turned the car around, going the wrong way on the interstate, hoping to put some distance between him and the shooter, but there was more gunfire. A bullet knocked out a tire, making him skid and lose control.

The skid threw Krista against the door. They were going to go off the road ... into a ravine.

The firing stopped, and Ryan looked out the back window. The truck was in reverse, backing up. Turning around, it came toward them again, rammed Ryan's car, making it slide to the edge of the embankment.

Who *were* these people?

His tires lost traction, and he felt the slide. His head rammed against the window as the car flipped. Airbags blew out, and he managed to touch Krista's back, as if his arm could protect her as they rolled and bounced ... and crashed at the bottom of the ravine.

When the Jaguar came to a halt and stopped moving, they both hung upside down. Blood rushed to Ryan's face as he looked at Krista. "Are you all right?"

"Yes." She was gasping for breath. "Are you?"

He steadied himself on the roof of the car, which was now on the ground, and unbuckled his seat belt. "I'm okay," he said. "We gotta get out now. It could blow up."

He helped her get her seat belt open, helped her right herself in the car. "Out your side, so they won't see us."

She tried to open her door, but it was bent and stuck. Her window was partially broken, and Ryan looked around for something to break through the glass. An umbrella was wedged between the seats. He yanked it out and rammed it into the window, knocking out the rest of the glass. Thankful it was still dark, he urged her through the hole first, then slid out behind her.

Protecting Krista with his arm, he pulled her along, away from the car and into the dark woods. He couldn't see where he was stepping. Twigs tore across his skin. She hit a tree branch with her forehead and ducked, stumbled. He helped her back up.

They heard gunfire again from the road above them, then a sudden *whoosh.*

"Down!" He pulled her to the ground and covered her body as fire swelled from the car like a greedy demon. The gas tank exploded in a thunderous bolt.

"They must think we're in there, dead."

The fire from his car illuminated their path, and he grabbed her up and ran deeper into the brush. He turned and looked up at the road. The truck's headlights turned as it righted itself in the lane. As it drove away, he let out a grateful breath.

"God help us, they were trying to kill us."

Krista was trembling, and she struggled to catch her breath. "Who ... who was that?"

"Had to be two people — the driver and the shooter — but I didn't see their faces."

"Could it be Ella's killer?"

"Maybe," he said. "Or someone who didn't want us doing that interview."

"Your board members?"

"No, couldn't be. They're businessmen, not killers. Just because they fired me doesn't mean they want me dead."

"I want to get out of here in case they come back," she said. "Do you have your phone?"

Ryan reached into his pants pocket and pulled out his phone, grateful it hadn't gotten smashed in the wreck. He made the call to 911. But he knew that by the time the police got there, the shooters would be long gone.

forty-three

Ryan sat in the ambulance with Krista, watching out the open back doors as police and fire fighters worked around his smoldering Jaguar. His chest felt as though a vice was clamped over his heart. The smell of burned leather, rubber, and metal wafted up from the ravine, and smoke still hovered like a low-lying cloud.

Krista shivered as if she sat in subzero temperature, and the red knot on her temple signaled a possible concussion. The EMT turned off his pin light. "I don't think you have a concussion," he said, "but you need to be checked out by a doctor. We'd like to transport you to the hospital."

"No, I'm fine. It doesn't even hurt. I want to stay here and talk to the police."

"The police can interview you at the hospital."

Ryan squeezed her hand. "You have to go, Krista. I'll come with you."

She turned her fierce gaze to him. "But those guys are still out there, Ryan. They tried to kill us. We have to give the police all the information they need to find them, now."

"But ma'am, you were both thrown around pretty good. As a precaution—"

"We don't have time for this!" Krista got out of the ambulance.

Ryan followed her. "Krista, are you sure?"

"Where's the officer in charge?"

Ryan looked down the embankment and saw an officer with a camera. "Maybe there. Krista, I want to make sure you're all right."

"I'm fine, just like you! The Jaguar has great air-bags." She stormed over to the cop who'd questioned them originally.

Ryan didn't know why his brain seemed so sluggish. His thoughts moved in slow-motion, as though the live-stream video of his life had hit a snag. But Krista was right. They had to help the police find that truck.

The ranking officer, Sergeant Rutherford, had them sit in the backseat of his car, where he could question them.

"When did you first notice that you were being followed?"

Ryan tried to steady himself. "I'm not sure. Maybe at my house, when I was pulling out of my driveway."

Krista looked at him. "Really? You didn't say anything when you picked me up."

"I didn't think they were following me then. I just remember noticing headlights behind me, and thinking someone else was up and at 'em kind of early. I didn't notice them behind me all the way to your house, so they must have kept their distance."

"So it's possible that they were waiting for you to come out of your house?"

"I guess so, but how would they know I was leaving then? I had the interview for this morning, but I didn't tell anyone except Ian. Krista, you probably told your dad, right?"

"Yes. No one else."

Sergeant Rutherford shook his head. "Actually, I saw a promo about it late last night when I was getting ready for my shift."

Ryan met his eyes. "A promo?"

"That's right. The *Today Show* mentioned you were one of their guests this morning."

Ryan raked his hand through his hair. "That explains it. Word got out, and someone who didn't want me talking did this."

"Who didn't want you to talk?"

He gave him a list of the men who sat on his board.

"Did you recognize any of them in the truck?"

"No. It was dark. I didn't recognize the truck, either."

He gave him a description of the truck, but half the population of Texas had trucks like it. Since they didn't have the tag number, they were hamstrung in finding the shooters.

"If I were you, I wouldn't go home," Rutherford said. "You might not be safe there."

Ryan thought of the truck turning around and driving off after the car went up in flames. "They think I'm dead. They didn't see us get out of the car before it blew. That's why they took off."

Rutherford scribbled something in his notebook.

"Maybe it would be a good idea to let them keep thinking that until we find them."

Krista shook her head. "I can't let people think I'm dead! My dad has been through enough."

"And Ian." Worried his friend would hear about his accident, Ryan pulled out his phone, dialed Ian.

It rang four times, and he expected voicemail to pick up, when Ian finally answered. "When are you going on the air, man? I've seen enough beauty secrets and recipes to last me a decade."

"Not going on," Ryan said. "Someone tried to kill me. My car exploded."

"What? *Who?*"

"We don't know. It could be related to Ella's case ... or it could be someone at GrapeVyne. No matter who it was, you need to leave my house. If they get word that I survived the crash, they may come there to finish what they started."

"Wow." Ian hesitated a moment. "All right, I'm packing it up right now. Guess I'll keep working at my house."

"No, that may not be safe either. Watch for a black truck, man. They have guns."

Suddenly, Ryan heard a crash over the phone line, and Ian cursed. Then the phone clattered, and he heard Ian yelling.

"Ian!" Ryan yelled. "What's going on? Ian!"

There was a sound as loud as a freight train, then the phone cut off. "Something just happened," he told Sergeant Rutherford. "I've got to get to my house."

"I'll take you," the cop said. As he called dispatch to get a car to Ryan's house, he started his car.

As the siren came on, Ryan and Krista hooked their seat belts. Ryan stared out the window as they drove toward his house, praying that Ian was safe, that he'd only broken the phone. That was possible. He could have knocked the lamp over. The crash could have been the base breaking. Maybe he dropped the phone when he tried to pick it up.

Krista's soft eyes contemplated Ryan as he tried to call Ian back. But there was no answer.

"They got to him," he whispered. "They did something ..."

They were silent as they flew through town, siren roaring. Radio transmissions crackled back and forth, but Ryan couldn't understand what they were saying.

As they rounded the curve to Ryan's house, he leaned forward, hands gripping the front seat. As his house came into view, his chest closed tight. He couldn't breathe.

Flames engulfed his home.

Ian!

Ryan was out of the car before it came to a complete halt. The police officer who'd beaten them to the scene stopped him from running toward the house. "You can't go in there."

"But my friend is in there! We've got to get him out!"

"Over here, buddy!"

Ryan swung around and saw Ian sitting in the backseat of a police car. His laptop was on his knees.

Ryan almost collapsed in relief. He went to the car and slapped his hands on both sides of Ian's face, smacked a kiss on his forehead. Then he looked into Ian's bloodshot eyes. "What happened?"

Ian shook his head. "No idea. I was talking to you on the phone when something came flying through the window. It rolled across the floor. A grenade or some kind of bomb, I guess. I dropped the phone and ran out the front door, and I saw a black truck taking off. Just like you described."

"Did you see who it was?"

"No. I tried to run after them to get their license plate, but I lost them. When I came back, the house was on fire."

Ryan tried to think. "It had to be Willow. They were trying to destroy everything we had against them. Maybe they knew you were snooping last night."

"Well, they didn't get everything." He held up his laptop. "I was holding this when it happened."

"Guard it with your life," Ryan said.

Ian gave a nervous laugh as he hugged the laptop to his chest. "I think I just did."

forty-four

The interview room at the police station was too cold, as if the city leaders had decided not to spend money on heat. Krista sat next to Ryan, unable to control her shaking.

He put his arms around her, rubbing her arms to warm her up. He looked at the two detectives across the table. "Do you have a blanket anywhere?"

Pensky, the detective who was investigating Ella's, Megan's, and Karen's cases, left the room and came back with a blanket.

Ryan took it and draped it around Krista.

"Why are you working on this case?" Krista asked the detective. "Do you think it has something to do with Ella's killer?"

Pensky looked at Detective Sanders, assigned to Ryan's case. "We don't think it's related, but Detective Sanders asked me to join the investigation to make sure."

241

"But this is about me," Ryan said, "not her. It was my house that was burned. Krista was just an innocent bystander."

"That looks to be the case," Sanders said. "We have a car on your street now, Krista, watching to make sure nothing is attempted there. But I wanted Detective Pensky to know the details, just in case there's any crossover." He shifted in his seat, glanced at his notes. "We're working on questioning the board members of Willow."

"If it was any of them, they'll have alibis," Ryan said. "They wouldn't do it themselves. They have plenty of money. They'd hire someone."

"So if you're right," Sanders said, "and they're the ones who wanted you dead, what were they trying to cover up?"

Ryan told them about Ian's suspicions. He knew it was over their heads. Though these men seemed competent, cyber crimes were probably out of their league. He urged them to call in the FBI's cyber crimes unit.

"Is there anyone else you can think of who might want you dead? An old enemy from outside the company? A competitor?"

"No competitor would consider me a threat after yesterday. But yeah, I might have enemies. You don't run a billion-dollar business and not have a few enemies here and there. But I don't think they'd go as far as wanting me dead."

"Who's next in line for your position?"

"Well, Ian would have been, but he got fired too."

"Did Ian blame you for his firing?"

Ryan stared at him. "No, not at all."

"But he knew when you were going for the interview this morning, right?"

"Yes, he was at my house when I left."

"And he was still there when the explosion happened."

"Yes." Ryan leaned forward. "Where are you going with this, Detective?"

"We just have to consider every possibility. You two built GrapeVyne together, right? Yet you were considered the owner, and you were the one who got a hundred million when you sold it."

"That's because I invented it, wrote most of the code that got us off the ground, and I got the funding when we were getting started. I've been the owner from Day One. He's never had the slightest problem with that."

"That you know of."

"Look, he got pretty rich too. He was given a huge bonus to stay on when I sold the company. He has a seven-figure salary."

"Had."

Ryan grunted. "You don't know him. He's my best friend. He knows we can start over with something even more innovative than GrapeVyne."

Someone knocked on the door, and a female officer stuck her head in. "Detective, we just got a call that Ian Lombardi's house was robbed this morning. Some officers went by there with him on the way here, and they found the place had been ransacked, computer equipment taken, all of his files, financial records ..."

Krista gasped. Ryan turned back to the detectives. "See? He's a victim too!"

"Robbery's a far cry from a murder attempt and a bombed house. We're not saying he had anything to do with it, but he could have staged this. We have to question him."

"You're way off-track, man. Can't you just consider that everything I've told you is true, and they hoped to kill him in my house? His car was there, man. They knew he was inside."

He looked at Krista, saw the doubt in her eyes.

"Ryan, he had access to Ella's and Megan's pages."

"Don't even think it," he said. "Ian's my best friend. He would never do this to me."

forty-five

David's alarm went off some time after Krista left the house. Throwing off the blanket she'd covered him with, he got up and went into the kitchen. The coffeepot was full of hot coffee. He poured himself a cup and turned on NBC, hoping he hadn't missed her interview.

He zoned out as they were doing a cooking segment outside Rockefeller Center, debating whether to use charcoal or propane.

He thought of Krista in the television station, getting her hair and makeup done, and going on TV to talk about Ella's death. How could she do it? The death was so fresh to him, the wound still so wide open, that he could never go on national TV and answer questions intelligently.

He thought of how sweet she'd been to him lately, how she'd made him meals and covered him with the blanket this morning. He was like an old man at only forty-eight, wandering around the house with his mind turned to mush. She'd be better off without him.

He thought through his options for suicide. Ideally, he would find the murderer and kill him, then turn the gun on himself. But what if he never found the killer? Could he go on, knowing he was out there somewhere?

The knowledge that he didn't have to endure the pain much longer was the only thing that made life bearable. So how would he do it?

He had to think of Krista. He didn't want her to find him, so he couldn't do it at home. He'd do it somewhere else, in a way that was least traumatic for whoever did find him. He thought of driving down to Galveston and shooting himself on the beach. But what if a child came along and discovered him? That would traumatize them for life.

Maybe pills were the way to go. He could just fall asleep in a hotel room somewhere. But where would he get the pills? And what if someone found him and revived him? Pills could cause him some kind of lifelong disability that would linger and make life even worse.

He could drive off a bridge, but that might kill others. No, he didn't want Krista to have to live with that too.

The thought of his suicide's effect on others was getting in his way. There was no way to do it without hurting someone. For the first time it seemed mean, and he'd never been a mean person.

Ryan Adkins' name on TV snatched his attention away from his fantasy. He turned up the volume.

"We've just learned that two of our guests this morning, Ryan Adkins, formerly of GrapeVyne Corporation and Krista Carmichael, sister of Ella Carmichael who was found dead in Houston a few weeks ago, were in a car accident

on the way to our Houston affiliate. We've also gotten a report that Ryan's house was burned in a fire this morning. We have no information on the condition of Ryan or Krista, but we'll keep you updated as we know more."

David's heart bolted. He grabbed the phone off the wall, tried to think of Krista's number. What was it? He dropped the phone and reached for his cell phone, pressed his speed dial. It went straight to her voicemail.

He grabbed the phone book and tore through it, looking up the number to the closest hospital. He dialed it, then asked the lady who answered if Krista Carmichael had been admitted. After a delay while she looked, the woman told him she hadn't.

He didn't know what to do. He tried Krista again, but it still didn't ring through. Quickly, he looked in the blue pages for the number to the police department. Which precinct would work this case? He finally just called the one closest to the television station.

When someone answered, he blurted, "This is Krista Carmichael's father. She was in an accident. I'm trying to find her—"

"Hold on, I'll transfer you to the officer working the case."

The case. He held on, waiting, praying that Krista had survived.

"Detective Sanders."

David's voice came out hoarse. "This is David Carmichael. I'm looking for my daughter Krista."

"Yeah, she's here with me."

"Then ... she's alive?"

"Yes, she's fine. Want to talk to her?"

"Yes!"

His heart almost leaped through his chest as Krista took the phone.

"Dad?"

"Krista, I heard on TV—"

"Dad, I meant to call you, but then the thing with Ryan's house fire distracted me ... We were run off the road and someone tried to kill us."

"Who did this?"

"We're trying to figure that out now."

"Krista, you get away from him! I'm coming to get you."

"Okay," she said. "I'll wait here for you."

He hung up the phone and dropped into his chair. Was he going to lose his last family member? He didn't know if he had the strength to deal with that.

He threw on some fresh clothes, then headed to the police precinct. As he drove, sorrow crushed him, and the joy of finding Krista alive wasn't enough to pull him out of it. A sense of more impending doom floated over him like a thunder cloud.

The nightmare wasn't over yet.

forty-six

When the police finished questioning Krista, she went home with her father. Tension rippled as she got into his car. Was it rage? Fear? Despair?

She hooked her belt. As he started the car, she looked out the windows, wondering if any black trucks lurked nearby. No one seemed to be watching them, and no one was in any of the cars parked along the streets.

"I'm still shaking," she whispered. "I was so scared."

David's jaw muscle popped. "I don't want you around that man."

"Ryan? Dad, he didn't cause this."

"No TV, no speaking engagements. Just keep a low profile for a while."

"But Dad, there are other girls out there who might fall into predators' traps. I have to tell them—"

"No, you don't have to tell anybody anything!" he shouted. "Let someone else tell them."

"But God gave this to *me*! It gives purpose to Ella's death."

He slammed his hand on the steering wheel, making her jump. "There *is* no purpose! This wasn't part of some grand plan by God, for anyone's good. This was pure evil, and that evil is still breathing on us. You think you're immune, just because you're trying to do the right thing? You're not immune."

"Dad, this just makes me more determined to fight."

"They have guns, Krista! Grenades, bombs. They're out of your league!"

She watched him for a moment. The pain on his face was etched deep, and there was more gray in his hair than he'd had a month ago. He was a man in physical anguish, and his emotional scars were raw. "Dad, I'm sorry I caused you more pain."

Tears sprang to his eyes. She wondered if it was wise for him to drive. "Then don't do it again," he said. "I don't want you going on television. Do you hear me?"

She knew she could do whatever she pleased. She was an adult, after all. But she didn't want to hurt him more or cause him anxiety or stress. And she believed in the commandment to honor her parents. He was the only one she had. And she was all he had.

She was quiet for a moment.

"Krista, please. What would I do if something happened to you too?"

She couldn't deny him. "Okay, I won't."

He blew out a breath of pained relief. "And whatever you do, don't fall in love with that guy."

"I have no intentions of falling in love."

forty-seven

Ryan waited outside the interview room as the police interviewed Ian. It was going on too long. Were they trying to pin this stuff on him? How could they even think his friend would do something so deadly?

Two hours passed as Ryan paced the stained concrete floor. He hoped Krista was safe. The police had someone watching the Carmichael house, so maybe the guys who'd done all this would leave her alone.

He sat back down, elbows on his knees, and dropped his face into his hands. His house, his car, everything he owned ...

How could this happen?

He thought of the board members who'd been so delighted with him until recently. They'd respected him, appreciated him. He'd played golf with Henry, stayed in

Marvin's Colorado condo, had dinner in all their homes. He knew their wives, their children. Would one of them really hire a killer to eliminate him?

The interview room door opened, and Ryan looked up. Ian came out, looking like he always did—unwashed and unkempt, and utterly sleep-deprived.

"You okay?" Ryan asked.

"Yeah," Ian said. "That was big fun. It's just hard to beat a murder attempt, a robbery, and an interrogation, all in one day."

"Got that right," Ryan said.

"They questioned me like I was the one who broke into my own house. And why would I firebomb your house, Ryan? Why would I try to kill you?"

"I know. It's nuts."

"Whatever. Let's just get out of here."

"In what?" Ryan asked. "I don't have a car anymore."

"Well, I do. My car's out front if you're not afraid to be seen in it."

Ryan thought about that for a moment. "I think we both need to get new cars. You're in as much danger as I'm in. Maybe we need to head over to a car dealership right now."

Ian couldn't argue. Ryan followed him out. As they both got into Ian's red Mercedes Cabriolet convertible, Ryan looked at his friend. "We're homeless millionaires, man. Who woulda thought?"

"You're homeless. I'm not."

"True." Ryan settled in his seat. "So what did they take?"

"Anything that even looked like I might have stored files there. They cleaned out my file cabinet, took my backup backup external hard drive. If this doesn't have Willow written all over it, I don't know what does."

"So after we buy cars, we'll check into a hotel and get on the Internet. We're going to get to the bottom of this."

They were quiet as they drove to the car lot. When they pulled in, Ryan glanced at Ian. "Not telling you what to buy, but I'm getting a car as nondescript as I can. No more Jaguars. They're too easy to identify."

"But I really, really like my Cabriolet."

"If you want your car to blend into a hotel parking lot, I wouldn't get one."

"Even if it's a different color?"

"I'm just saying ..."

Ian sighed. "I hate these people. They're ruining my life." He pulled into the space at the front of the lot. "I'm going to ruin theirs as soon as I can."

....

It took two hours to buy the cars, which Ryan thought was ridiculous, since they were both paying cash. But the paperwork went on forever, and then the dealer insisted on detailing the cars before they drove off the lot.

Ryan had chosen a black Pathfinder, opting for an SUV for added protection from the next person who tried to run him off the road. Ian couldn't downgrade quite that much. He chose a white Lexus SUV, something he could get excited about. When they finally owned their new cars, Ian cleaned all of his belongings out of his beloved Cabriolet, and loaded them into his new vehicle. "So where are we going to bunk tonight?"

"How about the Hampton Inn near Rice?"

"No way, man. Hampton Inns don't even have room service."

"Room service could get us killed."

He sighed. "All right, whatever. I'll follow you there."

When they reached the hotel, Ryan sent Ian in to get the room, since no one was likely to recognize him. Ryan had been the front man for GrapeVyne, the one who'd done countless interviews over the years. He didn't want some hotel clerk spreading gossip that Ryan Adkins was staying in his hotel. That could get them killed too.

While he waited for Ian to get the key, Ryan called NBC. They were enthusiastic in their agreement to put him on for the next day. He didn't know if Krista would join him. Her father would probably handcuff her to keep her from going anywhere with him again. But he thought he'd give her the chance if she wanted. He called her as he waited for Ian.

She sounded glad to hear from him. "Ryan, is everything all right with Ian?"

"I guess so. They let him go. We just bought some new wheels. Checking into a hotel now."

She was silent for a moment. "Are you sure you can trust him?"

He bristled. "Yes, Krista, absolutely. I trust him like he was my own brother."

"But there are a lot of coincidences. The police seemed suspicious."

"It's their job to be suspicious. But I know him. He's my best friend. I have nothing to fear from him, and neither do you."

She didn't answer.

"But listen, NBC wants us on tomorrow."

Again, quiet built a wall between them. "I can't do it, Ryan."

"Come on, Krista. It'll be so much more powerful with you."

"My dad is freaking out. I could buck his authority, but he's so fragile. I don't want to give him any more reason to be upset."

"What if we can get a police escort or something? If I do that, would you be willing to come?"

"No. He doesn't want me on TV. He thinks it'll bring more trouble on us. We've had enough, Ryan. I know it seems cowardly ..."

"Hey, wait a minute," he cut in. "Nothing about you is cowardly. This isn't about your lacking courage."

She sighed. "Maybe it is. I'm not feeling very strong or courageous right now."

"Well, neither am I."

Ian came back out, brandished the key cards, and slipped into his own car. "I'll call you later. Ian's got our hotel keys."

"Be careful, Ryan."

"I will. I have some shopping to do this afternoon. I have to buy my second computer in two days. And clothes, shoes, underwear ..." As Ryan spoke the words, the reality of it all came crashing down on him. "I don't have anything left, except money."

"Get a gun, Ryan," she muttered.

"Yeah, good idea."

She paused, and he could hear her breathing. "I'm so sorry."

He knew she really was. "It's okay. I'll call you later."

Ian pulled around to the back door, the one Ryan assumed was closest to their room. His friend got his laptop and the bag he'd packed when he discovered his ransacked house. At least he had clothes. They followed him into the elevator, and found the small suite Ian had booked.

The moment they got into their suite, Ian plopped down on the couch and flipped his computer open.

forty-eight

Megan sat at the back of the lecture hall, her leg propped on a folding chair. She tried to concentrate on what the lecturer was saying. Dr. Landrum was one of the best English professors in the university, and she'd waited years to be in her class. Now the professor made about as much sense to Megan as Charlie Brown's teacher.

Never before had she sat in class zoning out like this. She'd always loved learning. While her friends in high school passed notes, texted, and flirted with each other, she'd been distracted by the algebra problems on the board or the literature her teachers analyzed. Homework hadn't been a chore; she'd found it a pleasure.

Though she'd always maintained a very active social life, Megan had goals and aspirations, and her hard work was paying off with the job she had waiting for her.

But now, she found herself distracted by the backs of the students' heads. There were probably a hundred people in this class, some of them older. Some of the men had brown hair like the killer ... the same shoulder breadth. Though she felt certain she would recognize her assailant again, was it possible that he'd disguised himself and slipped in among these students?

She tried to shake those thoughts free and focus on her teacher.

Her phone, lying on her desk, lit up, signaling that she'd gotten a text. She glanced at it.

Miss you, Megan. Enjoyed our time in the woods.

She gasped and went rigid. The next text flashed up.

Karen was almost as good as you, though she wasn't fond of me.

She felt her throat closing, her heart racing, her hands sweating. She grabbed her crutches, intent on getting out of there and finding someplace safe. How did he know her number? She'd changed it. Only her closest friends had it. How would he have gotten it?

She got to her feet, dropped a crutch. Bent to pick it up.

"Miss Quinn? Are you all right?"

She shoved the crutch under her arm, then stuffed her books into her backpack.

"Miss Quinn?"

The class turned to stare as another text bubbled up.

I'll see you again soon, Megan. Sooner than you think.

She pulled her backpack over one shoulder and tried to crutch toward the door. But the pack kept sliding off, throwing her balance off.

"Someone help her," Dr. Landrum said.

A couple of guys got up and came toward her, but she hobbled faster. "No, I'm fine. I just … need some air."

They retreated and she got into the hall, stopped and adjusted her backpack. She tried to breathe as she groped for her phone. Trembling, she called Detective Pensky.

forty-nine

The police's suspicions of Ian had niggled on Krista's mind since she'd left the police station. Could it be possible that he'd had something to do with the shooting or the fire? Her phone rang, making her jump. Megan Quinn's name flashed on her screen. She'd probably heard what happened.

Krista clicked on the phone. "Megan."

"He texted me again," Megan blurted. "I'm at the police station. This is a new phone number, Krista. How did he get it?"

Krista felt sick. "What did he say?"

As Megan told her, Krista closed her eyes. "Who did you give the number to?"

"Just my very closest friends."

"How did you give it to them? Face-to-face, or did you text it to them?"

"I sent it through my GrapeVyne email—privately, to just five or six people. It was the last thing I did before I deactivated my account. They promised not to give it out to anybody, and I trust them."

Krista closed her eyes and tried to think. Even Friends on GrapeVyne didn't have access to each others' private email accounts. How could the killer have gotten her phone number?

"I'm coming to the police station, Megan. How much longer are you going to be there?"

"I don't know, it could be an hour or two. They have me looking at more pictures while they try to figure out where the text came from this time."

"All right, I'm on my way." Krista clicked off the phone and shivered as she thought of Ian again. Too many things were stacking up against him. He had access. Even though he'd been fired, he could have hacked into GrapeVyne and viewed Megan's emails. He would have been able to see the cell number she was having her GrapeVyne emails forwarded to. He had known when Ryan was leaving to go to the television interview. He'd been there when the house was bombed.

Despite Ryan's defense of Ian, she couldn't escape the feeling that he could be the killer. There was one way to find out. She got her laptop, did a search for Ian Lombardi, and found a recent picture of him. She copied it and put it on her computer's desktop, where she could find it again easily. Then she headed to the police station to show it to Megan.

·····

Megan's eyes were swollen from crying. Though her

bruises were healing and weren't as dark, her face was still discolored and disfigured by stitches that hadn't quite dissolved.

They let Krista into the interview room, where the two of them sat while the detectives worked on finding out where the text had originated. Again they said it was a disposable phone, difficult to trace to an owner.

When the detectives had left the room, Krista opened her laptop, pulled up the picture of Ian. "Megan, I have someone that I suspect could have done these crimes. Could this be the one who attacked you?"

She turned her laptop around, and Megan looked. There was no change in her eyes, no recognition on her face.

"Megan, is that him?"

Megan burst into tears. "No."

Krista frowned. "Are you sure? Absolutely positive?"

"Yes, I'd remember that face anywhere. It wasn't him."

Krista breathed out a sigh of relief, glad that Ryan's best friend wasn't to blame for Megan's attack. But this stalker clearly had access to GrapeVyne. He'd read Megan's emails to her friends, gotten her phone number off of those private postings.

He could still be someone who worked in the company. Maybe they were getting closer.

When the police let Megan go, Krista gave her a ride back to her dorm. When they got there, Megan sat still for a moment. "I think I'm going to have to withdraw from school." Her voice shook as she stared at the wall between the parking lot and the door to the building. "My parents were right. I just can't do this."

"I know, Megan. It's hard. And I don't want to counsel you to be brave and courageous. Lord knows, I've done that enough, without a clue what I was talking about." Her voice broke off. "Pretty lame thing for someone whose life is as easy as mine was, to tell someone who lives in mortal fear every day of their lives. This morning when I almost got killed, I didn't feel strong or courageous. I just wanted to run away. So I don't blame you if you go home. At least then you'd be miles away, and it wouldn't be so easy for the killer to track you."

Megan wiped the tears under her eyes. "I don't even want to spend the night here tonight. I'm so scared."

"You can stay with me."

Megan shook her head. "No offense, Krista, but I don't think you're any safer than I am. Not after what happened today. I'll be all right tonight. I'll pack up, and I won't leave the dorm. Then hopefully tomorrow I'll be able to fly home."

"Let me take you to the airport," Krista said.

"Sure. My friends will all be in class, anyway. It would be really sad to have to say good-bye to them. In fact, I may not tell them I'm leaving. I might just leave a note."

"That's probably the best thing," Krista said. "Then word won't get back to the killer until you're gone."

"I deleted my GrapeVyne account. I'll have to find another way to keep in touch with my friends."

"There's this new invention called the telephone."

Megan didn't manage a smile. She opened the door, got her crutches out of the backseat, and started toward the building. Krista got out and walked her to the door. When Megan was inside, Krista went back to her car and sat in it, staring through the windshield. Her father had asked her not to go back on television. She wouldn't violate her promise to him. But she could save lives another way. She could meet the guy who was stalking her online. Stand face-to-face with him. Get a picture.

She opened her glove box, checked to make sure her gun was where she'd put it.

If this was taken care of tonight, then Megan wouldn't have to go home. Her goals wouldn't be put on hold. The impact the killer had had on her life would remain, but at least she could try to move forward.

Krista went and parked at a coffee shop that had wireless Internet, opened her laptop, and pulled up Maxi's Grape-Vyne account. Typing rapidly, she sent Steven an email.

> Great news! I can get to the Highland Village
> Mall this afternoon at 4:00. How about we meet
> in front of the Jambo Juice at the food court?

She waited, breath held. In minutes, his reply came through, even though he was supposed to be in school.

> Sounds great. Can't wait to meet you and see if
> you're as gorgeous as you sound.

Her heart raced as she typed back:

> I'm assuming you look like your picture. So I'll
> recognize you, right?

He wrote back,

> Sure. I'll have a red bandanna sticking out of
> my back pocket just in case. And I'm wearing a
> light blue Polo shirt today.
>   ....

A red bandanna. That would be the sign.
Steven asked:

> How will I know you? I can't tell that much from
> your picture.

She wrote:

> I'll be wearing a pink top.

She closed her laptop, checked her watch. It was only an hour and a half away. This thing could be over tonight.

Or she could be in more trouble than she ever dreamed.

She thought of calling Megan back and asking her to go with her so she could identify the killer if he was anywhere on the premises. But seeing her would make him flee. Besides, it was too much to ask of the girl. No, she would do it herself.

Be strong and courageous.

In her heart, she felt she would know when she laid eyes on the man who'd murdered her sister.

fifty

Krista pulled into a space in the mall parking lot and sat staring at her face in the mirror. She looked nothing like the profile picture she'd posted of Maxi Greer. If Steven were in fact the killer, he wouldn't be looking for her. He'd be looking for the young, stupid girl who'd broadcast how lonely she was and how often she was alone, and agreed to meet a stranger at the mall. So if they were both frauds ... then she wouldn't see Steven.

Would the killer recognize her as being Ella's sister?

She put on her sunglasses and pulled her hair up into a ponytail, hoping she wouldn't look familiar to him. She put her phone on camera mode, ready to take a picture of whoever appeared to be waiting for her.

Her throat went dry, and she thought of her sister fighting for her life, being beaten and raped and dragged into a shallow grave. She thought of Ella lying there for days, weeks, before she was found.

Her stomach burned at the thought of going in there alone. She opened her glove compartment again, slipped the gun into her purse.

She locked the car and started toward the entrance where the food court was. She was a little early, so she bought a drink and fries. She sat down at a table in a cluster of people, and pretended to be texting. Behind her sunglasses, her eyes scanned the crowd for evil. As four o'clock approached, she began to sweat.

And then she saw him come in. It was Steven, the boy in the GrapeVyne profile. He looked just like his picture.

Her heart sank. He was real.

He was around five-eight, and had the same little soul patch under his lip that the kid in the pictures had. He went to the counter, bought a Jambo Juice, then turned and leaned back against a wall, watching everyone who came in.

So this wasn't the killer. He wasn't a fraud at all. *She* was the fraud, using GrapeVyne to lure him.

This was wasted time. She got her purse, dumped her wrappers and cup into the trash, then left.

As she got into her car, she plotted bolder ways of drawing the killer out. She would have to get more aggressive.

fifty-one

It was Krista Carmichael. He might have known.

From where he stood in line at the most popular vendor in this despicable food court, he saw the boy who was here to meet the lovely homeschooled Maxi. But she hadn't shown. As he'd waited for her himself—a wonderful potential next victim—he saw the blonde sitting at a table alone.

He'd recognized her immediately as Krista Carmichael, though she looked like she'd made an attempt to disguise herself. Had she been the person behind Maxi Greer's persona?

Could she have been baiting him?

He had to chuckle to himself as he got his drink. When he turned back around, the boy still stood there, waiting for someone who would never come. Krista got up and did the good citizen routine, throwing out her trash. Then she walked out.

Adjusting his own sunglasses, he followed her out. He was parked several rows over from her, but he watched as she got into her car and sat there for a moment, staring at nothing. Finally, she pulled out of her space.

He followed her at a distance, gleeful that he had this chance. Ella had delighted him. Her sister might even be more fun.

fifty-two

M orning had the feel of danger. Ryan had made the
decision to go on television without Krista, risking
lawsuit and another attack to expose GrapeVyne and Willow. Lives were at stake.

But NBC had agreed to keep his appearance quiet until
he was on the air. Ryan had hired an armed escort to go
with him to the TV station—two black SUVs like in the
president's motorcade, with linebacker types who were fully
armed.

As they followed the same route he'd taken yesterday,
Ryan kept looking in his rearview mirror, making sure
there had been no security breach. When he got to the NBC
affiliate, he was greeted enthusiastically and quickly ushered
back to the makeup room. Ryan had done this dozens of
times before. Normally he was cool and calm, talking about

GrapeVyne's popularity and stock bursts, but today he was nervous. He didn't know how much time they were allotting him, how fast he would need to talk, what questions they were going to ask to drive the interview.

When the makeup lady had finished prepping him, Ryan saw a man approaching him in a suit and tie. "Mr. Adkins?"

Ryan extended his hand to shake. "Yeah, how you doing?"

The man didn't smile. "I'm George Barnett from Barnett and Lewis Law Firm." He handed him a large envelope. "You're being officially served."

Ryan looked down at the envelope as the man walked away. "Well, here we go." Opening it, he pulled the papers out.

"What is that?" the makeup lady asked.

"It's a lawsuit that GrapeVyne has filed to shut me up."

"Oh no."

He scanned the page, saw the amount of damages. A hundred million dollars. The exact amount for which he'd sold the company.

It was a ploy, he thought. A warning. If he cancelled the interview and didn't talk, they'd leave his money alone ... and maybe his life. But if he didn't ... he stood to lose it all for defamation, commercial disparagement, and half a dozen contract violations.

"Do we need to tell them you can't do the interview?" the makeup lady asked.

For a moment, he thought of taking off the lapel mike they'd already put on him, and walking right back out of there. But then his thoughts returned to Ella Carmichael, Karen Anders, Megan Quinn ... Krista.

He thought of the bloodthirsty killer out there using his invention as an evil tool.

He thought of the board of directors who were illegally gathering way too many facts about the clients of Grape-Vyne. He thought of the attempt on his life.

And he decided it was worth it to take them down. If he lost everything he had ... well, so be it.

Be strong and courageous.

"No," he said. "Let's do it."

His face burned as they put him on the set under the lights, and linked him into the *Today Show*. He watched the monitor and waited stiffly for Matt Lauer to introduce him.

When he was finally on the air, Matt started by asking Ryan about the accident. "Ryan, on your way to your interview with us yesterday, you and Krista Carmichael, our other guest, were in a pretty bad accident."

"It was no accident," Ryan said.

"Is it true that someone deliberately ran you off the road and shot at you?"

"Yes, that's true."

"And that your house was later burned down?"

"That's right."

"Any idea who would do this?"

"Someone who didn't want me to talk to you about my firing, or the things happening at GrapeVyne."

"Well, let's get to that. You received quite a blow two days ago when your board of directors gave you a pink slip. Can you tell us a little bit about why you were let go?"

Ryan cleared his throat. "We had a little difference of opinion about some policy matters at GrapeVyne. I was concerned about the online predators that use the site, and the number of missing persons across the country who were lured into danger by people they met online. I wanted to put some more security measures in place to protect our clients and educate the public. They felt I was calling too much attention to the problems with the community, so they decided to replace me. Then someone tried to kill me."

"Are you suggesting the GrapeVyne board of directors was behind that?"

"I'm just stating what happened to me, not casting blame. But just before this interview I was served with papers for a lawsuit they've filed to keep me from talking to you."

"A lawsuit? Who filed it?"

"The board of directors of GrapeVyne Corporation."

Matt's eyes narrowed. "What's the amount of the lawsuit?"

"A hundred million dollars."

"Why a hundred million?"

"It's the exact amount they paid me for the purchase of the company."

Matt looked like he'd just uncovered the story of the century. "Ryan, what has made this such an important issue to you, that you'd literally risk your life and fortune to come talk to us today?"

"Because five weeks ago a fourteen-year-old girl named Ella Carmichael was beaten, raped, and buried alive. The killer found her through her frequent GrapeVyne posts. Not long after she was found, another Houston GrapeVyne client was attacked, and her roommate was murdered. Police believe it's the same assailant. He's still out there, and I want people to understand that everything they post on Grape-Vyne can be used to lead predators to them."

"Do you think the GrapeVyne killer is the one who tried to kill you and Krista yesterday?"

He hesitated. "It seems like two separate events to me, Matt. But the police are looking into the connections, if any."

"Ryan, do you feel responsible for the deaths of these girls, since you created GrapeVyne?"

"It was never our intention to create a tool for predators, and honestly, every social networking site has the same issues. None of us ever wanted to see our members dying."

"But aren't you afraid of losing your fortune because you're speaking out?"

Ryan paused, and realized that the money was incidental. "This message is more important than my bank account."

"So what is it that you would like for people to do?"

"Examine their social networks and take down everything they've posted that they wouldn't want a murderous predator to see. Don't post where you are, ever. Don't post where you live, or your school, or your town, or your church. Don't post pictures that identify places, like colleges or schools or particular teams you might be on. Never post your work schedule or your activities or your travel plans. And don't flood the site with pictures of yourself. You have no idea how much information a predator can get from those pictures."

"Well, we thank you for coming on with us today, Ryan. We wish you well and hope that millions of our viewers will pay more attention to what they're doing online."

"Thanks, Matt."

The link was cut off, and the affiliates turned the bright lights off. The stage manager crossed the set to take off Ryan's mike. "That's chilling," she said. "I'm going home and taking down every personal posting on my GrapeVyne account today."

"Good." At least one person's life might be saved. Sweating, Ryan stepped off the set and picked up the envelope he'd set in a chair. He pulled out the papers again. Unbelievable.

His phone vibrated on his belt, and he pulled it out and glanced down. The Caller ID said ABC News. Already the other networks wanted to interview him. He might as well go for broke.

fifty-three

So Steven was who he said he was. He obviously wasn't the killer, so Krista had spent the night studying the new Friends coming to Maxi's site, taking copious notes on any red flags that were raised. He was here somewhere. She knew it.

The police had ruled out all the friends Ella and Megan had in common, so those were dead-ends.

Systematically, she Friended everyone on her sister's Friends List. Some of them wouldn't bite—the ones who'd heard her speak at school the other day would know better than to accept a stranger. But the killer was there for sure, and how could he resist another young, vulnerable girl? Surely he would come.

Dozens of people had accepted her Friend request, giving her lots to work with. But it was slow-going. She went to each of their sites and read everything they'd ever posted, studied all their pictures and videos, articles they'd shared, their own lists of friends.

Even after hours of work, she was no closer to identifying the killer. Why had she thought she could do a better job than the police?

She had taken a break only to get a couple of hours' sleep, then got up to watch Ryan on the *Today Show*. His boldness lifted her spirits, especially after he'd been served with a lawsuit. His sacrifices for this cause astonished her.

As soon as it was over, she had gone back to the computer. Hours passed. She didn't even know what time it was, but her stomach growled, and she realized she hadn't eaten.

The doorbell rang, startling her. She wasn't expecting anyone, so she padded in sock feet to the front door and peered out.

It was Ryan. Aware of how bad she must look, since she hadn't done anything to herself all day, she opened the door. "Ryan, hi."

He smiled as if it did him good to see her. "Hey. I just wanted to come by and check on you. You weren't answering your phone."

Her phone. The battery was probably dead, since she hadn't thought to charge it last night. "Sorry about that."

"I know you probably don't want to be around me right now, after what happened the last time we were together, but I have a bodyguard in that black SUV on the street."

She looked past him, saw the vehicle in front of her house.

"They'll make sure no one throws any Molotov cocktails through your window while I'm here."

She knew he wasn't joking. "Come on in."

He came in and she shut the door behind him. "Did you see my interviews?"

"I saw the *Today Show*. You were amazing. Were there others?"

"Two others today, and I have more scheduled for tomorrow."

"You did great with Matt Lauer." She led him into the kitchen and put on a pot of coffee. She could use some. "So tell me about the lawsuit."

"GrapeVyne is suing me for a hundred million dollars, for defamation."

"And you went ahead with the interviews anyway?"

"It's the right thing to do. I knew after I did the first one, I'd get other requests. I even had a publisher call me today, wanting to talk about a book deal. I have a huge forum here. I'm not going to lose it because of GrapeVyne's threats. If they want to take me to court and let me expose the things I'm finding out about them, then they can bring it on."

She poured the coffee, brought him a cup, and sat down. "I'm proud of you."

"Thanks." He glanced at her laptop, sitting open next to her at the table. GrapeVyne was up, and she was on the page of a girl named Maxi Greer. "What are you doing on GrapeVyne?"

She closed the laptop. "Nothing. Just ... studying all of Ella's friends. Looking for anything strange, unusual. Anything that might lead me to the killer."

"Want my help?"

She looked at him for a moment. Though she didn't want him to know the dangerous game she'd been playing, he knew a lot more about the inner workings of the site than she did. Maybe she should let him help.

She showed him the legal pads she'd filled up with notes she'd taken on Ella's Friends. "I've put a big dent in it. But every time I think I've gotten close, I find something that legitimizes that person. Then I'm back at square one."

He touched her hand. "You're shaking. Why?"

She shrugged. "I don't think I've eaten today."

"Then let's order a pizza."

Glad to distract his attention from her GrapeVyne activities, she agreed. Food might make her feel better.

••••

Krista looked like she felt better after she'd eaten. Ryan was relieved to see the color return to her face, and she stopped shaking. She even seemed to relax a little.

But that haunted, distant look still glistened in her eyes. He wished he hadn't contributed to it. "Krista, I feel like I've damaged you. Made things worse."

"What? How?"

"Almost getting you killed, for one thing. I don't blame your dad for hating me."

"He doesn't hate you. He's just ... worried."

His eyes swept her face. "I want you to be all right."

Tears rimmed her eyes, and she turned back to the computer. Typing something in, she said, "If I could find the killer, I would be. If he weren't around to torment Megan or stalk any other women. If there were any chance of justice."

"There is going to be justice, Krista. You have to believe that."

"Do I?" She got up, poured some more coffee. "To tell you the honest truth, I don't really know if I believe that anymore. I'm not supposed to doubt God, but I'm weaker than I thought."

The look on her face told him how much the admission had taken out of her. "Krista, doubt is not the same as failure."

She whispered a laugh and sat back down. "Unless you spend every day trying to convince others that God is their champion ... their protector."

"He is their protector. You know he is."

"I know it in my head."

"But not in your heart?"

Her face twisted. "In my heart, I remember Ella half-buried in that makeshift grave, and I feel so much rage."

He leaned on the table and took her hands. They felt so small in his, and the urge to protect her swelled in his chest.

"I just . . ." Her mouth trembled as she struggled with the words, and her tears spilled over. "I always thought that the people I loved would be safe. That the ones I prayed for every day would be guarded. What have I got to give those girls at Eagle's Wings? How can I tell them that God will protect them, when my sister is dead? And if they can't turn to God, where can they turn?" She wiped her face. "There's this girl Jesse who comes to the center. Her life is a nightmare. What can I say to her? I can't throw out Bible verses and think it'll make a difference for her."

"Maybe God has just used this tragedy to make you understand that."

"But how can I have a ministry if I'm so confused myself? I've let her down already, by spouting out things I don't even understand. What can I tell her about the anger she must feel? What can I share with any of those girls?"

"You share their pain. It's something you couldn't share before. And what's that verse in the Bible about how we're not fighting people?"

"You mean Ephesians 6:12? Our fight is not against flesh and blood?"

"Yes, that's it. And if God can bring Bible verses back to my mind after all these years, then he can sure give you the right things to say to those girls."

She smiled through her tears. He hoped he was making her feel better.

"My mom used to say God has angels fighting for us," Ryan whispered.

"But Ella ... the horror of what she went through."

"Do you think God's making her live with that in heaven?"

She met his eyes, processing that question. "No. No, he wouldn't. I've never imagined Ella traumatized and grief-stricken in heaven. There are no more tears for her. Just for us."

As she melted into her grief, he pulled her into his arms. She didn't pull away. Instead, she lay her head on his shoulder, and he closed his eyes. It felt so natural to hold her. So right.

But he couldn't bear to see her hurting. As he stroked her hair, he prayed that God would comfort her. That he'd walk her through this darkness. That he'd bring her into sunshine again.

And that, when he did, he'd let Ryan be there for her too.

When her weeping was spent, she pulled back, wiped her face on a paper towel. Her soft gaze swept his face. "You're nothing like I thought," she whispered.

Heat flushed his face, and his heartbeat thudded in his neck. He pressed his forehead against hers. "You're exactly like I thought," he said.

When he kissed her, she didn't recoil. Instead, she responded as if she'd hoped for it ... as if she needed it as much as he did.

Then he heard the garage door opening, a car pulling into the bay.

They pulled back, stricken, and gazed at each other. He let her go, yearning to hold her longer. "Maybe I should go," he said. "Your dad probably won't be thrilled about my being here."

She dabbed at her eyes again. "Yeah, he's probably freaking about the SUV in front of the house."

As she walked him to the front door, her father burst in through the garage door. He stormed into the kitchen and saw them. Ryan felt exposed, as if David could read every thought on his face.

"Who is that in front of my house?"

Ryan cleared his throat. "Hi, Mr. Carmichael. That's a bodyguard I hired to escort me around town today."

"A bodyguard," he repeated, as though the word disgusted him.

"Yes. I came to check on Krista. I was just leaving."

Her father looked at Krista. It was clear she'd been crying. Mr. Carmichael probably thought he'd upset her.

Maybe he had.

David left without a word and headed down the hall. Ryan said a quick good-bye to Krista, then slipped out the door, hoping he hadn't caused more trouble.

••••

Krista closed the door and leaned back against it, thinking about the threshold their relationship had just crossed. It gave her comfort and hope ...

But Ryan had almost seen her Maxi Greer page. She'd managed to navigate away from it before he'd seen what she was doing. She went back into the kitchen to her laptop, signed back in as Maxi Greer, and pulled up her alias's GrapeVyne page. There were no new messages.

She was tired, so tired. She knew that she should go talk to her dad, but she didn't want to spoil the memory of Ryan holding her. No, she'd go and take a shower, and give herself a break.

She closed the computer, putting it to sleep. She could come back to it later. Maxi's friends would still be there.

fifty-four

When David heard Ryan leave, he stormed into the kitchen to find Krista. But she had gone into the bathroom. He stood outside the door, waiting for her, then he heard water running. He paced into the kitchen again, filled a glass with water, and drank it down.

How dare that guy come into his house? How dare he hit on Krista when she was so vulnerable?

What were they doing? He opened Krista's laptop, ran his finger across the trackpad. The display lit up with a girl's GrapeVyne page.

Maxi Greer.

He didn't recognize her picture, so he scrolled down. Then he saw a half-finished email.

How would Krista have access to this girl's email?

He heard her come out of the bathroom, go into her

room. Quickly, he navigated to Settings, pulled up her account. Maxi Greer's email address was the same as Krista's email at work.

Alarms went off in his chest, and he went back to her page, looked into her Sent mail, and saw the exchanges between Maxi and Steven.

His lungs stopped working. Krista was baiting the killer!

He bellowed her name out, shaking the house. "Krista!"

She shot out of her room and came into the kitchen. When she saw that he was at her laptop, she dashed forward and slammed it shut.

"What ... are you ... *doing?*" he yelled. "Luring some guy ... saying these things ..."

"Dad, I can explain."

"You were baiting him! Drawing him out!"

"But it wasn't him! I went to the mall to see if it was him, but it was that kid ... I just went home. I didn't do anything."

"He could have killed you!" He slammed his fist into the wall, breaking the Sheetrock, then turned back around with his teeth bared. "How could you do this? You've already been run off the road, almost murdered!"

She reached out for him. "I just want justice."

He shook her off. "I've lost total control of my family, of my life." He clutched his head. "I can't stand it."

"Daddy, come sit down. Let me fix you something to eat."

"I don't need food! I want my family back!"

"*I'm* your family." She stood there in front of him, weeping, but she feared he didn't see her. "Dad, I'm still here."

He leaned back against the refrigerator, his hands over his face. Finally, he slid his fingertips down and met Krista's eyes.

"I want you to still be here tomorrow, and the next day. I don't want to lose another child."

He did see her, she thought. She wasn't invisible. He dropped his hands, then reached for her. She fell into his arms, and they clung to each other.

"Daddy, it's going to be okay," she whispered. "I won't do it anymore. I'll cancel Maxi's account. It was stupid, but I thought—"

"Cancel it now," he said. "Tonight."

"I promise." Somehow, his despair comforted her. He really did love her.

He let her go and bent over the sink, dropped his head down. "We have to make some changes or we're both going to die."

She wiped the tears from her face. "What kind of changes do you want to make?"

"I've been thinking about quitting my job and moving," he blurted.

She stared at him for a moment. "Moving where?"

"I thought we could go to Dallas, and be closer to our family—my mother, my brothers. You could be closer to all your cousins."

"But Dad, we have lives here. What good would it do to move?"

"I want the danger to be over. I want to get you out of here. And I want to move to a place where I don't have to think about Ella every single minute of every single day."

She shook her head. "I want to stay here. I don't want to give up all her memories."

"The memories break my heart," he bit out. "Don't you understand? This isn't safe. We have to go before he takes more from you than he already has."

"Who? The killer, or Ryan?"

Her father shook his head. "Maybe both," he said.

fifty-five

When her dad went to bed, Krista stared at the hole in the kitchen wall. Tomorrow she would go to the store and buy some drywall mud, patch up the hole, and paint over it.

After deactivating Maxi Greer's GrapeVyne account, she went to Ella's room and lay down on her sister's bed, pulled the pillow against her. She breathed in the apple scent from the cologne that sat in a bottle by the bed. She brought it close to her face, squeezing her eyes shut and missing her sister.

She had never seen her father like this. She feared he was right. The crushing grief would kill him. Maybe even by his own hand.

Maybe he *should* move and start over fresh. It might save his life.

She thought of being in Dallas, getting a new house, a new job ...

Everything new.

But it wouldn't fill the void Ella had left, or distract them from their grief.

And what about the girls at Eagle's Wings? If she dropped out of their lives, would anything really be lost? Especially now, when she had so many doubts about what she could offer them.

Ryan's words tonight echoed softly through her head. *Doubt is not the same as failure.*

But wasn't it?

She thought of Jesse, the girl who'd lost her brother and mother. She'd failed her. What difference had her work made in Jesse's life? Her last conversation with her had left Jesse empty.

Still, Krista didn't know if she could walk away. She loved those girls. They needed Christ, and someone to tell them they were beautiful and important. Someone to remind them they had purpose and hope.

Because they did. Even with evil stalking, hope shone a beacon light.

For I know the plans that I have for you.... plans to prosper you and not to harm you, plans to give you hope and a future.

Jeremiah 29:11–13 had been her life passage for years. Now, even after so much tragedy, she found she still believed it.

Then you will call upon me and come and pray to me, and I will listen to you. You will seek me and find me when you seek me with all your heart.

Maybe Ryan was right. Maybe she could understand the girls better now that she shared their pain. Maybe she was still called. Maybe God would rebuild her strength and courage, so she could help build it in others.

But her father would never understand. So her choice came down to doing what might be best for her dad, or doing her best for God.

And then there was Ryan. She'd never expected good to come out of her suffering ... but wasn't that how God worked? This thing with Ryan was new, but their bond was already tight. His kiss tonight had opened floodgates in her soul. His touch was healing. She couldn't walk away.

Later, she went to her own bed and tried to sleep, but her conversation with her father played over and over and over in her mind. Sleep never came, and finally she got up and went to the kitchen to wait for morning.

When it did, she heard her dad rustling around. When he came into the kitchen, she poured him some coffee.

"Have you been up all night?" he asked.

She nodded. "Dad, I just keep thinking about what you said last night."

He took the coffee. "Yeah?"

"I can't move to Dallas with you. I've questioned my calling over the last few days, but it's real, and my work is important. I want to stay. I want to keep working at Eagle's Wings."

He leaned back against the cabinet. "Krista, I can't go without you."

"Then don't go. It's not going to make the grief go away."

He blew out a long sigh, pulled out a chair, and dropped into it.

If only they could find Ella's killer. Then maybe her father would have the peace that justice would bring. Maybe then he wouldn't want to dismantle his life ... and all his memories. Maybe then they could all move on.

fifty-six

K rista did her best to patch up the hole in the Sheetrock with the things she scavenged from the garage. As she waited for the mud to dry, her cell phone rang. Megan's name appeared on the Caller ID.

She answered it quickly. "Hi Megan."

"Krista." Megan sounded stopped up, like she'd been crying, and Krista could hear the grief in her voice. It was similar to what her father had sounded like last night, and the way she'd sounded herself with Ryan. "I just wanted to tell you that I've packed up and made my flight reservation. It's for three this afternoon."

Krista didn't answer for a moment. Though she'd expected the call, the sense of defeat crushed down on her. "You're sure you want to go home?"

"I have no choice."

"I know," Krista said. "I just hate for this man to rob you of your dreams and goals."

There was a long moment of silence. Then Megan said, "I don't have dreams anymore, Krista. I think he beat them out of me."

Krista would never get over the tragedy of that. "Will you still let me take you to the airport?" she asked Megan.

"Sure," she said. "My flight's not for a few hours, but I'm all packed up."

"All right," she said. "I'm heading over to get you right now. You can hang out with me until it's time to go."

fifty-seven

Krista Carmichael had stayed in most of yesterday, from what he could tell. He had watched from his car for several hours, parked on the curb several houses down, trying to determine if she was alone. It was hard to tell, because they kept the garage door closed, and he couldn't see if her father was there or not.

Since he couldn't watch her house constantly, because of his work and the expectations of others, it was possible her father had left at some point during the day. But since he hadn't seen him go, he'd had to wait.

Now he saw her garage door going up. He started his car, watched as she backed out of her driveway. When she drove toward the neighborhood entrance, he followed at a distance.

The baseball cap and sunglasses he wore provided some

cover, though he knew she wouldn't know who he was even without them. No, when he finally had her where he wanted her, she wouldn't know what hit her. She'd searched so hard for Ella's killer. She'd finally fulfill her dream of meeting her sister's killer. Wouldn't she be surprised to learn she was his next victim?

He followed her across town, his heart pounding with the thrill of the hunt. He was ready to force her into his car if she got out in an isolated area. But he was a patient man. If not today, then tomorrow.

If it couldn't happen today, he was all set up to make his hunt easier. If he couldn't get to her without being seen, he'd wait until she parked her car. Then he would put a transponder under it, so he could track her via his computer. He'd know where she was at all times, even when he wasn't nearby.

She took the exit for Rice University, which gave him pause. Where was she going? He slowed as she pulled onto the campus and headed to one of the dorms.

His mouth went dry. This wasn't a safe place for him to be. If Megan Quinn saw him, she could identify him.

He didn't park, but circled the dormitory as Krista went in. He came back around, and thought of parking somewhere some distance away, and taking the opportunity to put the transponder on.

But it was too dangerous for him. No, now wasn't the right time.

When he came back around the block a second time, he saw her at the trunk of her car with another girl.

His heart jolted. Megan Quinn.

So this was where she'd moved. He had no idea that Krista and Megan knew each other. But of course they would. They had a lot in common.

He slowed as he drove the block again. Megan was on crutches, and Krista loaded luggage into her trunk.

Was Megan going home to New York?

He'd hoped to find her and kill her before she identified him. It was just too good to be true ... having them both together like this. He laughed out loud as he came around the block again and saw them pulling out of the parking lot.

Now he had a new urgency. He had to act while they were together. Almost giddy, he followed them back to the interstate.

fifty-eight

Krista's phone rang as she and Megan pulled onto the interstate. She checked the Caller ID. "It's Ryan," she said to Megan. "Do you mind if I get it?"

"No," Megan said. "Go ahead."

Krista clicked it on. "Hey, Ryan."

"Hey there," he said, his voice soft. "I just wanted to check in with you. See how you're feeling today."

She thought of last night, the kiss, the way he'd comforted her. "I'm better today," she said. "I'm with Megan. She's decided to withdraw from school and go home. Her flight's in a few hours."

Ryan paused. "I'm so sorry we haven't been able to figure out who the killer is yet. I wish we could have given her that peace."

"Me too."

"But this morning Ian downloaded the GrapeVyne and Willow employees' directories, with the pictures they have on their badges. I was thinking that maybe Megan could come by and look at them all, and see if she recognizes anyone. Would you mind bringing her here to do that before she leaves? We're staying at the Hampton Inn."

She glanced over at Megan and started to repeat the invitation. But Megan had heard him.

Her eyes rounded with hope. "Yes, we can go. Can we do it now?"

Krista nodded. "All right, we're coming," she said. "See you in a few minutes."

fifty-nine

Ryan hung up the phone and rubbed his eyes. They felt raw as he tried to focus on his computer screen. He and Ian had been up all night, reading every article they could find on each of his board members, trying to determine if any of them had been behind his murder attempt. Then they'd finagled a way to download the employees' directories and had begun to research the other top executives at Willow, to see who might want them dead.

"The idea of it being a conspiracy that involves several people is just too preposterous," Ryan had told Ian last night. "No, whoever wanted us dead has to be only one person ... or two at the most."

"I don't know," Ian said. "It's bizarre that the dude who's been texting Megan Quinn might have some connection to GrapeVyne or Willow, and here we are looking for another person who tried to have us killed. It's just too coincidental."

Ryan mulled that over. "Maybe it's not really a coinci-dence. Maybe it's the same person."

Ian shook his head. "Don't think so, man. We've got a crazed predator who's killing girls ... and an angry board of directors that's mad because we're uncovering some industry secrets. I don't see how the two can be related."

"What if it's not the industry secrets that they're really mad about? What if it's something deeper?"

"That they're murdering girls?"

"Not they. Him. Maybe one person."

"So how does the Data-Gather stuff fit in?"

Ryan stared at his coputer.

"Maybe this person is using that information to find and stalk his victims."

Ian had stared at him for a long moment. "Dude, I think you're onto something."

Now he hoped Megan would be able to help. Maybe when she scanned the faces of the Willow and GrapeVyne employees, she would find her attacker.

Ian came out of the hotel bathroom in a pair of jeans and a T-shirt, his hair wet from his shower. "Did you find out anything else while I was showering?"

Ryan shook his head. "No, but Krista's bringing Megan over to look at the directories."

Ian looked distraught. "Chicks? Why don't you tell a guy so he can shave?"

Ryan looked around. The small suite was a nightmare of clutter. "Pick something up, will you? They'll be here in a minute. I can't let them think we're pigs."

....

Outside, the killer was watching from across the parking lot as Krista got out of the car at the Hampton Inn. Megan got out with her, hobbling toward the door on crutches.

Who could they be visiting here? Were Megan's parents staying here? Maybe they had come to get her.

The parking lot was too visible from the street, so he couldn't make his move here. But he was pretty sure he could get under Krista's car without being seen. There was a security camera on one corner of the building, but if he parked around the corner and came at the car from the other side, he wouldn't be seen.

He opened the box on the seat next to him. He got out the transponder, mounted on a magnet to hold it in place. Opening his laptop, he checked to make sure it was working. A map came up on the screen, with a triangle pinpointing the transponder. Yes, it would work beautifully.

He pulled on gloves, just in case the transponder was found and fingerprinted, and wiped it down with a handkerchief.

He pulled around the corner, parked, and got out of his car. He bent as though looking for something, making sure he was hidden by the cars he passed as he made his way to her Kia. Then he knelt, and quickly placed the device inside her wheel well.

He checked to see if anyone had seen him. There was no one near, and none of the traffic passing by had slowed enough to watch him. Heart racing, he went back to his car. He got in and opened his laptop, and checked the device again.

Perfect.

He would always know where she was, even when he couldn't follow her. He could trail her without ever getting close enough to be detected. And sometime soon — sometime in the next few hours — he would be able to make his move. Megan was the icing on the cake ...

As he entertained the possibilities, his appetite intensified.

Soon it would be satisfied again.

....

Ryan was startled by Megan's appearance as he let them into the hotel suite. He had expected her to be more healed from her wounds, but she looked almost as bad as she had in the hospital. The brace on her leg, the crutches, the bruising and stitches ...

Krista looked like she still hadn't slept, and her skin had a chalky, pallid color. Ryan wondered if she'd eaten anything since the pizza last night.

He smiled at her as he let her in, and Krista's cheeks blushed pink. He gave her a quick hug. But Megan's body language was stiff and unaccepting, so he only patted her shoulder.

"I'm glad you guys came by," he said. "Megan, this is Ian. He helped me start GrapeVyne."

Ian gave her an awkward salute. "Hello."

"Nice to meet you," she said softly. "I'm sorry about your firing."

"Yeah, well." He combed his fingers through his wet hair. "Sorry for being all wet. I just showered. Didn't know we were having company." He moved his laptop off the couch, set it on the table. "Have a seat."

Megan and Krista sat down. "Can I see the directories?" Megan asked.

Ryan handed her his laptop and sat down on the other side of her. She opened it while he explained. "There are thumbnail pictures of everyone here that you can scroll through," he said. "If anyone looks familiar, click on the picture, and a larger view will open."

She swallowed and began scrolling down, looking intently at each face.

As they waited, Krista looked at him. "You guys okay? Has anything else happened?"

"No, I think we've managed to keep our whereabouts a pretty good secret."

"You should change hotels tonight. Just in case."

"Yeah, we were thinking about that."

Ryan glanced at Megan as she scrolled through the faces.

"And you haven't heard anything from the police?" Krista asked.

"No, nothing. I hope they're working on it."

Suddenly, Megan sprang up, dropping the laptop.

"Whoa!" Ryan caught it before it hit the floor.

Megan's face turned crimson. He thought she was choking. "You okay?"

Pointing, she said, "Him."

"Who?" Ryan asked.

"That man ..." She sucked in fast, shallow breaths. "It's him ..."

Krista's face went white, and she grabbed the computer. "Him who? Which one?" She saw where the cursor was on the screen, clicked the thumbnail picture. A face came up, with a name beneath it.

"Henry Hearne?"

Ryan's heart jolted. "*What?*"

Megan was hyperventilating. "Call ... call the police."

Ryan couldn't grasp it. "Are you saying he's the one who attacked you?"

Ian took her shoulders and looked into her face. "Megan, are you saying Henry Hearne is the killer?"

Megan's legs wilted under her, and she leaned against Ian and almost fell. "Yes!" she whispered.

Krista grabbed her phone out of her purse and began to dial.

"Bathroom," Megan gasped. "Gonna be sick."

Ian pointed. "In there."

Krista thrust her phone at Ryan and helped Megan into the bathroom.

Putting the phone to his ear, Ryan stared at Ian. "Henry Hearne."

"No way," Ian said. "No stinkin' way. If he's the killer, and we were uncovering all the data he was collecting ... then he's the one who wanted us dead too."

As Ryan heard Megan purging her terror, the detective answered. "Detective Pensky. Hello?"

Ryan tried to steady his voice. "This is Ryan Adkins," he said. "We know who the killer is."

sixty

Henry Hearne heard the sirens as they approached the Hampton Inn. Were they coming for him?

He pulled out of the parking lot and drove away as fast as the speed limit would allow. He stayed away for fifteen minutes, but then curiosity compelled him to go back.

He drove past the hotel, saw four police cars in the parking lot. None of the cops loitered there, so they must have gone in.

Maybe it wasn't about him. He kept going and parked in the lot of a grocery store a few blocks down. Watching that triangle on his laptop, he waited for Krista to leave.

Finally, the triangle began to move. He pulled out in traffic and followed her route. When he went back by the Hampton Inn, the police cars were gone.

The uneasiness returned.

He followed a mile behind her, watching the triangle on his computer navigate its way down streets and around corners. Finally, it came to a halt.

As it did, he realized where she was. The police station.

Something had happened. Had they figured out who he was? Surely not. He had covered all his bases, and there was no way they could trace him. He had used different vehicles for every incident. He'd even hired thugs to chase down Ryan. He kept a low profile, despite his money and his position. He hadn't had his picture taken in years, and he never did interviews.

Megan would have no way of stumbling upon his image.

No, she probably just wanted to talk to the cops one more time before she left town. If her parents were indeed the ones she'd gone to see at the Hampton Inn, then maybe they had called the police to encourage them to look harder for him.

It was nothing to be afraid of, and he wouldn't let it distract him from his goals.

It wasn't wise to go to that area, so he turned at the next red light and headed back to Krista's house. He would wait there, watching to see when her father left home. If he did, he would go inside.

Maybe, if he was lucky, Megan would come home with her.

sixty-one

The revelation of who the killer was sent the police department into a tailspin. Krista sat with Megan, Ryan, and Ian, as the police chief himself questioned them. He seemed reluctant to believe that a man as rich and powerful as Henry Hearne could have done such horrific things.

But it all made sense. Hearne had gathered all the data he needed to target the girls he would torment. That data had made him aware of Ella. And she had played right into his hand.

The knowledge gave Krista no relief. Instead it inflamed her grief, and she wanted to go sit in a dark room and rail out her anger to God. At some point during the questioning, she called her father and told him. Within minutes, he was at her side. His hand was icy as he held hers, yet sweat glistened on his face. His eyes looked glazed and haunted.

When the questioning died down and the police force had been dispatched to pick up Henry Hearne, Krista had the presence of mind to ask Megan if she still wanted to fly home.

"I think so," she said. "The flight's not for three hours."

"We can wait at my house for word," she said. "You can put your leg up and eat something. It'll be more comfortable than sitting here."

Megan agreed, and the two of them left. Her father stayed behind to talk to Detective Pensky. Ryan and Ian were being interviewed by the FBI about the information they'd uncovered.

As Krista and Megan walked out to her car, Krista fought the rush of emotion. She didn't want to upset Megan more than she already was. But as she got behind the wheel, tears assaulted her.

"I'm sorry," she whispered. "It's just all hitting me. That man ... what he did to my sister ... to you and to Karen. And who knows how many others?"

Megan's eyes were red and puffy from crying. "I hope they put him in the worst prison with the most vicious criminals. I hope he gets a taste of what he's done."

Krista started her car. "I hope he gets the death penalty." She pulled out of the police department's parking lot and started home. By now, they may have already found him. Maybe he was at work when they arrived at his office. Maybe they'd paraded him out of Willow in handcuffs. She hoped the press would show up and capture his stunned expression.

Soon everyone would know.

"So much makes sense now," Krista said. "Ryan said Hearne never does media for Willow, so his face hasn't been on the news or in the papers. He keeps this low profile, acting too humble for the limelight ... When all along, he was hiding from people who could identify him."

As she drove, she tried to think how he did it. Yes, he'd learned of Ella's and Megan's whereabouts by reading their Thought Bubbles, but he hadn't been on their Friends Lists. He'd been watching from behind the scenes, not even needing to masquerade as a Friend. That was how he'd gotten Megan's new phone number. He'd read her private Grape-Vyne emails.

Megan leaned her head back and closed her eyes. "If they find him, if they can keep him, maybe I can stay. Maybe I can finish my degree."

"Oh, if they find him, they'll keep him. Between your identification and the evidence Ryan and Ian turned over about his activities with GrapeVyne, he won't get away with it. Maybe now we'll all have some closure."

Megan looked out the window. "I have a feeling closure is not all it's cracked up to be."

Krista turned onto her street. "It won't undo anything. You're going to need counseling. But it'll help. Just knowing there really is such a thing as justice ..."

She pressed the button on her garage door opener, then pulled into her garage.

She got out and helped Megan out, got her crutches from the backseat. She followed Megan to the door, then unlocked it, and let her in.

Her father had left the light on in the kitchen, and the television on. She imagined him dropping everything and racing out of the house when he got her call.

As Megan lowered into a chair at the kitchen table, Krista changed the channel to a local station. "Maybe they'll cut in when he's arrested," she said. "This will even make national news because of who he is."

"Is the press going to hound me?" Megan asked. "Because I honestly don't think I can talk about it."

"You won't have to." She filled the coffeepot and started it percolating, then sat down next to Megan.

She heard movement in the other room, a subtle shifting of air, the tap of a footstep. Was her father home after all? Where was his car? She turned toward the door and called, "Dad?"

A shadow moved into the doorway from the living room. She stood up slowly, took a step toward it ...

Megan screamed.

Henry Hearne stood there with a smile on his face. He was holding a gun.

sixty-two

K rista couldn't seem to draw in a breath. Her gun, she thought. Where was her gun?

She'd left it in the glove box in her car.

Sweat broke out on her skin, beading on her lip, dripping down her temples. "What ... do you ... want?"

His eyes were pure evil. "I enjoyed your sister, so I thought I'd come and see how much you're like her."

"You evil monster ..."

He turned and looked at Megan, who sat frozen, no color in her face. "And Megan, what a joy to find you here. I've always detested unfinished business."

Megan got up, took a step, then wobbled, and dropped to the floor. Krista fell to her side. "They know about you!" she bit out. "The police are looking for you right now. They know who you are."

He laughed. "Nice try. But they don't know me. Megan doesn't even know my name."

Megan's eyes fluttered open. "You're Henry Hearne," she said. "I told them what you did to me!"

The glee left his eyes, and a flicker of fear passed over his face. "Even if that were true, they wouldn't believe you. I'm a powerful man. I own people."

"It is true," Krista said. "If anything happens to us they'll know it was you. There'll be nowhere for you to hide. Your money will be useless."

She noticed a tremor in the hand holding his gun. The news shook him. "But if you leave us alone right now, you could walk out of here, disappear, and access your money before they freeze your accounts. You could get out of the country."

For a moment, he seemed to consider it. Then the grin returned to his face. "Once the only eyewitness is dead, they'll never be able to pin this on me. Get up, both of you!"

Megan's face twisted, and a low, deep moan came from her throat. Krista helped her to her feet.

Hearne wiped his forehead on his sleeve. "We're going to your car," he said. "You're going to drive, Krista ... and Megan will sit in the passenger seat. I'll be in the backseat ready to put a bullet in her brain."

"Where are you taking us?" Krista asked him.

"Somewhere private," he said. "Somewhere where we'll have plenty of time."

Yes, Krista thought, if they got in her car, she'd be able to get her gun.

But Megan was trembling so fiercely that Krista doubted she could walk. She held her close to herself and helped her limp to the door. She turned the knob, praying her father would come.

When she opened the door, his bay was still empty. Where had Hearne left his own vehicle? How had he gotten in here?

"Don't open the garage until we're in the car," he said.

Krista's mind raced. Maybe she could get someone's attention. A neighbor ... the mailman ...

"Both of you. In the car."

Krista felt the barrel of the gun in her back, and she opened the passenger door. "Get in, Megan," she whispered.

"I can't," Megan sobbed. "I can't do it."

He rammed the gun against Krista's kidney. "Now, Megan, or I'll finish my business with you right here."

She sucked in a breath and got into the car. He got into the backseat, his gun to Megan's head, as Krista went around and slipped into the driver's side.

"Now, open the garage and pull out slowly. And if you do anything to call attention to yourself, you're both dead. I have nothing to lose by taking two more lives."

She pushed the button, and as the garage door came up, Krista glanced toward her glove box. If she could just reach it ...

She met his eyes in the rearview mirror. "Let's go," he said.

She started the car and backed out, praying that God was watching. He knew the number of her days, just as he'd known Ella's. She prayed Henry Hearne's wouldn't be the last face she saw.

sixty-three

Ryan had spent so much time at the police station lately that he knew most of the staff by name. Today he and Ian had spent hours with the detectives and the FBI, going over the details of the Data-Gather program and the access Henry Hearne had to GrapeVyne sites.

When they were finished with him, he learned Krista and Megan had left moments before. He called Krista to make sure she was okay. Her phone rang through to voice-mail. That didn't make sense. She would have her phone with her, waiting for them to tell her when they'd made the arrest.

He decided to drive over to her house and check on her. She was probably grieving more than any day since Ella's body was found. He wanted to comfort her.

When he pulled into her driveway, the garage door was

up, but there were no cars in the bays. Alarm bells rang through his mind. Every time he'd been there before, the garage door was closed, even when they were home. She wouldn't have left it open.

He knocked on the front door, but there was no answer.

Maybe she had taken Megan to the airport. Her phone could have died. Maybe in all the excitement, she'd forgotten to close the garage door.

He'd turned to go back to his car, when her father pulled into the driveway. David shot him a harsh look as he pulled his car around Ryan's and into the garage. Ryan waited for him to get out.

David slammed his door. "What are you doing here?"

Ryan almost winced at his tone. Identifying the killer hadn't changed the man's attitude about him. "I was looking for Krista. She told Detective Pensky she was going home, but she's not here. And she's not answering her phone. I'm worried about her."

David stared at him. "How did you get the garage open?"

"I didn't. It was open when I got here."

David's brows drew together as he looked at the door. "Krista knows better than that. She always closes it." He pulled his phone out of his pocket, dialed her on speed dial.

When he lowered the phone, Ryan said, "No answer?"

"No."

Ryan felt sick. "This isn't right." He walked down the driveway, looked in both directions for ... what? A police car? Henry Hearne?

David followed him. "Ryan, you don't think—"

Ryan walked out into the street, looked to the left. No cars were parked on the street in that direction. He turned to the right. About eight houses down, he saw a black SUV, like the one Henry Hearne parked in his reserved space at Willow. "No, don't tell me ..."

He started running toward it.

David's feet pounded the blacktop behind him. "Ryan!"

Ryan reached the car, looked in the window. Hearne wasn't there. He tried to open the door, but it was locked. On the seat, he saw a laptop.

David was out of breath as he caught up to him. "Ryan ... what are you doing?"

"I think this is his car," he said, going from one door to another. They were all locked. "It's Hearne's SUV."

David's jaw dropped. "Aw, no ..."

Ryan grabbed a large rock from the garden near a mailbox. He picked it up and slammed it into the driver's side window, cracking the glass. Rearing back, he crashed the rock into it again, this time shattering it.

David froze as Ryan reached through the broken glass and unlocked the door. He dusted glass off the seat and got in, grabbed the laptop and opened it.

A map of the area filled the screen, and he saw a moving triangle, curling down the interstate. "That's them!"

David's voice was hoarse. "What is?"

"He must have a transponder on Krista's car. He's been following her."

"Then ... where is *he*?"

Ryan got out of the car with the laptop. "I don't know. Maybe he's with her. Come on, we have to go after them."

They ran side by side, back to the house. Ryan reached his car first, and he popped the lock. "You drive, Mr. Carmichael."

David took Ryan's keys and got in, started the car. Ryan slipped into the passenger side and opened the computer. "Head toward Avery Boulevard."

He called the police, told them what they'd found, and where the car was. "Don't touch anything," the dispatcher said.

"I already have. I have his computer that's tracking Krista's car."

"Just wait there until the police come."

"No!" he yelled. "I'm using it to track them. You've got to help us. They're traveling north on Firon Street in a navy blue Kia."

David screeched around corners like a stunt driver, until he reached the interstate. "The police haven't picked him up yet?"

"No, not yet."

He stomped the accelerator and flew at a hundred miles per hour, weaving in and out of lanes, with no patience for traffic. "Please, God ..."

Ryan kept the phone to his ear as the dispatcher put him through to Detective Pensky.

"Ryan, what's going on?" the detective asked.

Ryan told him as he watched the triangle make a turn. "They're going east on Hampstead Road."

"There's nothing there!" David said. "Just trees. He's going to kill her."

Ryan thought of the terror Krista must be feeling right now, and the added trauma for Megan, if she was still with her.

Lord, please protect them!

Would God allow Krista to be snatched away now, when he was falling in love with her?

No, that couldn't happen.

Jesus, stop this! Help us find them ...

David flew through the city, screeching around corners, until he reached Hampstead Road. He soared down the long, lonely road, shaded by bare branches of oak trees.

"They're turning," Ryan said, watching the green tri-angle slow and move across the screen. He zoomed in on the road name. "It's Carson Street."

David slowed enough to read the signs. When he finally got to Carson Street, he turned.

"They're turning again," Ryan said.

"Where?"

Ryan tried to zoom in, but there was no street where they had turned. "I don't know. It's off the road somewhere." He looked up as they flew past trees. "Slow down. Look for a dirt road, a driveway, anything ..."

"Where are the police?" David yelled.

sixty-four

The dirt road was long and winding, made more for three wheelers than for a car. As Krista drove down it, bushes and branches scraped and beat her car.

Behind her, Hearne kept his gun to Megan's head.

Maybe there was a house back here, or someone hunting. She prayed that God would intervene and not let him murder them.

No one knew where they were!

They went about a mile into the dense forest, and the path ended at a creek. As she stepped on the brakes, she scanned the area, looking for an escape. If they could just get out of the car, maybe she could run. But not without Megan.

Megan covered her head, wailing, traumatized. The gun was still in the glove compartment, just in front of Megan. If Megan could just grab it . . .

Hearne opened his car door, and got out on Krista's side, moving his aim to her head as he reached for her door.

"Megan," she whispered quickly. "Glove compartment. Gun."

But Megan was too distraught, and she didn't hear.

Hearne opened her door. His eyes looked wild, anxious.

Megan moaned, rocking back and forth as though comforting herself.

"Please ..." Krista said, looking up at him.

He pulled something out of his pocket. White plastic ties.

"Put your hands together at the top of the steering wheel," he said.

She hesitated.

"Do it!"

Krista grabbed the top of the steering wheel.

"Megan," he said, bending in. "If you keep wailing like that, I'm going to put a bullet through your brain. Is that what you want?"

She hushed, but kept clutching her head and rocking.

"Megan, take this tie, and wrap it around Krista's wrists."

Megan shook her head no. "I can't."

"It's okay, Megan," Krista said, trying to keep her voice calm. "Go ahead. Do it."

With shaking hands, Megan took the tie and wrapped it around Krista's wrists.

"Slip it through the hole, and pull it tight," he said. "Hurry."

She did as he said and pulled it. The insides of Krista's wrists touched each other, but it wasn't too tight.

"Now, take this other one," he said, giving it to Megan. "And put it through the first one, then tie it to the steering wheel."

"Can't," Megan muttered. "I'm gonna be sick."

"Come on, Megan," Krista coaxed. "Please, just do what he says."

Megan pulled the tie through so that it bound Krista's hands to the steering wheel.

Hearne grabbed the end of each tie, yanked them tighter. Krista thought her wrists would snap. He leaned in and got her car keys, slid them into his pocket. Then he went around the car to get Megan.

"Glove compartment," Krista bit out. "Megan, open it!"

But Megan snapped, and lunged out of the car, trying to escape before Hearne could get to her. Because of her leg brace, she hobbled more than ran. Krista screamed as Hearne descended on Megan and knocked her to the ground.

The gun ... she had to get to the gun.

Megan was screaming, fighting, but her fight seemed to delight Hearne. He was going to rape the girl again. He was going to murder her this time. Then he would do it to Krista, and bury them both.

God, you've got to help us!

She tried to free her hands, without success, and she shook the steering wheel, tried to curl her hands and slip them out. But the ties were too tight.

She slipped her right foot out of its shoe and groped at the glove compartment. She managed to pull the handle with her toe, and the small door opened.

She could see the gun. She just couldn't get to it. *Please God!*

He'd gotten Megan to her feet, ripped her brace off her leg. She kicked and screamed as he tried to control her.

Grunting, Krista lifted her leg again, and with her foot, managed to slide the gun out. It hit the floor on the passenger side of the car.

Hearne got Megan down again, swung to hit her with his fist, but she foiled his swing. Somewhere, Krista heard dogs barking.

She slid partially off her seat, moving her right leg around her console, to the other floorboard. She felt the gun, but only pushed it away. No, she had to reach it ... pull it.

But it was too far. As she groped for it with her foot, she heard Megan's bloody scream.

....

As David drove, Ryan searched for any sign of tire tracks going off the road. But he saw nothing. Where had they turned?

He watched the triangle on the computer. "It's still up ahead. We haven't passed their turnoff yet."

"How far?" David asked, breathing hard.

"Maybe a mile."

David sped up as Ryan spoke to Pensky again. "How far away are you guys?"

"We're almost to Carson."

"We've lost them," he said. "We don't know where they turned off." It looked as if they were coming closer to the triangle. "It's somewhere along here," he said. "They turned left. There has to be a road or driveway ..."

"There's nothing," David cried. "He's going to kill her!"

....

Krista slid sideways on the seat, hands still bound to the steering wheel. She managed to touch the gun again with her foot, and this time pulled it toward her. Afraid it would go off accidentally, she got it to the hump between the seats and managed to pull it over.

Megan screamed outside the car, long, blood-curdling screams that racked through the forest. The gun fell onto Krista's side of the floorboard. Straightening, she looked out the windshield.

Megan had gotten to her feet and was running again, each step on her right leg making her lunge. Hearne was on her heels, grabbing her hair, throwing her back down.

Krista slipped her other foot out of its shoe, kicked the shoes aside, then swept the gun between both of her feet. She lifted her legs, trying to get it up to her bound hands. How would this ever work?

Sweat trickled into her eyes, though cold wind swept through the car. She worked at it again, moving her knees apart as her feet came up with the gun. Grinding her teeth, she leaned back and pulled her feet up, trying to twist her fingers down so she could grab it. She couldn't reach, so she dipped her head and clamped her teeth over the barrel.

She pulled it up, placed it in her hands, turned it around.

Megan was flailing, scratching Hearne's eyes, kicking with all her might. He held his gun tight in one hand, but let her go and grabbed a fallen branch. Holding it like a bat, he reared back to swing.

Getting both fingers over the trigger, and aiming through the windshield, Krista squeezed . . .

The gun fired.

....

"I heard a gunshot!" David said, rolling his window down. "He's killing them!"

"There!" Ryan said. "A dirt road. Fresh tracks!"

David slowed, muttering prayers under his breath.

"We found a road," Ryan said into the phone.

"Leave a marker," Pensky said. "Your shirt or your shoes . . . Anything to show us where you turned."

The shirt could blow away, but not his shoes. He pulled them off, tossed them out the window as they turned onto the dirt.

The road didn't seem wide enough for a car, but there were broken branches, and the tracks they saw appeared as wide as Krista's car. Bushes and limbs scraped the SUV as they pushed through. He heard screaming, and his heart slammed against his chest.

Was Krista still alive?

....

The bullet missed Hearne, but it startled him enough to make him step back. He looked at the car, saw Krista aiming ...

Dropping the branch, he raised his gun to fire back, but she pulled the trigger again. It hit the tree next to him, splintering wood.

Megan took the reprieve to get to her feet again. She limped away, into the trees.

Hearne fired, shattering Krista's windshield, hitting the seat next to her. She ducked down, trying to get her head under the dashboard, and fired blindly.

When she peeked over, he was walking toward her, cocking his revolver. She leaned toward the door as his gun fired. Pain tore through her arm, hitting nerve and bone, knocking her back. She dropped the gun.

....

The screaming had stopped, but the gunfire went on. Ryan felt sick. He wanted to get out of the car and run toward the sound, but knew they could get there faster by car.

"Let him know we're here!" Ryan yelled. "Your horn."

David pressed his horn as he wound down the path. It blared through the woods, and birds fluttered out of trees.

....

Just as Hearne cocked his pistol again, Krista heard the sound of a horn coming closer. It stopped Hearne, and he looked past her, down the dirt road.

Someone was coming!

Hearne took off then, into the trees, running away like the coward he was.

Screaming for help, she looked in the rearview mirror. She saw an SUV ... her father driving.

He slammed to a halt behind her, and he and Ryan tumbled out and ran to her.

Thank you, God!

Her father reached her first, saw the blood pooling on her blouse and her seat. "Dad! I dropped the gun," she gasped. "Get it and go after him!"

He picked up the revolver. "Krista, you're shot!"

"I'm okay ... Please, don't let him get away ..."

Ryan opened the passenger side door, knelt on the seat, and pulled his belt off. He wound it around the top of her arm and made a tourniquet. "Are you sure you're all right?"

"Yes!" she cried. "Please! Megan's out there too."

David checked the cylinder for bullets. There were seven left. Ryan pulled a pocketknife out of his pocket and cut her loose. Her hands fell.

"He went that way, Dad. *Go!*"

....

Megan's knee ripped more with each step, but she tried to double back toward the road. She saw a broken branch on the ground and grabbed it in case she had to fight again.

But she didn't hear him behind her.

When she heard the horn and the sound of the car, relief flooded through her chest. Someone was coming. She kept moving, trying to get back to the road, but she figured it was at least a mile away.

Gunshots fired back and forth ... and she prayed that Krista wasn't hurt. She heard her screaming. She was still alive.

Then she heard sirens, distant at first, moving closer, louder. Help was here. She turned and started back toward the dirt road.

....

In the woods, David saw a footstep here and there, and followed Hearne along the creek bed. Had he crossed? No, if he had, he would have seen his footprints in the mud.

He kept going, seeing broken twigs and smelling the scent of sweat. He heard barking from somewhere.

Hatred dug its cleats into his soul, driving him on to kill Ella's killer, to destroy the man who'd just shot his only remaining child. Hearne would not get away. David would gladly give his own life to take down that monster.

And then he saw movement just ahead of him, heard a grunt. The barking grew louder.

Behind him, he heard sirens. But he couldn't wait for the police. He had him now.

He raised Krista's gun and moved closer. Hearne was at the edge of the creek bed, and two dogs were snarling and taunting him. Hearne tried to fire, but his gun was empty.

David froze, Krista's .22 aimed at the back of Hearne's head.

"Back ... boys ..." Hearne dropped the gun and held his palms out, as though he could keep the dogs back. "Good boy ..."

But one of the dogs lunged, and the other followed. They attacked, mauling and tearing through flesh, ripping through Hearne with rabid, ravenous appetites. Hearne screamed and shook them off, fought and fell back.

David didn't move, for fear of drawing their attention. For a moment he watched as Hearne was tortured, tormented, murdered slowly, as he'd murdered Ella and Karen ... as he'd tortured Megan ... as he'd intended to torture Krista ...

It was too much to watch. The dogs foamed at the mouth, raged and tore as if Hearne's own demons had turned on him. Unable to take any more of the bloody scene, David fired.

One of the dogs fell back; the other kept raging.

He fired again ... once ... twice ... killing the second dog.

Hearne lay there, limp, bleeding from his face and throat, his arms, his legs ...

Yes, there was justice. David took a step toward him, another ... until he could see the man's face.

Bloody eyes looked up at him, beseeching. David moved the gun, aimed between those filthy eyes ...

"Kill me," Hearne said through his teeth. "Just pull the trigger."

David thought how it would feel to pull the trigger, to watch the life drain out of him. But it might be mercy for this perverted excuse for a man. It might put him out of his misery.

And David didn't want that.

Instead, he kept the gun on him and called out, "I've got him! Over here!"

By the time the police had made their way to them, Henry Hearne was dead, like the dogs who lay beside him.

sixty-five

The Eagle's Wings center had filled up today, and girls lined the tables in the big room. Anticipation hung in the air, but their faces were somber, and the usual chatter had fallen silent. Pachelbel's *Canon in D* played softly over the speakers.

Krista stood at the front of the room, her arm bandaged and stabilized in a brace against her chest. "So we're here today to create a memorial for someone we've lost. Whether it's a brother who died ..."

She looked at Jesse, and the girl looked down ...

"Or a mother, or a father, or cousin ... or a neighbor or friend. Or maybe you've had to say good-bye to some part of your life that's died ..."

Her gaze drifted to Megan, whom she'd invited to join in.

"You've brought symbols of those experiences from home. Be creative, be courageous, and honor them today. And as you're working, thank God for the time you had them in your life."

The girls got to work, and Krista looked at Jesse, who had a stack of her brother's CDs that she was hot-gluing together into some kind of art piece. She glanced at Megan, who was making a memory box for some of her childhood things.

Krista went to her own table, where she had dozens of fragments of a broken mirror. It was the mirror that had fallen out of Ella's purse the day she was abducted. Pieces of it had sprinkled the ground, evidence of a struggle. Since Henry Hearne's death, the arrest of the two thugs he'd hired to help him, and the conclusion of Ella's case, the police had returned Ella's personal effects. In a Ziploc bag were the mirror pieces that symbolized darkness and evil. Krista had carried them for a while, searching for a way to repurpose them so that they honored her sister's life. Finally, she'd thought of this way. She'd broken another hand mirror from Ella's room to give her more fragments to mix with those from that horrible day.

Now, as the soft music played, the girls worked quietly, wiping away tears. Krista made a mosaic that she glued to a foot-wide floor tile. As she placed each piece, she imagined seeing Ella's face in it, smiling back at her, fixing her pretty hair, rounding her eyes as she checked herself out.

She smiled through tears and kept working, carefully placing each piece of glass.

••••

Later in the day, when the sun was about to set, she and her father stood at Ella's gravesite. The tombstone had been placed, and at the center of the stone cross was a one-foot square indention for her tile. David held the tile as Krista swept the adhesive onto the stone. Then she took the tile, knelt, and set it in place.

Getting up, she dusted off her knees. David put both arms around her, and whispered, "I love you, honey." The two hugged desperately as they turned back to the stone. David kissed the top of her head, then read the inscription on the marker. " 'For now we see through a glass, darkly; but then face to face ...' — 1 Corinthians 13:12."

Krista wiped her tears. "Thank you, God, for letting us hang out with Ella for fourteen years. She was such fun."

She heard footsteps behind her and turned to see Ryan approaching them from the car, holding three bundles of pink helium balloons. He'd taken time off from the new Internet security business he and Ian had launched to come here with them, but he'd given them a few minutes alone. Now he joined them, and she and her father each took a bundle of the balloons.

David cleared his throat. "Ella loved pink. If we would have let her, she would have dressed in pink every single day. Her room was pink on pink. Her bike was pink. Her toenails and fingernails were pink. Even her skin was a little pink ..."

Krista laughed softly.

"Most of Ella's days were good days, thanks to Krista, who saw to that." He smiled at her as tears flooded his eyes. "You did good, honey. I couldn't have raised her without you."

"Thank you, Daddy."

Ryan set his hand on the back of Krista's head, stroking her hair. He kissed her temple as David went on. "So now it's her mom's turn to enjoy her. And she's with Jesus, who adored her already. He has the same photo albums we have. I know he's thrilled to have her." He drew in a long sigh, looked up to the heavens, and said, "Lord, please tell Ella we love her."

Then he released his balloons, and Ryan released his. Finally, Krista let go of hers.

The wind caught them, scattering pink across the sky, lifting them toward the light. Krista imagined Ella looking down, waving as she scooped them up, laughing as she ran and tumbled across vast perfection. Joy seeped back into her heart.

When darkness came and memories crushed, Krista would remember the weightless wonder of pink dotting the sky ... and smile for the joy of knowing Ella.

A Note from the Author

I have a problem with gratitude. While I have so many things to be thankful for, I never seem to dwell on those much. I rarely talk to God about them. I dwell on the negatives in my life, and those are the things that occupy most of my prayers.

Today it occurred to me that God sees all of the suffering in the world, and then he sees me with my whiny little prayers that seem so urgent to me. Last night I got a cramp in my toe, and I couldn't get it to go away. It literally occupied my every thought. I prayed and whined and put compresses on it, and asked God why.

But how does that sound to God? I tell him my foot hurts, and I beg him to make it feel better. He sees people who have amputated feet, people who are paralyzed, people who have flesh-eating bacteria on dying limbs. He hears their passionate prayers for healing, and then he hears mine. "God, my toe is really killing me. Can't you fix it? I don't want to hurt." And he knows that my pain is nothing—absolutely nothing—compared to theirs.

I pray for my back pain, which can be significant for me. He hears my prayers, but he also hears those millions across the world from people with backs that have rendered them quadriplegics, backs with debilitating nerve damage, backs that keep them doubled over, unable to look up. He feels the pain of all that suffering, and then he feels mine. While he's compassionate, I can't help wondering if he's sad that I'm not more grateful that I don't have cancer eating me from the inside out, that I can walk upright and move my hands and do the things I want.

I complain of having migraines, but there are people whose brain chemistry has been out-of-balance for years. I complain that my house isn't big enough, yet there are people who sleep under bridges. I complain that my job is difficult and stressful, yet there are people who walk miles for water and do desperate things in order to support their families.

I complain about my church, how the air conditioning is too cold, how the pews are too hard. And God sees people across the world who are risking their lives to assemble together in underground home churches, so anxious to worship God that they'd give their lives for it.

I imagine it's like spending time in a famine-ravaged country, where people walk around like skeletons, desperate for food. And then you come home to America and walk into your own home, where the pantries are stocked and the refrigerator is full, and your kids whine that there's nothing to eat. It would be more than irritating. Yet that's what God sees in us all the time. Yes, he still loves us, just like we love our own children when they're ungrateful. I'm sure he also realizes that we don't know how fortunate we are. Unless we've seen what he's seen, how can we know that we sometimes sound like crybabies squealing in his ears?

If earth is a training ground for heaven, then what should we be doing here? Revelation says that thanksgiving and praise will be a huge element of our lives in heaven.

Maybe that's because we'll then be able to see clearly all the good things that God gave us, all the ways he worked strength and endurance and perseverance into our lives. All the ways he prepared us for our heavenly work. We'll be overflowing with gratitude, because we'll know all the close calls he protected us from, all the devastation, all the heartache, as well as the help he gave us, and we'll learn how he used the things he allowed.

But we're not supposed to wait until we get there. We're supposed to train ourselves in thanksgiving now. "Pray continually; give thanks in all circumstances, for this is God's will for you in Christ Jesus" (1 Thessalonians 5:17–18 NIV). "Do not be anxious about anything, but in everything, by prayer and petition, with thanksgiving, present your requests to God" (Philippians 4:6 NIV). "I will give thanks to the LORD with my whole heart; I will recount all of your wonderful deeds" (Psalm 9:1 ESV). "Offer to God a sacrifice of thanksgiving, and perform your vows to the Most High, and call upon me in the day of trouble; I will deliver you, and you shall glorify me" (Psalm 50:14–15 ESV).

So how do we keep our prayers from being narcissistic and self-centered? We take time to focus on how fortunate we are. I know a lady who has ALS, otherwise known as Lou Gehrig's disease. Though her muscles no longer work (she's paralyzed), and she can hardly hold her head up or speak, she manages to go to the local jail to do prison ministry once a week. She has hired troubled women (who have been in prison themselves) to care for her during the day. And most of what she asks them to do for her centers around Bible study and praising God. As they're helping her, she's helping them. These women say their time with her has changed their lives. This lady will minister to others and praise God until her last breath. Through all her suffering (and it is extensive), her life is a testimony of praise and thanksgiving, because she knows Christ died to cleanse her of her sins, so that one day soon she'll be raised to new life—completely healed, with an everlasting life to serve the God she served here on earth. And since thanksgiving is already a way of life for her here, she'll enter his gates with even more thanksgiving, and live in joy and gratitude for eternity.

So let's be more grateful for what we have, and in our pain, be thankful for how God will use that pain someday. Let's remember those famous first words in *The Purpose Driven Life*: "It's not about you." If God never did another thing for us than send his Son to die a substitutionary death on the cross for us, so he could forgive us of our sins, he'd still deserve overwhelming gratitude. But he's done so much more.

"The LORD's lovingkindnesses indeed never cease, For His compassions never fail. They are new every morning; Great is Your faithfulness. 'The Lord is my portion,' says my soul. 'Therefore, I have hope in Him'" (Lamentations 3:22–24 NASB).

predator
Discussion
Questions

1. Do you have a profile on a social network? Has this book made you rethink what information you supply and whom you have contact with while online? Do you think social networking has had more of a positive or negative influence on your life? On society?

2. When Ryan is reluctant to make changes to GrapeVyne that would help protect its members from online predators, Krista tells him that by not taking action he might as well be a predator himself. Do you agree with her? What role does indifference play in the proliferation of evil?

3. Describe the different ways Krista and David cope with their grief. What negative effects do they each suffer as a result of their coping method? Do they eventually find solace and peace? If so, how?

4. Krista develops serious doubts about God for not interceding to protect Ella, and fears she will no longer be able to continue ministering to young girls. Do you think her fear is valid? Could her suffering eventually lead her to be a more effective witness, as Ryan suggests?

Can you think of someone whose suffering helped them proclaim God's glory in a way they wouldn't have been able to otherwise?

5. What good things is GrapeVyne used for in the book? Do you think Krista's desire to shut it down completely because of online predators is justified? How do you think Christians should approach technology that can be used in a dangerous or inappropriate way?

6. Describe how Ryan changes throughout the course of the book. What does he value most when Krista first meets him? What does he do to prove his values have changed by the end? What causes his transformation?

7. The verse inscribed on Ella's grave is 1 Corinthians 13:12: "For now we see through a glass, darkly; but then, face to face" (KJV). Do the characters eventually see any good result from their suffering? What questions are still left unanswered?

8. Has reading this book given you spiritual insight into personal suffering or doubt in your own life? If so, how has your view of these experiences changed?

Intervention

A Novel

Terri Blackstock,
#1 Bestselling Suspense Author

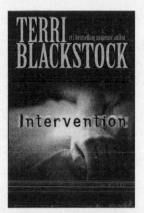

Barbara Covington has one more chance to save her daughter from a devastating addiction, by staging an intervention. But when eighteen-year-old Emily disappears on the way to drug treatment—and her interventionist is found dead at the airport—Barbara enters her darkest nightmare of all.

Barbara and her son set out to find Emily before Detective Kent Harlan arrests her for a crime he is sure she committed. Fearing for Emily's life, Barbara maintains her daughter's innocence. But does she really know her anymore? Meanwhile, Kent has questions of his own. His gut tells him that this is a case of an addict killing for drugs, but as he gets to know Barbara, he begins to hope he's wrong about Emily.

The panic level rises as the mysteries intensify: Did Emily's obsession with drugs lead her to commit murder—or is she another victim of a cold-blooded killer?

Available in stores and online!

Share Your Thoughts

With the Author: Your comments will be forwarded to the author when you send them to *zauthor@zondervan.com*.

With Zondervan: Submit your review of this book by writing to *zreview@zondervan.com*.

Free Online Resources at

www.zondervan.com

Zondervan AuthorTracker: Be notified whenever your favorite authors publish new books, go on tour, or post an update about what's happening in their lives at www.zondervan.com/authortracker.

Daily Bible Verses and Devotions: Enrich your life with daily Bible verses or devotions that help you start every morning focused on God. Visit www.zondervan.com/newsletters.

Free Email Publications: Sign up for newsletters on Christian living, academic resources, church ministry, fiction, children's resources, and more. Visit www.zondervan.com/newsletters.

Zondervan Bible Search: Find and compare Bible passages in a variety of translations at www.zondervanbiblesearch.com.

Other Benefits: Register yourself to receive online benefits like coupons and special offers, or to participate in research.

ZONDERVAN®

ZONDERVAN.com/
AUTHORTRACKER
follow your favorite authors